T0304809

Ice Town

Also by Will Dean

The Last Passenger
The Last Thing to Burn
First Born

The Tuva Moodyson Thrillers

Dark Pines
Red Snow
Black River
Bad Apples
Wolf Pack

WILL DEAN

Ice Town

HODDER &
STOUGHTON

First published in Great Britain in 2024 by Hodder & Stoughton
An Hachette UK company

2

Copyright © Will Dean 2024

A CIP catalogue record for this title is available from the British Library

Hardback ISBN 978 1 399 71731 1
Paperback ISBN 978 1 399 71735 9
ebook ISBN 978 1 399 71733 5

Typeset in Plantin Light by Hewer Text UK Ltd, Edinburgh
Printed and bound in Great Britain by Clays Ltd, Elcograf S.p.A.

Hodder & Stoughton policy is to use papers that are natural, renewable
and recyclable products and made from wood grown in sustainable
forests. The logging and manufacturing processes are expected to
conform to the environmental regulations of the country of origin.

Hodder & Stoughton Ltd
Carmelite House
50 Victoria Embankment
London EC4Y 0DZ

www.hodder.co.uk

For @DeafGirly. You have been an integral part of Team Tuva from the very beginning. I suspect there is a trio looking out for Tuva Moodyson at all times: Tammy, Lena, and you. I am so very grateful.

'Deep into that darkness peering, long I stood there, wondering, fearing, doubting, dreaming dreams no mortal ever dared to dream before.'

Edgar Allan Poe, The Raven

Melanie Bairstow
Victoria Jayne
Brian Henderson
Zoe Bilverstone

Emma Kilner
Caroline Cobb
Helen Savigar
Luke Marlowe

John Duffy
Mark Brownless
Kestrel Carroll
Esther Fletcher

Sarah Walford
Caroline Rhodes
Graeme Young
Jo Poultney

Lee Matthew
Samantha Lamb
Elizabeth Morris
Anastasia Boulis

Jodie Spencer
Susie Price

Jason Locker
Kelly Forrester
Nicola Mackenzie-Smaller
Adam Ross Patterson

Wil Carpenter

Trish Hills
Suzy Grant
Peter Fleming
Kathy Sandison

Sarah Blackburn
Lesley Locker
Christine Mapp
Michelle Newton

Neil Tabor
Chris Stamford
Ian Purple
James John

Lisa Stevens
Chloe Slim

Sam Spencer
Shamiela Ahmed

Juliet Rean

Christine Taylor
Charmaine Azam

Jonathan Leaper
Stacy Walden

Jennifer Robson
Angela Pitman
Gabrielle Bray
Amanda Milner

Stephen Robertshaw
Jaynie Shedden
Chrissy Milburn
Breda Guy

Lindsey Cross
Karen Grikitis
Scott Whitney

Emma Armytage
Alison Reeve
Donna Gordon
Donna Gallagher

Chloe Brown
Kate Newey

Sally Milton
Gail McGuinness

Laura Jayne Breed
Jonathan Osborn

Antonella Gramola-Sands
Tracey Harriman
Thanhmai Bui-Van
Darren Paterson

Paul Smith
Sol Loredo

Caroline Chapman

Alison Blundell
Natalie Freeman
Alison Richards

Sue Manley
Robert Moore
Kevin Anderson
Stella Wright

WELCOME TO

ESSEBERG

Population: 85

1

Gavrik, Sweden

An elk runs along the snowploughed road searching frantically for her lost calf.

Panic in her eyes. Myriad headlights picking out that panic.

The thick scent of exhaust fumes.

I slow my Hilux truck and switch on my hazard lights. The traffic on the other side is still moving, drivers desperate to exit these bleak winter roads and retreat to their apartments, their twenty-first-century caves.

The calf looks light as air. It is running, legs long and fragile, and it is desperate to be reunited with its beloved mother, its sole protector in this cold, dark wilderness.

A Volkswagen slows and hoots its horn. A teenager hangs out of the back window filming the towering mother elk on his phone. I look down on this behaviour and yet, at the same time, I know I will likely be using that same footage later this evening for the paper, crediting the very same teenager.

Complicit.

The cow elk summons an ungodly noise and runs onto the asphalt, falling, scrambling to stand back up, the calf lost among the mayhem, the halogen-lit chaos. A man yells something unintelligible from his lorry cab. The calf stops dead for a moment. Its mother trots down into a ditch, nostrils steaming, and someone overtakes me, beeping like this whole scene is an inconvenience, and I am struck, not for the first time, by the spectrum of priorities I witness from my fellow humans. Money, power, convenience, comfort, kindness. White light split through a prism into its many constituent parts.

A grey Saab on the other side of the road skids on a patch of black ice and then recovers. The cow elk makes one last effort to run across the road, to risk everything for her offspring, and a Ford pick-up brakes hard, swerving, missing the beast by a fraction. The elk bolts across in front of me. The Ford crashes down into a ditch, dirty slush-water erupting from its bonnet, red lights glowing through the mist at head height.

The elk family are lost to the forest in seconds. Running, together, nature corrected, back into the shadowy world of Utgard forest. You might try to search for a larger, denser forest than Utgard, but you will likely never find one.

The driver of the Ford is okay. Wet and cold, but okay. I have already called Thord at the police station, my hearing aid synched to my phone. He will probably drive by for ten minutes but this is more a job for a tow truck than law enforcement.

Traffic resumes. I make a turn and head back to Gavrik town, my home, the place the world forgot. A marginal settlement surrounded by vast forests. Hunters and salt liquorice. More than our fair share of darkness.

We haven't had much news these past two years, truth be told.

Quiet place.

Time to heal.

I drive between McDonald's and ICA Maxi, the two gateposts of Gavrik, and snow begins to fall. December flurries are always welcome. Check back again in March when my fellow Swedes are dreaming of moving south to Spain, or maybe Malmö. I moved here years ago when Mum was ill. After she passed away I just kind of stayed. Don't ask me why. No, in fact, do ask me. Because the people I care about live in this desolate place. It is as simple and as complicated as that.

I go on.

Pensioners wearing more layers than most people on this planet would ever contemplate: merino wool as life support. Streetlights forming halos within pale clouds of snowflakes. A young man pulling his weekly shop home on a sledge.

The long-stem weeds on the roadside, despised all summer, are admired now that they are adorned with ice crystals.

I spot Tammy's food truck in the distance. She will be in there listening to nineties dance classics and slicing chilies and spring onions. My best friend in the world. My sister in all but blood. Tammy will be refining her bone broths and cleaning out her rice cookers. Working culinary magic inside a van in the most inauspicious corner of a car park. An unlikely hero but a hero nonetheless.

Past Benny Björnmossen's hunt shop, the stuffed brown bear looking back, judging me. Hunting is the main pastime here in Gavrik so Benny does well, although he'll never say as much. Past the police station and through the long shadows cast by the twin chimneys of the Grimberg Liquorice factory, our largest and oldest employer.

Welcome to Toytown, population: 8,000 souls. Most of them lost, or on their way there.

I head into *Gavrik Posten* and the bell above the door tinkles. Lars looks up from whatever Jedi-level Sudoku he is currently working on.

I start peeling off layers and slipping off my snow boots. My blonde ponytail feels more dishevelled and dry than it usually does and that is saying something.

'Elk out on the Utgard road. Almost hit a truck.'

Lars, as a general rule, takes a while to react. He used to be the sole full-time reporter here until I took over, and he's much like an old-fashioned vinyl record playing at half speed. I take my gloves off and then, after a moment, he says, 'Elk?'

'Cow with her calf on the other side of the road. Both looked panicked.'

'Almost hit a truck?' he says.

'Truck's in a ditch. Everyone's okay.'

'Everyone *is* okay,' he repeats, like he's trying to reassure himself of the fact.

Lena is back in her office fixing for the print and Nils is in his trying to sell ad space to the same poor axe shop owners and hairdressers he's been trying to sell ad space to for years. Swedes don't bother so much with hair styling in the dark months, you see, not in rural parts. If you have your skull encased in a woolly hat all day every day why would you even bother?

The office smells of coats drying out.

I open up my last file and turn down the volume on my new hearing aids. They are superior to my old pair in almost every way – battery life, interference, water resistance – but they hurt. Every night when I return home I pull them out as soon as I open my door, and the relief is immediate.

One piece of breaking news grabs my attention.

It scrolls across the base of my screen.

Deaf teenager goes missing in Esseberg.

Police believe he has no money with him, or contacts outside of Esseberg town.

Mountain rescue are launching a search party but conditions hinder their efforts.

The deaf teenager is described as vulnerable.

The tunnel is being kept open all night as an exception.

2

It takes me all of two seconds to decide I will dedicate myself to this story. No, that's not true, it's more a gut reaction than a decision. I act because how can I not. This guy needs all the help he can get. Missing, alone, up in the vast, frigid Jämtland mountains – a region that makes my green Värmland forests appear civilised – in the bleakest, iciest days of midwinter.

I knock on Lena's door.

She grunts.

I open it.

'You got a second?'

She takes off her glasses and looks up.

'Sure.'

'Deaf teenager gone missing. Described as vulnerable.'

'Okay. Is Chief Björn or Thord on it? Any more information? Missing could mean took a day trip to Visberg and she didn't tell anyone.'

'This isn't Gavrik news, Lena. Up north.'

She frowns. 'How far up north?'

'Jämtland. The empty mountains west of Åre. Small town called Esseberg. I'm going up there.'

Lena runs her hands through her afro. She's keeping it shorter these days. 'You sure this is for you, Tuva? *Jämtland*, really?'

I do not hesitate. 'I am sure.'

'It's a long way. Do you know if it's a—'

'It's a deaf kid, Lena,' I say, cutting her off.

I wait.

'You want to take Lars with you as backup?'

'Seriously?' I glance back at Lars, still working through his Sudoku puzzle, his fleece-lined slippers tucked neatly under his chair, his backside resting on a donut-shaped haemorrhoid cushion. 'No, I'll be fine. Listen, I know you worry about locals not wanting to read news from other places, and I get that, but we haven't had a real crime in Gavrik for two years now.'

'You say it like it's a bad thing.'

'You know what I mean.'

She glances over her shoulder at my *Journalisten – Thirty Under Thirty* award on her shelves. I refuse to have it out front. I do not feel comfortable with the thing, especially as I'm not actually under thirty anymore. I am grateful to the judges but I wish it was kept private. When I was awarded it, I received two less than positive messages from old schoolfriends via Facebook. One said: *thirty isn't a widely used cut-off point for good reason. It's usually forty under forty. Enough time for real achievements.* The other told me her British aunt had just been awarded an MBE from the Queen. Why are people like this?

'If you need anything I'll fly straight up,' she says. 'Deal?'

'Deal.'

Nils emerges from his corner office, his hair in spikes. He has to dye it now because he won't accept the inevitable, and it looks like he's poured a tin of blue-black paint over his head.

'Heard about the moose on the Utgard road. Some school teacher crashed into a ditch, right? People don't know how to drive in winter these days.'

Lena looks at him and says, 'You reversed into a bus last month.'

'That was a malfunction,' he says, pulling back his shoulders. 'I told you. Camera had a glitch. It was a technical malfunction.'

'*You're* a malfunction,' I say under my breath.

He narrows his eyes. 'It was the reversing camera. I couldn't see properly.'

'Couldn't see a damn *bus*?' I say.

'What are you insinuating?'

'Who taught you that word? Was it Lars?'

'Nils,' says Lena, smiling. 'Tuva is off up to the mountains of Jämtland for a couple of days to work on a missing-person story. So be nice to her.'

'We've got the budget for that but no budget for my new laptop?'

He looks triumphant, like he's caught her in a cunning trap.

'Exactly right,' she says.

I leave the office and drive home, the scent of salt liquorice hanging in the frosted streets. Takes me all of ten minutes to pack. There are no pets or dependents to check on or leave food out for. I can hardly leave food out for myself.

In addition to my standard gas-station scrapers I bring along a long-handle snow brush, the one Benny

Björnmossen gifted me last year after Noora's funeral. He said it was a late Christmas present, a *very* late Christmas present, but I understood from his eyes that this was his way of saying *I am sorry for your loss*. He's not a man to hug or console, but that gesture, that simple and unspoken act of protection and care, spoke volumes.

I set off due north.

Sweden is a country that can trick you if you are not careful. Here in Garvik we are a solid twenty-hour drive from the southern tip of the country. And yet this is only *central* Sweden. Today I'm driving north out of Gavrik on the E16 motorway and my Toyota GPS tells me I'm nine hours south of my destination. And yet, that destination, Esseberg, or *Ice Town* as it is commonly known, is *also* in central Sweden. You can drive another twenty hours north from there, deep into the Arctic Circle, and you *still* won't reach the border. The vastness and wildness of my homeland astonishes me.

An hour in and I am settling into the drive. Sparse traffic. An occasional eighteen wheeler carrying dead pine trunks, each one amputated just above the ankle, and trucks passing down the other way laden with steel and paper products. Not a single police car on the road.

The snow falls in light flurries and the horizon is a milky blur.

I drive into that blur.

I remain inside of it for a long time.

A monochrome world. Johnny Cash playing on a loop. His sad, beautiful voice.

The arbitrariness of my job strikes me as I pull into the slow lane. Spotting that news story on my laptop screen. A scroll of words most of my peers would ignore. The story would simply pass them by. I know by now that missing-persons cases – or as some people call them, *misper* cases – are a dime a dozen. Humans go missing: they always have and they always will. Some want to go. Others never have a chance to explain what happened to them. My job, as the sole full-time reporter at *Gavrik Posten*, is to investigate and report. I have a responsibility to do both things.

Sadly, a person with no discernible characteristics goes missing and the world carries on regardless. But you have a beauty-queen kid or a bandy champion or a spelling-bee superstar go missing, someone real photogenic, or with a story attached, and that's different. It is clickable; and mark my words, people click. Ad revenue will be generated. The whole cursed machine will creak and grind on for another day more.

If the missing teenager turns up I will head back down to Gavrik. But I can feel something in my belly about this case. An ache. A warning.

I overtake a snowplough, salt spewing from its illuminated rear end.

The only time I've heard anyone speak of Ice Town, apart from YouTube Shorts displaying the one-way entry tunnel that closes each and every night, was from the mouth of my late mother. She used to talk about a friend she had from Esseberg, a friend she knew before she met my father. She told me she'd never visited because she was afraid of the place. She said she refused to be enclosed in that way.

I am the cow elk from the Utgard road. Frantic. On the other hand, I am still the calf. The first time I babysat little Dan, my neighbour's son, for a whole night, I panicked I wouldn't be able to hear him if he screamed out for me in pain or anguish. So I didn't sleep that night. I stayed awake with my hearing aids in waiting for his cries. I felt the burden of that unique obligation, the same as the elk mother did, and yet mine was only for one evening. I do not know how parents deal with that night after night.

I turn down my heated seat a notch.

Minus eleven on the dash.

After Noora died I would drive around after work. I was a *night-driver*, lost, empty, numb, trying to make sense of it all. My girlfriend left this world and I was vague rather than sad. I had already devoured all the sadness and it had devoured me. Months and months of caring for her, wondering if she would wake up, guessing if she could hear my voice and the voice of her parents. I was cold and alone, driving backroads and motorways, letting streetlights bleed through my windscreen, thinking, remembering: desperate to feel something.

Four hours in, I pull off the motorway into a Preem gas station. I top up my tank and check my tyre pressure. Most people learn these skills from their dad or else their mum. Well, my dad died when I was fourteen and Mum rarely went outdoors from that day on, so I learnt it from Lena. This and a thousand other things. In a strange way I would never communicate to anyone, especially her, my editor has become an augmented version of both my parents.

Melted slush all over the floor. I catch sight of my reflection in a drinks fridge door. A tired ghoul with a scraggly blonde ponytail. Have I stopped taking care of myself since Noora died? No. I didn't take much care before.

One hot dog.

A Nordic energy drink that tastes like someone dropped a car battery into a blender.

Three hours more driving.

Blackness. No more snow. The same Johnny Cash album. It has become a background hum for me now. I feel it more than hear it.

For the final stretch I listen to a YouTube travelogue about Esseberg, aka Ice Town, my phone tucked into my coat pocket, the words streaming through my hearing aids thanks to the miracle of Bluetooth.

I don't pick up every word but I get the gist.

Minus sixteen on my dash.

I turn off the motorway.

No traffic whatsoever to look at.

Ice Town, I am told, has eleven-hundred residents. It is twinned with a rather unusual one-building town in Alaska, due to the fact that both towns are only accessible via a deep mountain tunnel. Ice Town has two key employers: a power station that burns garbage to generate electricity for the region, and a state-pension administrative office. *Trash and old people.* The town used to be a popular ski resort until the much larger, more accessible ski centres of Åre and Sälen took over.

Gale-force crosswinds buffer my Hilux and I spot

other Toyota and Mitsubishi pick-ups parked up, sheltering under the shadow of a bridge.

I do not join them under the bridge. Instead I drive on past warning signs.

Tunnel Ahead.

I sit up straighter in my seat trying to steal a glance of it.

Elk crossing.

I slow down.

Danger – Falling Rocks.

What am I supposed to do with that information?

The video in my pocket keeps replaying so I can catch the details. The narrator explains how, in the 1700s, the remote valley was taken over by adventurous prospectors from Stockholm and Uppsala, uprooting the indigenous Sami population who had lived there peacefully, and sustainably, for countless centuries.

I drive on, the chill wind whistling through my air vents.

The GPS map tells me, in a somewhat ominous tone, that I am approaching a tunnel.

Turn around where possible.

The narrator talks of a myth he says is rooted in fact. How when the nomadic Sami people were displaced from their ancient lands, from their mountains and boreal forests, the deep glacial lake at the base of the valley froze all the way down to the bed. The narrator explains how the following spring, when the ice finally melted, tens of thousands of perch and pike floated up to the surface, where they duly rotted in the bright Nordic sunshine. The town became practically uninhabitable for a while due to the intense and lingering odour of putrefying fish.

Some say the smell has never fully disappeared, and that around the Easter festivities it can still be detected by local children.

Lights up ahead.

The agape mouth of the Ice Town tunnel.

3

Esseberg – Twinned with Whittier, Alaska

I stare at the buckled metal sign, and at the electronic sign above explaining how the next transit slot through the tunnel will be in eleven minutes. According to the YouTube narrator, this is an antiquated unidirectional tunnel only as broad as a railway engine, so it opens for cars one way at a time. It closes to traffic completely whenever a freight train laden with garbage needs to pass through. According to the sign, in Swedish up top and then in Sami underneath, the tunnel shuts down entirely from 11 p.m. to 6 a.m. No one in and no one out.

Perhaps that's what Mum meant all those years ago by not wanted to be enclosed.

Green light.

We start to slowly drive in.

The tunnel is carved out of granite rock and it is almost two kilometres long. It devours my truck. Darkness. The speed limit is 40 kph and suddenly I feel very insignificant. Bolted to the rough-cut roof are whirring ventilation fans. They drone as I pass underneath with my windows cracked open. The uneven rock walls are slick with moisture and they are streaked with brilliant seams of white quartz.

Will my truck be okay on railway tracks? I try to drive to the right slightly to avoid the metal studs of my winter tyres grinding on the steel tracks. Metal on metal is never a good thing.

Halfway. I can't see natural light behind or in front, and although I have my Hilux, which I trust like a suit of armour, and although the tunnel is well-illuminated, I am still driving with my heart in my mouth. Uncomfortable memories of Rose Farm, and Andreas's assault course from two years ago. The *casket,* in particular. I have nightmares every few months where I wake up sweating, bolt upright, fighting for air and space.

Light, up ahead.

I breathe.

When we emerge from the vast mountain I am confronted by a range of snowy peaks, a jagged-edged cauldron, with Ice Town down in its centre, on the valley floor. The frozen lake from the myth appears like spoilt milk at the base of a cereal bowl. The train tracks turn smoothly to the left and I continue straight on.

And I thought Gavrik was small.

On my right-hand side, past diminutive, red-painted timber homes, is a bar of sorts. There are black motorcycles parked under snow shelters and there is a man wearing leather shovelling snow in front of the entrance. The bar is called *Wrath.*

I go on.

Mountain peaks all around. We are hemmed in. Encircled. A ski chairlift to my left, set back a little behind a church, rising up steep pistes and rocky cliffs to the famous old-world hotel high on the summit.

I get to grips with this place in the time it takes me to drive to its centre. I have a knack for this, I guess. One supermarket: a mid-sized Willy's. Almost a decade ago, my UCL roommates in London never believed one of our largest supermarket chains is called *Willy's*. They also doubted we have chocolates called *Plopps* and rich tea biscuits called *Finger Marie*.

I pass by a Vårdcentral doctor's surgery and a hairdresser and three tattoo parlours. Sorry, make that four. This one is half tattoo place, half coffee shop.

These people are locked in every single night of their lives.

Locked in and locked down.

There are two accommodation options in Esseberg, which, to be fair, is one more than Gavrik. There is the expensive hotel on the mountaintop, which, and I am being generous here, does not fare well on Tripadvisor. The other is the Golden Paradise B&B, which is reviewed marginally less unfavourably. It is also considerably cheaper and I know Lena is budget conscious – that's probably the main reason our newspaper is viable when so many others are not – so I drive there and park in the generous car park. Not much of a facility to boast about, but it's the only one they list on their website. It literally says: Golden Paradise B&B, Esseberg. Facilities: Parking.

What the website didn't tell me is that the building also houses a solarium. One radiant patron strolls out as I walk inside. He glows orange like a cheese doodle as I search for the entrance to the B&B.

The overpowering aroma of tanning lotions.

Past the stand-up sun beds, I find the door. Its sign says Golden Paradise B&B. The sign also says, in a different font, *No Breakfasts.*

'Seventy minutes for the price of sixty and you get a free lotion. New promotion.'

I turn. Her diction is excellent otherwise I wouldn't have heard her so clearly. Perhaps it's also these new aids. She has white hair, brown eyes, jeans and a jean shirt. She looks like a kind and well-meaning crocodile.

'Actually I'm here for a room.'

'You booked?'

'I booked online.'

'You did?'

I nod.

'We got two rooms.'

'I only need one of them.'

She takes a minute and then checks the computer.

'Room Two,' she says.

I smile and follow her.

There are literally two doors beyond the Golden Paradise B&B door. One and Two.

'Room Two is this one,' she says, pointing to the door with the number 2 on it. 'You here for the podcast?'

'Podcast?'

'No, I guessed not. Johan usually books rooms for guests himself, pays for them as well. He covers all their travel expenses. Do you know how people earn money from podcasts?'

I could engage in conversation, but I've had a long drive so I say, 'Sorry, could I have the key, please? I'm tired.'

'Adverts,' she says. 'For all sorts of things.'

'Yep.'

'Sponsors, you see. Advertising money.'

'My key?'

She hands it over.

'No breakfasts,' she says.

'You need to paint over the second B.'

'What?'

'The second B. You should consider painting over it.'

'No. Sometimes we do breakfasts.'

'Right.'

I go back to my Hilux and collect my bag. She watches me suspiciously the whole time.

'I'm here because of the deaf teenager who has gone missing.'

'Peter?'

'I don't know the details.'

'His name is Peter.'

'Last name? Do you know where he lives?'

She scowls at me.

'I'm a journalist for a newspaper in Värmland.'

'You're a long way from Värmland.'

'Last name?'

'You're interested in Peter?'

I point to my hearing aids.

She shouts, 'I said, *you're interested in Peter?*'

I nod and step back a little.

'I'm not one to spread rumours.'

No, of course you're not. I don't say a word, I just look at her. One of Lena's tricks.

'Odd character, Peter was, if I'm totally honest. Boy was always an outsider. He never did me any harm but he wasn't one with friends or hobbies, you know? My cousin's neighbour was in his class at high school. Said he was a loner. Difficult and withdrawn, you know the type. Used to draw disturbing pictures in his school books. I've heard people in the town say he might have ended his own life out there in the mountains.'

4

After I raid the vending machine in the solarium I retreat to my room and crank up the thermostat. Something about long drives and creeping darkness chills me to my bone marrow.

Strong cup of coffee, bar of *Kex* chocolate wafer, the rump of a bag of wine gums I opened somewhere in Dalarna. Email from Lena, checking I made it all the way up here in one piece. What other boss would ask such a thing?

My original plan was to hit all the major 'nightspots' in town tonight, which should be feasible in fifteen minutes. Gas station, the biker bar I passed on the way in, possibly the coffee shop slash tattoo parlour if they stay open late. Then Willy's for bread, fresh milk and digestives. But checking local news and Esseberg-specific social media I discover there is a volunteer search for the missing teenager, Peter Hedberg, and the meeting place is the Evangelical Lutheran Church of our Lady.

Five years ago I might have called in first to the local police department. Rookie mistake. In my experience you gather more information, more *colour*, from placing yourself, however uncomfortably, directly in front of locals on the ground as soon as you can.

One more cup of strong coffee. I pull on all my outer clothes and set off to find the church.

I am not sure what I was expecting of this locked-away place but this certainly isn't it. Doesn't fit the dictionary description of a town. This is a village at best, just one with a power station and a multi-storey pension office. The mountains all around are jet black, invisible in the thick snow-haze. All except one. The mountain with the hotel is part-illuminated: floodlit pistes, and, snaking down each one, the chairlift connecting the town to the peak.

Few people out on the streets. Back in London, or even in Stockholm, you would find folks eating and drinking outside pubs and restaurants, even in December. They'd have scarves and recently styled hair, and they'd be laughing with friends over a glass of overpriced wine. Not here. Nothing of the sort. You finish work and you scrape your Volvo windscreen and set the heater running. Then, after the required wait, you move off stoically, hoping you don't skid on sheet ice, back to your insulated home, and then you damn well stay there until the next time you're forced to leave. If you're unlucky, you head out in your moon boots and your fur hat and you keep your face down away from the biting wind and you make your way from here to there with as little deviation as possible.

A gritter-tractor passes me by and the driver is wearing a green camouflage-pattern balaclava and an anti-glare ski mask.

The town has three streets.

Three.

No map required. No phone navigation app. I can see it all. You could fit this so-called town into one wide-angled photograph.

On Fredriksgatan, outside the church, thirty or forty people gather in clusters like children in a kindergarten playground. There is something infantilising about the puffy winter clothes we must don to stay alive each winter. Our bodies are hidden. We are reduced to insulated and anonymous shapes: amorphous collections of fleece and Gore-Tex.

You might expect this to be awkward. New town, new region, no contacts to rely on. But it is not awkward. Quite the opposite. Put me with a new group in a loud bar and I'd stand no chance. I would be unable to decipher voices, to follow conversations. But out here in the snowy gloom, if and when I chat with locals, it will be one-to-one. Focused. Scarves away from mouths. Conversations will be conducted on my terms.

There is no priest announcing search protocols or emergency procedures. No military veteran taking control and organising us into teams. There is only the natural, unspoken hierarchy of such occasions. For I have seen this many times before. The fittest and most able cleave off. They wear cross-country skis and they look like they do this kind of exercise most evenings for kicks, the sick bastards. Then, there are the rest of us. The pasty and the timid and the ones afraid of slipping over. My team, even though many of them are eyeing me suspiciously. *Outsider.* We set off in a large huddle and spread out, searching back alleys and long paths, each one unfurling out into nothingness. I thought Utgard forest was desolate in the wintertime but it is nothing compared to this. There is a special kind of murk that accompanies snow and extreme chill up here. A unique variety of silence. The mountains are at once blank and glowing. They stand resolute, surrounding us, leaning in, giving the impression they overhang the town, and then, when I turn to face the distant nature, I see nothing at all.

At least that is what I tell myself.

I spot the priest or deacon or vicar at the far end of the crowd for a moment, a broad-shouldered man with a group of parishioners circling around him, but then he is gone.

They know what I know. That a missing deaf teenager with no money or contacts is something to worry about in a place like this. Something to fear.

We all understand the odds.

I strike up a conversation with a local environmental consultant. After initial frostiness, she tells me her brother used to teach Peter, the missing boy. She calls him a *boy*. I guess eighteen is an awkward age: for the individual concerned, and for society at large. When does a child become an adult? The demarcation is as arbitrary as any other. A child soldier is no such thing. They have adulthood thrust upon them. And then I have known boys in their mid-thirties. Boys, not men. Overgrown children. They thought they were all grown up but, irritatingly for them, we all knew better. The tragedy is that deep down they probably knew it themselves.

A pair of older women in moth-eaten fur coats struggle with the heavy hatch of a garbage dumpster, and then they peer inside. They are doing the right thing but the action unsettles me. They are being realistic. They are expecting the worst from this rarely visited place. Why else would they check in that filthy, hidden container?

'Oh, he's back,' says the consultant, prodding me with her well-insulated elbow.

She gestures to a young man with blonde hair and no hat. He is holding up a vlogging camera with an integrated ring light and microphone, and he is recording as he walks.

'Local journalist?' I say.

'Local celebrity piste-basher,' she says. 'You don't know Johan?'

'I don't think so.'

'He has the podcast. But he still grooms the pistes in season, God knows why. He certainly doesn't need the cash. Guess he likes being out and about at night. You must know his podcast, you must have listened to it. *True Crime North.* You know?'

'Oh, sure,' I lie.

A small drone flies overhead, buzzing. Two cross-country skiers, each wearing neon vests, pass in front of us and disappear along a trail leading to the shadowy side of the valley, to the deep-frozen lake.

We search for another hour. A black leather glove is found by a bloodhound named Balthazar. It is placed inside a paper bag.

'I haven't seen any police,' I say, rubbing my gloves together. 'Where's the station?'

'In Esseberg we have no police,' she says, her eyelashes frosted with ice crystals. 'Once the tunnel's locked for the night we are left completely on our own.'

5

Post-search party *glögg* mulled wine is served in the church youth centre. I stay for five minutes but then weariness hits me: one wave after the other. Also, hot festive wine with dried fruit and nuts feels to me like an inappropriate way to conclude an unsuccessful search for a missing person.

I shuffle back to the Golden Paradise B&B via Willy's, my hood tight around my head. The store is almost empty. People are sweating in their layers, pushing carts full of canned soup and Styrofoam-packed elk mince. A couple argue animatedly in the frozen fish aisle, and then their son gets involved and starts moaning and the mother turns to him and says, 'Who shit in your eggcup?' and the argument promptly fizzles out.

I buy polar bread and ice-cream and chocolate and three bottles of Coca-Cola. Noora would have given me side-eye. Tammy would probably sneak lettuce into my basket.

Nobody else out on the walk home. *Home*? For now. Streetlights glowing through floating ice crystals, and the absence of any moving vehicle whatsoever. A town in stasis. Cryogenically frozen. I trudge through hardened slush and consider the laws of thermodynamics, which are, in my opinion, among the most poetic of all the physical laws. Entropy, especially. The phenomenon of everything slowing over time. Losing energy. Cooling. All of us: you, me, and everything else in the universe. Grey hairs. Calming down. Fading away. The blessed, gradual finality of it all.

I do not fall asleep like you would. Not if I am in a strange place, and especially not on the first night. Before switching off my bedside lamp I check for anchor points: a strip of faint light beneath the door, the red flash of a fire alarm on the ceiling. Anything to navigate by if the main lights fail and I need to evacuate. With no visibility and no hearing aids I rely on these details.

Eight hours of deep, dreamless sleep.

With thin walls like these, a hearing person may experience a disturbed night.

Not me.

Coffee, shower, more coffee. I have morphed into a Scandinavian trope since Noora died. But this is to replace the rum, you see. I drink too much coffee now. Far too much. Sue me.

Before I make it outside into the new day, the fresh darkness, I edit a piece on a hunting accident in Utgard forest that resulted in a hand amputation, and send it to Lena. I check in with Tam, send her a revolting little meme, and then, once I have judged the hour to be decent, I check Eniro for contact details of the missing teenager's family. No parents listed in the household, just a grandmother. With a little research, I discover his mother died years ago and, according to an interview he gave to an ice hockey blogger from Norway, he has never met his father. I make the dreaded call.

'Hello?'

'Mrs Wikström. My name is Tuva Moodyson. I'm a journalist trying to help find Peter.'

'Hello?'

I speak up a little. 'Can you hear me, Mrs Wikström? Could I meet with you for ten minutes today, please? Buy you a coffee?'

'You're helping find my Peter?'

'I am.'

She coughs. 'Thank you, dear. He never leaves me. He never would.'

'Can we meet? It would help if I knew more about him.'

'I can't go far.'

'I can come to you if that's easier? I'm here in Esseberg.'

'You're here?'

'It's a lovely town.'

She doesn't say anything to that.

'When would suit you for me to visit? I can bring coffees?'

'Can you come in an hour, dear? Is that too soon?'

'An hour is fine.'

'No need to bring anything. I have coffee in the pot.'

Once I am dressed in my life-preserving gear, I take an indirect route to her apartment. The sun is struggling to illuminate this concealed world. It never rises above the mountaintops this time of year. Esseberg has indirect light, sure, but never sunshine. I expect you will find locals standing outside their houses and offices in March to soak in the first direct rays of the year. We do that in Gavrik, so God knows they'd need it here.

I pass a red-haired man wearing shades of orange and brown. He is walking around with a bag of nuts and he asks me if I have seen the squirrel. I break it to him that I have not.

There is a ski lift running from behind the church car park up the mountainside. It is a rather old-fashioned chairlift and it creaks as it moves. There isn't a single person using it. This being early December, perhaps it is too soon in the season.

A queue has formed outside the tattoo place and as I walk closer a police car slows. It has a thick, mattress-size layer of snow on its roof. Two officers step out and I can tell by their uniforms that one of them is the chief here. I jog over to her.

'Excuse me, sorry to bother you, Chief. My name is Tuva Moodyson. I'm a journalist.'

'We're buying coffee,' she says, gruffly. 'Busy morning.'

She looks Sami. Like my maternal grandmother. Grey hair and intelligent, urgent eyes.

'Mind if I queue with you?'

She glances over at her colleague but they don't say anything, so I take that as a positive sign.

'I joined the search party last night.'

Again, they say nothing, which is not unusual up here. Only the Finns say less.

The queue shortens by one and we move forward.

'I was wondering if I could ask one of your officers some questions about the case? I work closely with my local police force back in Värmland.'

'Värmland?' she says.

'Gavrik town.'

'Never heard of it.'

Few have.

We move a step closer to the counter.

'I'd share whatever I can about the case, of course,' I say. '*Quid pro quo.*'

'Listen,' she says, unzipping her jacket a little. 'What would you know about this town? Our history? Our people? No offence, but we have our own journalists.'

'I want to help.'

'You want to sell newspapers.'

We move to the front of the queue and they order coffees and two cardamom buns.

'I'm deaf,' I say. 'I want to help find him.'

The chief takes a deep breath, pays with her card, then turns to face me. 'Tuva, right?'

I nod.

'We're overstretched. My patch covers more square kilometres than you can imagine. I've got two officers down with flu and another one just called in saying his daughter's off school vomiting so he can't come to work. Again, no offence, but you stick to your work and we'll stick to ours.'

I've had worse starts.

There's a chink of light there. Something I can build on.

On the walk to Mrs Wikström's building I check the stats on the *True Crime North* podcast mentioned last night. Over one thousand episodes. Reviews mention its adversarial approach, the tension on livestreams, unorthodox methods, not shying away from confrontation or sugar-coating the truth, and having multiple guests to ensure a lively debate. It appears regularly in the top-ten download list in Sweden and it is run by Johan Gustav Backman of Esseberg. Photo of him in a turtle neck looking mighty pleased with himself.

I reach the block of flats. Grit outside. A woman shovelling snow wearing a fleece-lined baseball cap and an XL ice-hockey shirt from a local team.

I buzz and she lets me in.

Her door is ajar.

'Mrs Wikström?' I say, smiling, offering her my hand.

She wipes her cheek with a tissue and says, 'Have they found him, dear? He's ever so afraid of the dark. Have they found Peter?'

6

Mrs Wikström's apartment is neat and old-fashioned. A dark wooden bookshelf, glass case of ornaments, and a walker parked in the corner. She has a small countertop dishwasher next to her sink with a rubber hose leading to the taps.

She signs to me that I am welcome.

'Oh, I'm sorry,' I say. 'I'm not fluent signing.'

'That's okay, dear.'

'I should really learn.' I want to. I'll take a course.

'Tuva,' she says. 'Such a pretty name. Unusual.'

'Thank you.'

She forces herself to smile but I can see in her eyes that she is deeply saddened that this conversation needs to take place.

'A cup of coffee?'

She starts to move to the kitchen slowly and I say, 'Can I bring the pot over? Save you the bother?'

'Would you, dear? My ankles.'

I bring over the pot, sugar bowl, cups and saucers, and a small jug of milk standing out next to a fruit bowl. Five years ago I wouldn't have felt comfortable doing this, but age, and caring for a loved one who could no longer care for herself, forces you to learn how to do what's needed.

She pours two cups.

'Is that Peter?' I ask, pointing to the framed photo on the coffee table.

'Taken last year,' she says. 'I've given a copy to the police, but it doesn't do him justice, really. Photos never do him justice. He's such a good boy.'

'Do you mind if I record?' I say, placing down my Dictaphone on the armrest of my chair.

She smiles and sips her coffee. 'They were out looking for him last night, all around the town and the surrounding pathways. Dozens of them even in that weather.'

'I saw them,' I say. 'So many people helping. A real community pulling together.'

'I wish I could do my bit,' she says. 'He's out there in the cold at this time of year. He takes walks every day, has done ever since he stopped training at the rink, and he strays from the pathways even though I tell him not to. He strays because he says the untrodden snow feels different under his boots. He likes the sensation of it. The vibrations, I suppose. I ask him to stick to the lit areas but he doesn't. He's never late, though. Not once. He knows I wait up so he's never home late. And now I worry his hearing aids will be running out of power. They might be off already. He's out there and people are screaming his name trying to help him and he can't hear them.'

That image gives me chills.

'Did Peter have his phone with him, Mrs Wikström?'

She shakes her head. 'He's been leaving it at home more and more. He's had some bother from other boys, old teammates. He left it here and now the police have taken it away to Åre.'

I make a note of that.

'Does he have any close friends I could speak with?'

'He put that up,' she says, ignoring my question and pointing to the artificial Christmas tree in the corner. 'Decorated it the day before he disappeared.'

'How did he seem at that time?' I ask. 'Any signs he was anxious or upset?'

She shakes her head sternly. 'No, it's nothing like that, dear. He was in a good mood. He was fine. It isn't that.'

I nod.

It could be that. It often is, and sometimes loved ones have no clue. One of the many terrible things about missing-persons' cases is their sheer number. Thousands each and every year. Many are solved within a few days. People have breakdowns. Some take a new lover. Others are lost. They are the good cases, relatively speaking. Then there are the unsolved stories. Some have fled overseas or taken new identities. But in reality there are a number, an incomprehensibly large number, who die alone or at the hands of another person. Chief Björn said to me last year how the criminals they catch, those I eventually write about in the *Gavrik Posten*, are the least competent ones. The smart criminals are still out there hiding in the shadows, or, more likely, in plain sight. Waiting to do it again.

'Look at his trophies,' she says, pointing to the top of the bookcase. 'He won't have them in his room anymore. Says they make him upset.'

'What happened?'

'You don't know? Peter was an ice hockey star in this town. Esseberg under fifteens top scorer two years running. He trained so hard.' She crumples a tissue. 'Ever since he was a little boy our bathroom's been full of his gear, smells awful it does, and the bathroom is small to begin with.'

'Impressive trophies.'

'Didn't last,' she says, pulling a new tissue from her sleeve. 'When he moved up a year early to join the under eighteens they never accepted him. He was proud as punch when he joined them for training but it wasn't long before they stopped talking to my Peter. They got frustrated he couldn't hear the commands and codes, I think. After training he couldn't follow their stories and he'd ask them to repeat themselves but they'd have already moved on. You know what teenagers are like.'

I do.

'Is there any chance he could have become lost? In a snow flurry, perhaps. How comfortable was he in the wilderness?'

'He's not lost,' she says. 'He was a scout. He knows his way around. And it wasn't bears or wolves, either. Someone on the telephone asked about that. He grew up here. He knows how to stay safe.'

'Are you his legal guardian, Mrs Wikström?'

She closes her eyes for a couple of seconds. 'His mother, God rest her soul, passed when he was eleven. We never knew his father. Lisa made me promise her to look after him. She had a tumour, you see.' She points to her stomach area. 'And now I've gone and failed them both. Him and his mother. Where could Peter be for all this time?'

I move closer to her. 'Everyone's out looking for him. I'm sure there will be news soon. He seems like a strong young man.'

She nods. 'He is strong. Strong like his mother.' She closes her eyes again for a few seconds and I feel, deep within myself, the quiet grace and power of this woman and her generation. And I feel the sorrow of Peter. An orphan, trying to fit in as a deaf boy in a forgotten town. Trying to navigate through his awkward teenage years. I relate to him and I feel for him.

She takes another sip of coffee.

'Please don't be alarmed by this question, Mrs Wikström, but can you think of anyone who Peter might be afraid or wary of? Any enemies?'

She thinks about that for a long time. 'Not enemies, no. He's a sweet boy. There was the thing in the supermarket, but that's all in the past now.'

I nod and take a sip of coffee. Let the silence hang in the air.

'It was three years ago.' She takes a deep breath. 'A misunderstanding. I don't know. Peter had an innocent crush, I suppose you could say; on an older lady working in Willy's. He was stacking shelves on weekends and she was working on the tills back then, just part-time. Now she has a job I don't honestly understand, something on the internet.'

'Do you remember her name?'

'Khalyla, dear. Beautiful name. Easy to remember. She's from the Philippines.'

'Khalyla,' I repeat.

'Works on the internet now. Photographs and all sorts. Peter follows her, shows me her little video recordings sometimes.'

I make a mental note to check her out.

'She lives in the hotel now, up on the mountaintop. I used to go there once a year as a girl, at around this time, in fact; they'd have a festive *risgrynsgröt* party for us normal towns-folk. Vast pans of rice pudding with cinnamon and nutmeg, all for free. They'd let us children take the skin from the pudding for ourselves. Grand place, it was then. We'd ride up in our best clothes on the rack and pinion railway. Closed now, it is. They have to transport food and supplies up using the old chairlift. Such a shame. Khlalya lives in the hotel with the son of the last owner. Eric, his name is.'

'Do you know his last name?'

'Lindgren. The Lindgren family.'

Some journalists would move straight past this detail but the minutiae matters, especially in an unfamiliar town. These titbits enable me to layer up the place and, as if using a 3D printer, form a dynamic model of it inside my head. A web of interconnections and relationships. A foundation I can work up from.

'My husband knew his father,' she says. 'Worked up there replacing some of the lifts after the war. Never thought much of Eric's father.'

'No?'

'My husband would say he's the kind of man who might quote himself.'

I smile broadly. 'I know the type.'

She lets herself smile. 'Lots of them about, dear.'

'Would you mind if I took a quick look at Peter's room, if that's not intrusive?'

She frowns.

'Only it would help me to write a complete article and do him justice. I want everyone out looking for your grandson.'

'I suppose that's fine,' she says.

I don't go in, I stand at the threshold. An old PlayStation and a small TV. A laptop covered in NHL team stickers. Shoes and socks on the floor. Ice-hockey posters all over the walls. A winter-Olympics themed duvet cover too young for him.

'I've let down his mother,' she says, behind me. 'I promised her.'

I walk back to her. 'I grew up deaf with no father. And honestly I'd have given anything for a grandma like you. You mustn't blame yourself, Mrs Wikström.'

I use my phone to photograph seven or eight photos of Peter. I load the dishes into her small dishwasher and then I say, 'Do you need any bread or milk? I could pop to Willy's for you, it'd be no bother.'

'You're a sweetheart. No, my neighbour helps me. But thank you, Tuva.'

I leave and the air is bitterly cold, perhaps twenty below. It is too cold to snow, and the wind is whistling down each street and alleyway.

I turn the corner and the police car I saw earlier passes me by.

I watch it stop right outside Mrs Wikström's apartment.

I watch the chief step out of her car with a serious expression, and stand in my old bootprints.

She puts on her police hat and then takes a moment to straighten it.

Deep breath.

She rings the buzzer.

7

My instinct is to surge forward, to ask what they have found, check if Peter is okay, if he's injured, but I force myself to hold back. I would be invested in any other missing-person's case, but with this young man it's personal. He is very much living a version of my life; only he's a dozen years behind me. I remember vividly how it was back then. The isolation and self-criticism. The all-consuming loneliness. Worrying I'd never form a meaningful relationship. The distinct and pervasive lack of hope.

The door opens. I can't see Mrs Wikström. The chief says something and then she removes her hat and holds it to her chest and I almost collapse to the snow. I can't lip-read any of them from this angle, from this distance, in this light, but I do not need to. I see it writ large in their bodies.

They step inside.

Poor Peter. Poor Mrs Wikström.

I could be wrong, though. I have been wrong before. This might be an update, is all. A scrap of clothing found, or an eye-witness report. Could be his bank flagging an ATM withdrawal made in Skellefteå or Orebro.

The town is noiseless. I check my phone; browse the multiple Facebook groups of Esseberg I joined yesterday, and I refresh the Twitter account of the church and the regional newspapers here in Jämtland.

I pause, my thumb hovering above the screen.

I cannot swallow.

They have found a body in the snow.

I look up again to the distant doorway.

Tears flood my eyes but I force myself to stay composed. I never knew Peter. But, I did know him in a way. I *was* him. There is very little moisture in the air at twenty below freezing. The atmosphere struggles to form snow at these temperatures. I take a deep breath through my nose and keep scrolling. No details. No specific location. Police have not yet commented.

I walk to the timber church hall where we convened last night. Where I left early. Vaulted ceiling with old wooden beams. Candles in glass candleholders. There is an old man in a Christmas pullover with a name sticker that says *Bertil Lind, Choirmaster*. I ask him if there is any news about Peter. He smiles and says. 'Not yet. I am praying for the boy.'

I walk out. The simultaneous brightness and dullness of a mountain day at this latitude. The stillness of this shrouded town.

It might be someone else. An accident or a heart attack. That's what Lena would tell me if I was standing in her office right now. But she would also tell me to trust my instincts.

The lighter side of the valley has no skiers. Nobody riding the rickety chairlift up to the hotel. The darker side mirrors it, only there is no chairlift but rather a serpentine network of cables leading up from the power station over the peaks.

I email Lars asking him to dig deeper for me, asking him for a location of the body.

Then I head to what I judge to be the best place to glean information in this town.

Willy's.

Pensioners pushing desperately empty carts with discounted yet overpriced dairy products: sour *fil* milk and sour yoghurt and fermented (sour) kefir. Small packets of pastries and cakes. Instant-coffee granules. Cooked ham.

I ask a cashier if he has heard anything and he frowns and shakes his head. I ask another and she asks me where I'm from so I tell her. She looks me up and down and then says her daddy doesn't much like Värmland people. I nod, tell her I feel the same way. She suggests I try the Facebook group. Then she suggests I visit the tourist-information office.

I step back outside.

A tourist-information office in this town? I google it. Ninety seconds away. I walk along salted pavements and find a shed-size kiosk with an open hatch. A long-haired teenager in ski clothes plays a game on his phone. His screen is cracked and he seems surprised to see someone approach.

'Excuse me. Is there any news on the missing teenager, Peter Hedberg?'

The young man looks puzzled.

'Have you heard anything? I'm a journalist.'

'You're a journalist?'

'Do you know where they found Peter?'

'I'm here for tourism questions.'

'Do you know where they found Peter?' I ask again.

He points towards the tunnel.

'Where exactly?'

He sticks out his lower lip and says, 'About 7 km out of town, I'd say. No marked paths or ski routes that way. Nothing to show you where it is. Blank snow. No features at all to guide you. Follow the police tracks, I guess.'

I thank him.

'Good luck,' he mutters, returning to his phone.

I head out in that general direction and after a while I indicate to nobody and leave the main road and venture up an old lane that hasn't been ploughed.

I follow deep tire tracks like the kid suggested.

Everything around me is brilliant white. A dazzling, silent sea of nothingness.

In the distance.

One grey forensics tent.

8

The sky is empty.

Not a single bird or cloud.

Police enter the tent, careful not to afford me or the other seven people assembled on this side of the police tape a view of what is inside.

This place is otherworldly: an orderly crime scene on a lunar landscape. Hazy whiteness in every direction. Forensic specialists wearing white suits and white boot-coverings over their thermal underclothes. A harsh and challenging environment in which to enjoy a hot chocolate, never mind investigate a potential homicide.

Because that is what this is.

Have no doubts.

In San Francisco or Lagos this might turn out to be an accident or coronary. This might not be the missing person you're looking for. But in a place as cut off as Esseberg I will jump to a conclusion because it would be absurd to do anything else.

Five years ago I might have been sick to my stomach at this news. A deaf teenager in a marginal town who used to play competitive ice hockey. A beloved grandson. I am still shocked but I have seen too much to be sick. I'm here. Doing the job I am paid to do. Bearing witness.

I photograph the scene in as much detail as I can. Three police Volvos, one Volkswagen, and one police van. A man with a thermos and a Russian-style hat watching all this far away from the rest of us, steam rising from his cup. And then I video a woman in a white suit as she sprays something onto the snow, onto a footprint. Thord has explained this process to me. He has assisted highly trained forensic specialists from Karlstad on more than one occasion in the cold months, usually to maintain a scene and keep other people from contaminating it. The woman is spraying snow-print wax or something similar into the footprint depression. Then she mixes dental stone, or alpha-calcium hemihydrate, into a Ziploc bag. She uses her hands to squeeze and combine the contents. Then she pours the dental stone mix into the footprint indentation and walks away.

I take notes on my phone.

This kind of forensic science is not as bulletproof as DNA analysis. Not even close. But sometimes, if a print is clear, it can help build a picture. I have heard from Thord that the 'accidentals' can sometimes be more valuable than the tread pattern. I asked him what he meant by *accidentals* and he said it was the unique patterns created on the sole through wear. Those patterns can prove invaluable to the building of a criminal case.

I record more video.

'You shouldn't film them,' says the older woman next to me. 'It's disrespectful to the dead. We wouldn't do that around here.'

'I'm a journalist,' I say.

She doesn't respond. I take close-up photos of the tent.

She mumbles something else.

'Sorry, I didn't catch that.'

'I said you still shouldn't.'

'I know what you're saying,' I tell her. 'But the most disrespectful thing would be to not fight for the truth of what happened to that young man. My job is to write his story. To make sure as many people as possible read about what happened here in the hopes we can bring his killer to justice.'

She stiffens up. Takes a moment. 'Who said anything about a killer? You *know* he was killed? These temperatures, all the way out here, a broken ankle could end you.'

I think about that.

She's right, of course. This could be a fall or a brain haemorrhage. It could be a previously undiagnosed health condition: a congenital heart defect or aneurism. She is right to be cautious.

Text from Lena. Screenshot from an online news service.

Body found in deep snow outside Esseberg, Jämtland. Police say a male in his late teens or early twenties has been found. Police are calling the death suspicious. There were signs of a struggle. Police ask for anyone with any information to contact Åre police.

Late teens or early twenties.

Peter was eighteen.

He never had the chance to embrace adulthood, to grow into himself, to find his voice, to leave this locked town. He never made it out the damn tunnel.

A red-haired woman approaches. She seems to know the older woman next to me.

They talk.

I photograph the forensic specialist removing a stone-like cast from the snow now that it has had time to set. She places it carefully inside a cardboard box and carries it to one of the Volvos.

'I heard it was the boyfriend, most likely,' says the redhead woman. I suspect she's around my age. Maybe thirty or thirty-five.

'Peter had a boyfriend?' I ask.

Her eyebrows arch. 'I mean the boyfriend of one of the local girls. You wouldn't know. Peter used to, I don't know if I should say.' She turns to the other woman. 'You know about it, Marie. You know, right?'

The older lady nods her head disapprovingly.

'What?' I ask.

The redhead says, in a hushed tone, 'He had a reputation for, feels wrong to say it out loud, but locals said he'd make people feel uncomfortable. Girls, especially. I know there was trouble in the high school over it; Peter was in a fight with one of the hockey players, who accused him of flirting with his girlfriend.'

Jealousy and rage are powerful drivers. Lena has told me about stories she covered in New York of men killing because someone propositioned their girlfriend on the street. One case of a mechanic politely offering to buy a woman a drink in a city-centre bar, and her husband shooting the man in the head outside in the parking lot later that same night.

'My neighbour told me,' the redhead goes on, 'Peter would, and I don't want to speak ill of the dead, and I don't know much about sign language, but I heard from my neighbour he'd stare at girls' mouths, like, I don't know, flirting, unnecessarily, you know, unsolicited, and it made them feel ill at ease.'

'He was probably lip-reading,' I say, sternly.

The old lady steps away from me a little.

'I know,' says the redhead. 'Everyone knew that he did that. But the boys in the school didn't care. They said it was inappropriate.' She turns to the older woman. 'Marie, are you cold? I'm freezing out here. What do you say, should we drive back into town together? It'd be safer that way.'

Turning my head, I face the mouth of the tunnel.

I have a sudden urge to flee through it.

9

The mountains darken, as if retreating. Later this month – solstice, Christmas week – this town will reach peak winter. A few hours of milky daylight buttressed by long, inescapable stretches of gloom. A settlement lost in the base of a valley; the opening of the tunnel like some mythological beast's eye gazing wearily from the bedrock.

People exit the crime scene. Others arrive. Groups of locals in goose-down jackets shuffle their feet to keep warm. One statuesque woman wears a long white coat and no hat. It is unsettling to see someone without a hat on a day like this. Her hair is black and long and she wears white fur ear muffs. She looks on from the far side of the police, well away from the rest of us.

The people in white suits emerge slowly, cautiously, from the tent, carrying a stretcher. The corpse is zipped inside a dark-grey body bag. Usually you would see them move from bungalow or apartment building to ambulance or coroner's van by way of a wheeled gurney. The transportation of dead weight. But you can't use anything like that here in the wilderness. You have to carry your cadavers like the ancients did before us. The carriers take care with their footing, moving slowly through disturbed snow towards the open doors of the police van. And then, once the doors close, the deceased is taken away from this place.

I try to ask a question of the chief as she walks to her car with two other uniformed officers but she blanks me.

More people withdraw. It is not that they don't care or that they are not interested, but it is below minus 20 Celsius. It is necessary to leave. There is no other option.

A couple by my side talk about the elegant woman in white with no hat. One says, 'Good of her to grace us with her presence. I thought she only came down from the mountaintop if she was being paid for it.' Her partner says, 'She short-changed me once on my weekly shop. I never queued at her till after that.'

Police-car headlights illuminate the scene.

An officer walks towards us. He looks tired and there are crystals of frost in his grey moustache whiskers.

'Go home now, all of you. It's time for you to go.'

We do not leave.

'Go on, now. The night is falling. Go home.'

He has a point. It is indeed falling. Crashing down and shrouding us all: locking us down by virtue of the lack of available exit routes. A daily time bomb, regular as clock-work. *Tick-tock.* The night is falling upon our heads and all around us.

I climb into my Hilux pick-up and turn on the heated seat, heated steering wheel and main fan. It takes a while to warm up. I rub my hands together and catch sight of myself in the rear-view mirror. A red-eyed ghoul with frazzled blonde hair. This deep into the year I am as pale and unappetizing as rancid cream. A dry, flaky husk of a person.

I drive away, my tyres struggling to gain purchase.

A train emerges from the tunnel and follows the track parallel to the road. I drive with it. Two vehicles moving headfirst into oblivion. The wagons are full to the brim with non-recyclable domestic waste and the engine car is ensconced with graffiti, most of it black and red.

I keep driving.

The town is quiet. I suspect it is always quiet. Those who live elsewhere are fixing to leave for the night. Those who live within this steep-sided bowl of a mountain valley are completing their chores, buying their goulash soup in a tin, and heading off home with their necks bent against the gusts.

The authorities will need to allow the body to thaw before an autopsy can begin. Chief Björn mentioned this one time in Gavrik. A deep-frozen body, sometimes referred to as a *popsicle* by morgue workers, needs to be thawed slowly to room temperature so not to accelerate decomposition. I have to shake that image from my head.

You know what else is unnerving? Working in a town where I have no office or home. No base. I am not used to it. I walk through the solarium, some lizard of a woman passing me, sweat beading along the bridge of her nose due to the ultra-violet pummelling she has just paid money for. Good for her, to be honest: a rapid two week holiday condensed into twenty minutes of claustro-phobic grilling. A vacation in a can without the airport hassle. Maybe *she's* the one winning at life after all. I unlock my bed and breakfast (no breakfast) room.

Tiredness hits me in waves as I drag off each layer of windproof clothing. Peter. Eighteen. An ice-hockey player not welcome in the big team. A deaf student and friend. A boy. A man. A grandson.

Gone from this world.

I email Lena explaining how the story has developed. I tell her I need another day or two in this godforsaken town. It is up to me to do Peter justice somehow. To write about his short existence and still make it fill our pages. To bring him back to life in the minds of readers. This is my solemn responsibility. There is no other journalist here as far as I can tell. They may be on their way, but the ones who arrive will be those who picked the short straw. The journey alone is an endurance event. This young man's life will be barely reported on by reason of his geographical isolation. It was always going to be this way, and that makes my job all the more vital.

I dredge social media for Peter's connections. I try all the usual places but he had very little online presence. I send messages to several of his old school friends asking if I can speak with them.

A coffee. A half packet of gingerbread biscuits. Another coffee, this time with more sugar.

An email notification on my phone.

The mere sight of it takes the breath from my lungs. *Amy.* I only know one person called Amy. I don't even know her. We have never met. I start sweating. It is from Amy. My goodness. I never expected this so quickly. She asks if next Sunday would suit me. My fingers are trembling over my phone screen. I am not ready for this. I will never be ready. And yet I want to meet her. I desire it. I reply *Perfect. Thanks. 3pm?*

Part of me wants to hibernate like I did after Noora died. Hide away and cocoon inside my bed. But I make the effort to pull on my wet jacket and slushy boots and head out to face this place once again. I trudge over to the church hall because there are candles burning outside in the snow and that is a universal Swedish sign that you are open.

I venture in.

Twelve or so people sitting, drinking *glögg* mulled wine or festive *Julmust* soda. One is reading a newspaper and I am curious which one it is.

I pour myself a coffee. I know, I should cut down, add it to the list.

A place like this is vitally important to any small, cut-off town. Even as a cold-blooded cynical atheist, I can see it plain as day. Churches and their halls and community centres are life support. A quiet place of reflection, a food bank, a shoulder to cry on, a place where families come together for weddings and funerals and christenings. Places of worship, of all denominations and faiths, are lifelines.

The vicar's wife smiles and approaches.

'You're the newspaper reporter from out of town?'

'Yes. I'm Tuva Moodyson from the *Gavrik Posten.*'

'Hilda. You're very welcome here.'

I smile. 'I'm so sorry. About Peter.'

She nods. It doesn't make any logical sense that I say *sorry* to her, but she understands what I mean. Perhaps I lived in England too long. Their national sport of constantly apologising must have rubbed off on me. Hilda is, plain as day, a cornerstone of this hidden-away ice-encrusted town, and she accepts my clumsy token of empathy with grace.

'I have lived in this valley my whole life,' she says. 'Seventy years next spring. Peter was such a pleasant boy.'

'It's shocking.'

She wrinkles her eyes for a moment. 'When people say you have to keep the wolf from the door they mean it figuratively. When we say it here in Esseberg, we mean it *literally*. My husband, my neighbours, the teachers and carpenters, they all work hard to keep the wolves from our doors. They are out there, you see. Wolves come in many forms. We keep the bears from the schoolyard and the lynx from the nurseries. We have no choice. The bible talks of shepherds. Of protecting the flock. We are all brought up as shepherds and sheepdogs by necessity. We do our best to keep watch. And today, at this frozen, savage time, we failed, and a wolf broke through our ranks.'

10

A frail man wearing a long sheepskin jacket walks in, and the Deacon's wife goes off to sit him down and bring him a mug of something hot. I observe this church hall. A bookshelf serving as some kind of casual library, sparse tables from IKEA, radiators on full blast, a self-service table with buns and bread and soup. The kind of room we have needed for millennia. We may always need them.

The deacon's wife comes back over.

'Can I ask you a question?' I say.

She nods.

'Who do I need to know in this town?'

She looks around the room then leans in closer to me. 'You don't *need* to know any of us.'

I smile. 'You know those little dogs hunters send down holes to catch rats? I'm one of those. I never realised it until this past year. I go down the holes too tight for others to fit through and I come back up with useful things.'

She frowns at me.

'I will find out what happened to young Peter Hedberg. I have the patience of a wronged parent. I will not stop.'

'Somehow, I believe you.'

'Who should I be speaking with, Hilda?'

'My husband, when he has the time. You might also try Chief Skoglund, and Ulf Samuellson. He works the door at Wrath.'

'A priest, a cop and a Hells Angel walk into a bar . . .'

She smiles flatly. 'They do in this town.'

'Anyone else?'

'Bertil Lind, perhaps? He's our long-suffering choir-master so he's seen many of the locals grow up. Painfully shy but I can introduce you. Most people around here are tight-lipped. They are eking out a living and they don't welcome any trouble.'

'They've got trouble.'

She takes a sip of tea. 'We've had people go missing before. A few years ago. People care until they don't have the energy for it any longer. They need to keep moving forward. Stacking their firewood and paying their taxes. The person's still missing but locals need to prepare for winter, for the next unavoidable hardship. They move on and keep pushing.'

'Who else do I need to speak with?'

'There's Sven, I guess. He runs the power station. He's not the boss over there but he manages the men who do the actual work, most of them Wolverines. And then there's one of Bertil Lind's choir stars, at least back when he still had the voice of an angel. You probably know about Johan already. He has one of those new podcasts everyone is so interested in. All sorts of guests fly up here to speak with him. It's about awful crimes. Not my sort of thing at all.'

'Where can I find him?'

'Find him?'

I nod.

'You can find him driving a piste-basher every night. He grooms the slopes for the hotel. That's your best bet as he lives outside town. Now, if you'll excuse me, I need to check everyone's okay.'

She leaves.

They are not okay. They may think they are but I can sense an oppressive weight in this settlement, like a heavy chemical cloud weighing down on everyone from above.

Appropriately, it is foggy when I emerge onto the street.

I walk a few doors down to the ski-hire store.

The door bleeps as I enter.

'How can I help you?' asks the moustached blue-eyed man behind the counter. He's backdropped by racks of skis and boots.

'Can I buy a lift pass here?'

'You sure can.'

I approach. The store smells of boot sweat and air freshener.

'Day pass or a weekly?'

I check the prices on the board. Is it bad that for a hearing missing person I'd choose a day pass but for Peter I'm considering a weekly? It probably is bad. But it is also the truth.

'I'll go for a weekly, please.'

'Well, I'm happy to hear it. The powder is exceptional. You have all the equipment you need or you want to hire gear? I'm running a five per cent discount until Wednesday.'

Five per cent? This is typical in Sweden. One of Lena's neighbours asked her builder for a ten per cent discount on the cost of their new three-bedroom flat-pack home. The builder told them: *sure, ten per cent off is fine, but your house will be ten per cent smaller.* Scandinavians don't really negotiate.

'No need for gear. I want to check out the hotel on the top.'

'Are you going up there now?' he asks. 'In the dark?'

'The lift's open, isn't it?'

He looks out of the window at the inky mountains beyond and nods.

'Lift closes at eight prompt,' he says, his bushy eyebrows twitching. 'If you're not on the last run down you'll need to stay in the hotel, and it's pretty expensive up there. Eight o'clock is your last chance.'

He hands over my lift pass. It looks like a credit card.

'Got it. Thanks.'

I check my phone again. No mention of a police presser on the official website. No updates whatsoever.

It feels all kinds of wrong to jump on a ski lift and ride up a steep mountainside on the same day a young man's body was found frozen solid in the snow. In a city it wouldn't be so strange carrying on with your life following such an event, but in a place as intimate as this, it feels disrespectful.

Few people out on the streets. One man pushing a buggy: the kid inside covered in more layers of blanket and hi-tech fabric than your average climber on Everest.

The chairlift squeaks, causing piercing interference in my aids.

I approach the queue of zero skiers and present my pass to the barrier and it opens automatically. There is one man here supervising. He wears a bright red ski jacket and a matching red hat with ear flaps. I can see he has a tattoo of a cross on his right cheek, beneath his eye.

I move into position and someone arrives behind me suddenly, almost pushing me into the snow. She apologises. The woman is carrying two large fabric bags.

We sit together awkwardly on the chairlift and it lifts us off the ground. Two people on a chair built for three. She is in the middle seat and I'm on the far end. The whole thing is out of balance. Rushed. We're leaning quite severely to one side.

'Nice day for it.'

She doesn't know. Surely she doesn't know. But how could she not know in a town this small?

'You live here in Esseberg?'

'I was born here. Four brothers and three sisters. You're an outsider. I can always tell.'

I need to mine this lady wearing a misshapen fur hat for information. A captive audience if ever there was one.

'I'm Tuva Moodyson.'

The chair leans even more as she contorts herself to offer me a gloved hand.

I take it.

'Klara,' she says. 'Klara Svensson.'

'Your bags look heavy,' I say.

'They *are* heavy. Wine for the hotel. I bring it to them from the Systembolaget in Åre when they run low in the cellars. They stock expensive wines there. French grapes.'

I wish she was sitting in the far seat. But now it's too late to do anything about it.

'You want me to hold a bag for you?'

She eyes me suspiciously for a split-second and then says, 'Would you?'

I take the canvas bag. Six bottles inside. One of the labels says, 'Margaux.'

She has a pretty face but her mouth is broad and I can't help thinking, somewhat ungenerously, that it resembles a duck's bill.

'Very sad news,' I say.

'Peter Hedberg? Awful. His poor grandmother. He was her last living relative.'

'So sad,' I say. 'Who could do such a thing?'

'What do you mean?'

The chairlift rises dramatically up and over a vertical cliff of black granite.

It shudders.

'I mean,' I say, holding on tight. 'Assuming he was killed by someone. I heard there were signs of a struggle.'

'He was depressed, Tuva. I know about people because I used to work with the church youth programme. People talk. He didn't have many friends in this town. Peter was an outsider. I think he made this terrible decision for himself. Which is another kind of struggle, I know, and it is very sad.'

'I guess we'll find out soon. Is there anyone in the town who could have hurt him?'

'In this town?'

I adjust my grip on the safety bar and she says, 'It's high, eh? And in the dark, with the floodlights this weak. It's hairy, isn't it?'

I nod.

'Town keeps itself to itself, Tuva. We have the Wolverines to make sure of it.'

'You keep mentioning Wolverines. Who are they exactly?'

'They are the men who congregate at Wrath, the pub outside town. They're kind of like a team to keep watch over us all. The deacon keeps them in check, don't worry. We have no official police of our own in Ice Town but the Wolverines do their best.'

'I'd like to meet your deacon.'

'I bet you would. The deacon's a busy man. He doesn't tend to mix with people he doesn't already know.'

'Are the Wolverines a biker gang?'

She takes back the wine from me. 'I knew you weren't from these parts.'

'Värmland.'

'Southerner.'

Hardly.

'Wolverines are good men. Fair. They keep us safe.'

Not from what I can see, duckface.

'What's the hotel like?'

'The Pinnacle?'

I nod, and she puts on her ski mask against the cold. A mallard with goggles.

'Used to be a famous hotel. The King came here to ski in the forties. It still looks luxurious if you don't stare too close, but most of it's locked up now. Can't afford the heating costs. Eric wouldn't like me telling that to you, he's convinced he'll still find some Saudi or American money to inject into it just in time. A little delusional, my husband says.'

'Eric?'

'Eric Lindgren. He owns the Pinnacle. His family built it a hundred years ago and aside from his training at The Grand Hotel in Stockholm back in the day, he's been here his entire life. Eric's furious that all our ski custom went away when the major resorts became popular. Then his railway broke down, not the freight one, the rack and pinion that used to transport guests up to the hotel. Tremendous quote to fix it, there was. So now the only folks who stay are young snowboarders and such. You can't take a suitcase up there anymore so it's just young-sters with backpacks who ride this chairlift. They like the fact the mountains are so clear and challenging. I suspect Eric will be very displeased about all the police action today.'

'Displeased?'

She nods. 'He thinks of this as his family's private town. Some say he looks down on us all from his summit, but I think that's unfair. He will have been watching through his father's antique telescope and cursing all the atten-tion, though. If there's any news that reflects negatively on Ice Town and the Pinnacle, Eric tends to lose his temper.'

11

The anatine lady with the wine skis off elegantly to the rear of the hotel and I am left to trudge alone through the snow towards the main entrance. I can't see any lift supervisor up here. The whole place has the vibe of a safari park with no wardens, or a theme park with rides running all by themselves.

I turn around.

It is like being on top of the world looking down. Esseberg appears as a model railway village down there. It seems to come out of nowhere. Most places have motorways or lit roads leading in and out, connecting it firmly to the outside world. Not here. A dark mass of mountains all around, carpeted with thick snow, and then, as if placed down gently by some benevolent deity long ago, an illuminated self-contained town.

'Welcome,' says a booming voice just behind me.

I turn abruptly and say, 'Oh, hello.'

'Hello indeed. Welcome back to The Grand Hotel Pinnacle. Quite the view, isn't it?'

'My first time.'

'Really? I could have sworn I'd seen you before.' He looks down at the valley. 'Spectacular vista.'

'Stunning.' He ushers me closer to the entrance of the hotel and its revolving doors. I look up at the facade. Stone, in a style I would associate more with Colorado rather than Sweden, and then wood shingles from the second storey upwards. A Scandi version of The Overlook. Towering brick chimneys, and the hotel's name in gilt lettering.

'Please, do come inside.'

He has thin blonde hair with a side parting and pale blue eyes like mine. He's a little taller than me, fine-boned, with a slightly anglophile attitude, like he's impersonating a lord of the manor.

I follow him through the doors. Impressive flagstone floor, a roaring fire at the centre of the room, a pine reception desk with bell, and a brass luggage trolley on wheels.

'Let me show you to Reception,' he says.

'Oh, no, I'm only here for a drink if that's okay.'

He looks crestfallen but replies, 'Of course. Choose any table you like. I'll ask someone to come and take your order immediately.' Eric has an awkward warmth to him. He shows his disappointment outwardly and I can't help admiring that.

'What do you think of our town so far?' he asks.

'Scenic,' I say, trying to sound positive.

He smiles a rueful smile and I have to turn away. He reminds me of somebody.

There are no other people here. I have the whole place to myself.

After a minute or two Eric leaves to answer a call. He is replaced by a woman who approaches my table wearing cargo shorts with multiple pockets, a hammer hanging from her belt, and a blue denim shirt. The shirt emblem says, 'Grand Hotel Pinnacle.'

'What can I get you?' she asks, unsmilingly.

'A hot chocolate, please.' I've had enough coffee today to euthanise a small horse.

'Whipped cream?'

'No, I'm fine, thanks.'

She looks relieved. I guess her to be fifty or fifty-five, muscular and capable. She comes back through holding a mug of hot chocolate and places it down on my glass-topped wooden table.

'Lovely hotel,' I say.

She sighs. 'It will be when it's finished.'

I frown.

'We're doing a lot of renovations.'

'What's changing?'

'Most of it. We're modernising the place. Of course, the main improvement will be having the train operational again. Are you from Stockholm?'

'Originally, yes. But I live in Värmland now.'

'Lovely part of the world.'

Bizarrely, I find myself agreeing with her.

'When is peak season for you?' I ask.

She laughs and says, 'This is it, I'm afraid. Not easy competing with Åre, Sälen, and Hemsedal. But in my opinion we offer the best runs.'

'Best runs?'

She shifts her weight from one leg to the other, like she's in discomfort.

'Pistes. The purest downhill experience, particularly for advanced skiers.'

'Do you want to sit with me a minute? If that's allowed?'

She says no but then, after a few awkward moments, she sits down anyway and I can see she is relieved to take the weight off her feet. The fire in the centre of the room spits and crackles.

'We have the finest double black runs in Sweden,' she says. 'In all of Scandinavia, in fact. We've had Olympians stay at the Pinnacle. Slalom medallists. But these days it's usually thrill-seekers with backpacks.'

'No train,' I say. 'No suitcases.'

'Exactly,' she says. 'It's not easy. Our vintage chairlift isn't for everyone.'

'Have you worked here long?'

'Over thirty years,' she says, looking up at the ceiling for a moment. 'I knew Eric's father back when we were fully booked from one winter to the next.'

'You run the hotel?'

She cringes. 'No, I wouldn't say that. Eric runs the place. Mr Lindgren I mean. I manage reception, serve tables, cook in the kitchen. I organise for provisions to be brought up on the chairlift when needed. Oh, and I clean the rooms when we're short-staffed. You could say I wear a lot of hats.'

'Goodness. When do you sleep?'

'I don't sleep much, truth be told. I'm a genuine insomniac. Have been ever since I was a young child. I have the dark circles to prove it.'

I take a sip of the hot chocolate. It is rich and sweet. Delicious. She's grated fresh chocolate on top even though I asked her not to.

'Thanks for this.'

'You're welcome. Here on holiday?'

'Work. I'm a journalist. Tuva Moodyson.' I reach out my hand. I need to make contacts if I'm to dig deeper into this story.

She takes my hand. 'Karin Bates.'

'Bates?'

'American father. Minneapolis. Swedish mother. You're a journalist, you say? Web journalism?'

'No, the old-fashioned type. I'm looking into, well, it was a missing-person's case but now he's been found, unfortunately.'

'Awful business.'

'Did you know him?'

She shakes her head and I notice, out of the corner of my eye, an ornate chess board on the next table. It is set and the pieces look antique and hand-carved. 'I didn't know Peter Hedberg, no. But Khalyla did. She's Eric's partner. She used to work with Peter down in the town.'

I recall hearing about this.

'Friends?'

'I guess,' she says. 'I think the boy had a thing for her. Years ago, it was, when they both worked at Willy's.'

'Was there any bad blood?'

She strokes the claw of her hammer dangling from her belt. 'Bad blood? Oh, no, I wouldn't say that. Khalyla, unlike me, is a forgiving type. You could say she's moved up in the world. She's moved on from the stalking.'

12

As I stand up to leave, Eric Lindgren, the proprietor, approaches again and says, 'If you need anything else, a room for the night, a dinner reservation, let us know and we will do our very best to accommodate you.'

'You know what I'd like most of all, Eric? A brief tour.' He might know something. He's lived here all his life. 'Could you show me around?'

'Well,' he says. 'I'd be delighted, of course, but large parts of the hotel are closed for renovations at the moment. We are in somewhat of a fallow period, so to say.'

'It's just that I have a large readership at my news-paper down in Värmland. It might be fun to write a piece, perhaps early next year, about the town and specifically your hotel? I know lots of my readers are keen skiers.'

'Interesting.'

I seize my chance. 'And potential investors, too. People looking to buy shares or lend money to Swedish entre-preneurs. Gavrik is home to one of the largest pulp mills in Sweden as well as a privately owned liquorice factory. The other town I cover, Visberg, has plenty of old money sloshing around.'

His eyes light up. He wears his heart on his sleeve, this man, and I like that I can read him so clearly. 'Let's begin that tour.'

We walk and I notice the festive decorations for the first time. Pine-cone garlands draped around the fireplace. Knitted trolls, standing to attention, their eyes hidden by their pointed hats. Branches of spruce cut and set outside each main door like a green mat.

'We've been here ninety-eight years. We keep it in the family.'

'And before?'

'Before what?'

'Before the Lindgrens arrived.'

'Well, there was a small hamlet down in the valley, prospectors and miners, pioneers, hence the long tunnel. It was never really built for modern cars and trains, though. It's not fit for purpose.'

We pass through into a seemingly endless wooden hallway with uneven floorboards sloping down to the left, and he pauses next to a framed photograph.

'My grandfather's idea,' he says.

I look at the black and white photo and something is off about it. I can't put my finger on it.

'Your grandfather's idea?'

'Look closely at the image, Tuva.'

I look closely.

'Sorry, what am I looking at?'

'You are looking at a photograph taken in June. It is a Midsommar composition.'

'Late snow?'

'The piste is covered in salt, you see. Tons and tons of

sodium chloride. My grandfather invited his friends, regional dignitaries from Östersund, ecclesiastical relations, for the Midsommar festivities, and he managed to delight them all by miraculously, and at enormous expense, transforming summer into winter.'

I look again at the photo. There are wild flowers fringing the white piste.

'Extraordinary,' I say.

'Håken Lindgren was a truly unique individual. Despite being a religious man, a dedicated student of the Bible, he also had a frivolous side to his character. He installed the rack-and-pinion rail line as well, at great personal cost. It is my long-standing ambition to bring this hotel back to its former glory. The railway operational again, the lifts renovated, the pistes extended. If Åre and Sälen can jolly well do it then so can we.'

'Do you think the dead teenager will affect your plans in any way? I mean, that kind of news can be challenging for tourism.'

He scratches his blonde-grey hair and lowers his voice. 'Very sad. Only time will tell, I suppose. But we have endured tragedies here before. We've had our share of accidents. My own dear son perished on the black cliff when he was the same age as Peter Hedberg. The very same age.'

The black cliff? 'I am so sorry.'

He looks away. 'I still talk to him, you know; still argue with him sometimes.'

'What was his name?'

'Gustav. He was such a clever boy. Excellent chess player. In fact the rather eccentric, hand-crafted board out in the lobby was my Gustav's favourite object. He played a timed match on it with me the morning before he fell.'

'The priest's wife told me there had been dark periods in Ice Town over the years. I didn't realise you'd been affected so directly.'

'*Deacon.*'

'Excuse me?'

'We have no priest here in Esseberg. Sahlin is merely a deacon. There is an important distinction to be made.'

I nod.

'We're two years from our centenary here at the Pinnacle,' he says, opening the door to room 237. Is it unusual that a room with this number is situated on the ground floor? 'I intend to hold a celebration to rival those once hosted by my ancestors.'

We walk into the room and suddenly it is too small and Eric Lindgren too tall. He lingers in the doorway, between me and the corridor, and he says, 'I knew a Moodyson once when I was younger. Fond memories, in fact. She wasn't in Värmland, though. She was in Stockholm.'

'I'm from Stockholm.'

'It was before your time.'

I squeeze past him and head back into the main foyer of the hotel, the fire burning brighter than before.

'Have you met our Wolverines yet, Tuva?'

'The bikers?'

'Acolytes of the deacon, you could say. A most unusual set-up, I admit. They are his modern-day disciples, however unorthodox that may appear.'

We step outside. The snow glows blue and the sky is a pale pink. We are above some of the clouds and the town comes and goes in the valley below.

'Have you ever tried night-skiing?' he asks.

'I can hardly do it in the daytime.'

He smiles. 'Look down there. The cold air sinks and then it settles over the town. Snow everywhere: a beautiful eiderdown to hide sin; past and present. You cover a mass grave in enough snow and even that will appear scenic. Be careful down in the valley, Tuva. I was a parent once and I have never lost that protective instinct. There are tales to be told and there are local curses here dating back centuries. Stay out of the shadows and watch your back.'

13

The woman in white from the crime scene bursts out of the hotel and says, 'Eric, Eric, it isn't Peter. It's someone else. Thank God. It's not Peter.'

I gasp.

Eric looks pleased and then he looks at me and his smile fades. He walks over to her.

'That's ... thank goodness. Sorry, darling, this is Ms Moodyson. Ms Moodyson, my partner, Khalyla.'

Khalyla glances at me briefly and then turns back to Eric. 'I thought it was him. I thought Peter was gone.'

Eric shuffles on the spot and looks like he'd rather be anywhere than here right now.

'Do they know who it is down there?' he asks. 'The young man in the snow?'

I have a strong urge to grab my phone, to check the news, but that would be rude.

Khalyla checks *her* phone. She seems like the kind of person who isn't as encumbered by social norms. Hers has some form of elaborate selfie attachment at the rear. She says, 'I heard it from a friend but now it's all over social media. Nothing from the police. Rumours it was a young alcoholic. A Sami, most likely.'

'Well,' says Eric, deepening his voice. 'Let's not jump to conclusions.'

Damn right. And then I realise that I, also, have been jumping to conclusions. Lena would not have assumed the deceased was Peter. She'd have waited for a positive ID, for forensic results, for an official police statement. I let my mind run away with me because I am too personally invested in Peter. And because here in Esseberg I have no calm, experienced journalist in the next office to talk things over with.

Khalyla shows us her phone but she is too far away for us to see the screen clearly.

'I should go,' I say.

'Goodbye,' she replies, curtly.

Eric steps away with me for a moment and says, 'If you need a room you know where we are. Friends and family rates. And Karin will rustle you up a hot meal at any time, day or night.'

That makes sense. She told me she doesn't sleep.

'I'm sorry this is going on in your town. We've had similar tragedies in Gavrik and it always hits everyone in some way or another.'

'With any luck Peter will be found alive and well now, and we can all move on and make this resort what it used to be. So much potential up here, you see, Tuva. Best advanced slopes in all of Sweden.'

'So I've heard.'

'Of course, the Norwegians would disagree. But, they always do.'

'Reporter saying it was a drunk twenty-two-year-old from Vikböle,' Khalyla says, still looking at her phone. 'No name released yet.'

'I should go. I can still take the chairlift down?'

Khalyla doesn't look up from her scrolling.

'Yes, for another fifteen minutes or so,' says Eric. 'Try not to shift your weight around. Sit in the middle and keep the bar on your knees.'

Hardly inspires confidence.

I set off down the steep slope towards the lift barrier. Looking back to the hotel in all its former glory, part luxury hotel part dilapidated relic, I ponder what this kind of extreme isolation and disappointment can do to a person.

The chairlift squeaks and judders.

I move into position and brace myself and then it scoops me up and lifts me away. I pull the safety bar down but it won't budge. It is stuck. I look around desperately for help as I rise off the ground and descend down the mountain, up and down at the same time, and my boots feel heavier than usual. Like I'm being pulled lower. I heave the bar again and something gives. It crashes down and bangs hard onto my thighs with a dull thud.

My anxious breath clouds in front of my face.

Countless snowflakes falling gently between me and the town far below.

My teeth begin to chatter. The constant threat of northern climes: a quiet, unseen killer. You don't even know it is taking over. You slow down: entropy at work. The frog in boiling water, inverted. Hypothermia. You grow sleepy. And then you leave the world behind.

At the base of the chairlift, the man with the bright red coat and matching hat mumbles something I can't pick up as I dismount. The ground is icy. It sounds harsh through my hearing aids.

'Sorry, what did you say?'

He mumbles something else.

'I'm deaf.'

He mumbles again. Impossible to hear or lip-read in all our winter gear.

'I am deaf,' I say again. 'Can you repeat that, please?'

He walks up to me, right into my face, and with exaggerated diction, says, 'Careful. It's slippery. You could break your neck.'

I focus on the cross tattoo. The top section of the cross melts into the dark circle beneath his left eye.

'The bar needs fixing,' I say. 'It was stiff.'

He walks away from me mumbling again.

Meathead.

I continue briskly to the Golden Paradise B&B. I pour water from the kettle into my pot noodle and warm myself up from the inside. Best way. I don't have any bread left so I eat it with a croissant.

Back out there.

I walk towards Wrath, the biker bar, but receive a notification on my phone as I'm passing Willy's: *Police presser in the school gymnasium in forty minutes. Passes to be collected ten minutes before. No bloggers or internet journalists will be eligible for passes. Professional newspaper, radio and TV reporters only.*

A wood-panelled station wagon slows. Hazard lights on. Driver's side window down.

'Excuse me,' says a young woman my age. 'Do you know the way to the town school, please?'

In a city this would be a strange coincidence. In a town this small it's just what happens.

'Journalist?' I ask.

She looks apologetic and nods her head. I notice she is wearing two scarves. One burgundy, one navy blue.

'I'm heading there myself. Keep driving straight, left at the roundabout with the Circle K gas station. It's sign-posted before you reach the power station.'

'Don't I know you?' she asks, narrowing her eyes.

Another driver pulls up behind her and I make a gesture to apologise.

'Tuva Moodyson,' I say '*Gavrik Posten* down in Värmland.'

'Astrid Svensson,' she says. '*Norrköping Nyheter.* I don't think we've met but I recognise your face.'

The car behind doesn't beep, because we tend not to beep in tiny towns like this, but he does close the gap between the two vehicles.

'You'd better go,' I say. 'See you there.'

The road clears and I climb into my Hilux. I came here for a missing-person's case. Now I still have that same missing person, someone I desperately wish to find alive and well, but I also have an unexplained death.

The key question is: are the two linked?

14

On the way to the school gymnasium I find half a dozen kids on the lake playing evening ice-hockey. They are using piles of bags as goals and they're taking it in turns to fire a puck from their sticks. One wears a helmet with a Velcro patch on the back. It is an image of a Wolverine, white on black, within a red triangular border.

I drive into the school car park.

Mountains of ploughed and shovelled snow.

A pale brick building.

My stomach rumbles. Indigestion and angst.

The security lights burst on as I walk towards the door.

Warm air pushes my dry, brittle hair across my dry, brittle face as I step inside and I take a moment to push it back into place. I am tempted to put my hat back on to cover it up and save everyone the ignominy of having to avert their eyes.

Seven journalists seated.

One stands at the rear.

I take a seat on the second row. Back in Gavrik, Thord, my primary contact – an officer who used to be border-line incompetent but is growing more confident and useful with every year on the job – would have reserved me a seat right in front of the podium. Because I am the local reporter and almost a friend, but also because he knows I need to lipread.

I leave my bag on my chair and go place my Dictaphone next to the TV4 and SVT microphones already set up. I recognise one reporter, *Slickback*, a guy from Stockholm, and we nod to each other. The rest are most likely from Östersund and perhaps Strömsund. It takes a while to reach a place like Ice Town. I expect more of my peers will arrive tomorrow via airplanes and night trains.

The chief walks in and by her side is a younger guy with chinos and a striped button-down shirt. He has a name pass swinging from his neck but Chief Skoglund needs no such identifier.

'Thank you, everyone, for coming. Welcome.'

Her tone is more personable that Chief Björn's. He always looks like it's an inconvenience having us hacks inside his precious building. Perhaps she is less affronted because we're on neutral territory here. The realities of a northern town with no police station of its own. You use whatever public building you can.

She pours water for them both and we wait.

Flashbulbs as cameras capture the scene. Climbing ropes behind the stage. Some sort of pommel horse, and, surrounding it, dark red mats and pads.

She clears her throat. 'At approximately 13:45 yesterday Åre police department received a call from an Esseberg resident who had discovered an apparent body close to the tunnel while out walking her dog. My team responded, together with an ambulance from the local station. At approximately 14:30 the individual was pronounced deceased at the scene. We are treating this death as suspicious and have opened a formal investigation. The homicide team at Östersund police headquarters are assisting us with our enquiries, and we are also assisted by forensic specialists at Linköping National Forensic Centre. On behalf of Åre police I am requesting that anyone with information pertaining to this case come forward immediately.' She reads out the website, email and telephone details. 'Now, due to the ongoing nature of this investigation I may not be able to answer certain questions.'

She pauses.

The man next to her says nothing.

A journalist in front of me with a purple coat asks, 'Who is the man with you, Chief?'

'Sorry,' she says. 'This is Per Gustavsson. Per is the Investigator-in-Charge.'

He smiles. He does not look put out or slighted in any way.

Per steps forward. 'Thank you, Chief. This is an alarming discovery in a small community and my thoughts are with everyone affected. It is my understanding that door-to-door enquiries are being conducted in Esseberg and surrounding areas. We aim to work swiftly to discover what happened to this individual.'

'Chief?' says a tall man beside me. 'Do you have any suspects? Any idea of cause of death?'

She looks at the man by her side and then at us. 'I'm not going to comment on that right now.'

The man to my right goes on, 'There's talk the victim was found with a vodka bottle. That he was a local with addiction issues. Could this have been an accidental death, perhaps when taking into account the cold temperatures?'

The chief stiffens. 'No comment on the identity of the deceased at this time. I can say that the forensic teams are working diligently on toxicology, prints, trace evidence, footwear impressions and so on. CCTV evidence is limited due to the out-of-the-way nature of the scene, but it can help us piece together the individual's movements earlier in the day. Like you say, the cold weather is a complicating factor at this time of year.'

The tall man makes a note in his book.

Normally I would ask the first or second question but I judge I can gain more today from watching and waiting. I need to get a feel for the police, the investigator, but also for the local and regional journalists.

Astrid, the woman I gave directions to earlier, raises her hand. Her hat hair is even more dishevelled than mine, and for that reason alone I warm to her.

'Chief, there's a photograph circulating on Twitter of a mark around the victim's neck. Do you care to comment?'

I note that all the questions have been directed to the Sami police chief so far. This surprises nobody, least of all me. She has a quiet authority. Sometimes it is obvious who is in charge and this is one of those times.

'I won't comment on that and I'd urge you and your audience to treat any speculative content, photos included, with caution.'

I raise my hand.

She points.

'A question for both of you, if I may. The missing teenager, Peter Hedberg. Are there any updates? Is there a link that you know of between the two men?'

The investigator-in-charge adjusts his posture slightly, indicating he would like to answer. He says, 'That case is ongoing. I can tell you that Peter Hedberg didn't pack a bag or leave any note. No money has been withdrawn from his bank account. None of his cards have been used since his disappearance. He did not take his phone. We'd urge anyone with information on Peter's whereabouts to contact local law enforcement. Peter is not in any trouble, I want to reiterate that. His family are keen to know he's okay.'

His *family*. That sounds like a whole gaggle of people gathered around a Christmas table laughing and cheering, children and elders, everyone leaning on one another. Whereas in reality it is one elderly lady desperate to see her grandson again. The word has too much spectrum built into it, too much range. She is the entirety of his family and the vulnerability of that twists my stomach. It reminds me too much of my own childhood.

The man at the back of the room, the only person still standing, says, 'Accounts of Peter Hedberg walking around in the neighbourhood where the latest victim was found dead. Accounts of him walking and jogging there regularly with no headlamp or torch. Is it true that, in actual fact, Peter Hedberg is your prime suspect in this case?'

15

The chief wraps up the presser without answering the man's question. Once they have vacated the stage everyone chats among themselves about Peter Hedberg, or the body, or whether it is possible to get a decent meal and a bed for the night in this veiled place. It is all too much for me, though. I don't even feel guilty slipping out the door first. With so many voices coming at me all at once there is no way I can keep up.

The freezing air hits me as I exit. The barbarity of it. Snow and ice comes in myriad forms: this is the kind of breeze that carries tiny glass fragments with each gust. It burns, and it cuts deep into your skin.

The podcaster is lingering outside. I admire his resolve, honestly I do. He is talking into his digital SLR camera with a ring light illuminating his big, almost-handsome, heart-shaped face, picking out his grey-blonde stubble and blue eyes. As I pass, my head down, he pounces.

He does not ask permission to film me like a journalist might. He just includes me in his amateur performance.

'What's your theory on the body?' he asks.

My appalled face is clear to see in the tiny pop-out screen attached to the camera.

I can't say *no comment.* I'm not that much of a bitch. So I just keep on walking.

'The deaf teenager. Any views? Any leads?'

Does he think I'm police?

'Listen, hold up,' he says, moving to stop me in my tracks, blocking my path. 'Wait a sec, lady. You have your official pass and all; you have privileged access, but let me make one thing clear. Your newspaper in Jönköping or Lund or wherever it is you've come from; you'll get a few thousand reads, right? Five thousand, maybe. A few more if you're with a sensationalist tabloid, although most readers will skip right through your work, am I right? And yet you get prime access. Me, I regularly have hundreds of thousands of views and downloads. Sometimes millions. My shows are on average three hours long. And I don't receive a press pass with that kind of reach?'

Astrid, the reporter from the wood-panelled station wagon, joins me at my side. She says, 'Quality over quantity, bro.'

I can't help smirking.

'Legacy media,' he says, disgruntled. 'Have to move with the times, girls.' And then he walks away to hassle the other reporters.

'You want a coffee?' asks Astrid.

'No, I want a fucking beer.'

'There's a heavy-metal bar down the road,' she says. 'Only place in town, if I remember right.'

I smile again. 'Tempting, but I've got work to do.'

'Oh, please,' she says, narrowing her eyes. 'This *is* work.'

We walk out of the school grounds and she slips on ice.
I help her up.

'You okay?'

'You notice how this town smells *off*?' she says. 'Smells
metallic. No, it *tastes* metallic. Tastes like a damn
nosebleed.'

'It's probably all the garbage they burn.'

Astrid makes a face. She wears an unusual shade of
lipstick or lipbalm. Plum red.

As we walk west towards Willy's and Wrath we take a
break from talking for a block or two. I don't know about
her but I am digesting what the chief and investigator-in-
charge told us. How we now have a body *and* a missing
person, and how we don't know for sure if they are
connected. The thing is, in a town as miniscule and insu-
lar as Esseberg, they *must* be connected in some way.
Everyone knows it. It is up to me to work out how.

'Where are you staying?' I ask. 'The hotel up the
mountain?'

'Are you serious? I wouldn't stay there if they paid me,
and by the sounds of it, they'd need to. I'm at the Paradise
Gold. It's a B&B but they don't run to breakfast right
now. A dive, if I'm honest, but it's clean.'

I have to ask her to repeat herself once or twice because
of this incessant darkness, and she does so without
making me feel bad for asking. I appreciate that.

'I'm there as well. Golden Paradise.'

She glances at me. 'Figures.'

'Why do you say that?'

She adjusts her hat and says, 'The older faces at the
presser. They'll be staying on the other side of the tunnel

in Åre. Their papers might even have discount rates with Radisson or Clarion. No way they'd stay here after the tunnel locks down. Whereas us, on our budgets, we're left with whatever's left, and no way out.'

She's not wrong. Room 1 and room 2.

'I only got my reservation because someone else cancelled,' she says. 'Didn't realise it was in the middle of a sunbathing store.'

'People treat them like sad lamps,' I say.

'The patrons look like walking handbags. Dried-out mahogany skin in December. Tans that deep near the Arctic Circle in *December?* I mean, is that supposed to look healthy and natural?'

'Each to their own, I guess.'

'You're too generous,' she says, leaving the pavement to enter the gravel driveway of Wrath. A dozen or so Harley-Davidson motorbikes parked under snow shelters, a man-mountain bouncer at the door, and a dainty, flickering candle each side of him on the shovelled ground.

We walk up to the security guy.

'ID.'

'Bro, are you serious?' says Astrid.

He looks right over our heads like we're not standing in front of him. I reluctantly show him my driver's licence. Astrid does the same. He opens the door and an old Metallica song my dad used to listen to in his car seeps out to greet us.

Leather. Lots of it. Jackets, boots, and black cowhide banquettes. The scent of spilt beer. Tattoos. A bar with some kind of twisted metal and pipework art behind it, like a steampunk engine from a post-apocalyptic film set.

The bikers stare at us. Two blonde-ish, semi-frozen reporters from way down south. They react to us like they might react to a pair of stray cats.

We buy two beers and find a quiet table, relatively speaking. The music intensifies to death metal. Astrid tells me it is in fact Finnish *thrash* metal. I stand corrected.

'You think Deaf and Drunk are connected?' she asks.

'What?'

'You think they're linked? Think Deaf is the perp?'

'Don't fucking call them that. Jesus. Peter Hedberg is his name. You really just called them *Deaf* and *Drunk*?'

She holds up her hands. 'I'm sorry, okay? Seriously. I never meant anything by it.'

I move my hair aside to show her my hearing aids.

'Me and my big, stupid mouth. My big, stupid foot in my big, stupid mouth. I even knew you were deaf. We all know it. Tuva, I apologise. Gallows humour, I guess.'

The room vibrates from the speakers.

An anarchic cacophony of voices: conversations mixed and remixed into white, or perhaps black, noise.

She stares at me, waiting for my answer, and I have to look away.

After a deep breath I say, 'I don't know if they're connected. My gut says they are, but it also says Peter didn't kill the guy. My gut, for what it's worth, which isn't much, I've lost my edge these last two years writing about parking-ticket violations and school fights, says the body in the snow wasn't actually a murder.'

'The mark round his neck?'

I never saw any such mark. And anyway, grainy photos on social media can be doctored and filtered.

She takes out her phone and opens Facebook. She shows me the image.

'Jesus.'

'Yeah,' she says. 'He might have been an alcoholic, but he never deserved that. Someone strangled that guy out in the middle of nowhere. You have any idea the ice required in someone's heart to strangle a person with their bare hands?'

'Could it be a shadow or an old scar?' I say, zooming in. 'That photo was taken from quite a distance. It's not definitive.'

She answers but I cannot hear her. The music is more of a drone to me now, the beat shaking the floor beneath my boots. I have to focus hard to understand anything Astrid says and it strikes me once again that this is a particular type of exhaustion alien to hearing people.

A bartender drops a glass and cheers erupt, then four guys throw back their necks and howl at the ceiling.

'Chill place,' she says.

'Lives up to its name.'

'I heard there's a new search party going out with thermal imaging; a helicopter from Östersund if they can get it, and K9 teams.'

'Good.'

'Are they looking for a body, though?' she says, sipping her drink. 'Or are they looking for a person. And if they're looking for a Peter, is that because they fear he's at risk? Or is it to arrest him?'

16

When I wake from an angst-filled dream, it is pitch black in the room. I search around, my eyes blurry, searching for light, for my anchor points, for something to cling to.

I reach over to switch on my bedside lamp.

Click.

Nothing.

No light.

My heart starts to beat faster. The stale memory of rum on my tongue. I sit up and reach over for my hearing aids.

They're not here.

They are *always* here. They have to be. I can't hear anything and I cannot see anything. Taste, touch and smell don't really compensate for that.

I pull back the sheets and reach for my phone.

Nothing.

Is this a continuation of my low-grade nightmare, my tunnel drama, me being lost in these endless mountains in the dark, me screaming out for Peter and him screaming out for me and neither one of us understanding we're both freezing to death a hundred metres from each other in the central, deepest, unlit section of the tunnel?

My feet touch the floor.

Pulse racing.

I step over to the table and find my half-drunk bottle of Coke from last night. My underwear. My phone. My hearing aids. Thank God. I switch on the torch function and spin around with my phone. It's okay. I switch on my aids. My breathing slows. I pad over to the main light switch and the lights come on.

Three deep breaths.

I sit on the end of my bed sweating, trying to calm myself. There is nobody else to help so it is down to me. The realisation of adulthood. Of singledom. Of being a modern, uncategorised, unrecognised form of widow. Living solo. Nobody to place a soothing hand on my hip during a restless night, that light pressure, that support and gentle reassurance. None of it.

The bulb in my bedside lamp has gone. There are probably a thousand bright UV bulbs in the toaster oven of a solarium on the other side of the hall, and the bitter irony is not lost on me.

I step into the compact bathroom and wash cold water over my eyes.

December in Jämtland. It could be 3 a.m. or it could be 4 *p.m.* There is no discernible difference.

Last night I was talking to the formidable bouncer outside Wrath, the colossus doing a late shift. Imagine having to throw out bikers when they misbehave. He is a Wolverine, it turns out. We smoked cigarettes together while Astrid flirted with a random camo-covered snow-plough driver inside. The bouncer's name is Ulf. A solid Viking name for a guy twice my size who's skin is covered in dark green ink. We talked about the missing teenager.

Ulf told me he used to know Peter's mother; they went to Sunday school together. I asked him if he's still involved with the church and he told me he wasn't. It felt good to smoke outside the bar, to be away from the rage music and the many overlapping, incoherent conversations. I told him I was a reporter, working on a long-form piece, part of my new remit at the newspaper I work for, and he told me he was a poet. That's why you have to take the time to talk with people, I guess. Lena drilled it into me when she took me under her wing years ago. Listen, don't judge. The bouncer is a Sunday-school graduate and a poet.

It's 7 a.m. Far too early considering the night I had but it will have to do. I shower and pull on my ski underclothes, fourth day straight, and my tube socks. Six digestives and a pack of ready salted crisps for breakfast. Don't tell anyone. I find the other crisp flavours unconscionable so early in the day, but ready salted, in my opinion at least, passes for a deconstructed hash brown.

I step outside.

It is difficult to do the scene justice. The precise quality of this northern gloom. Occasional streetlights and headlights do their best to win a primitive battle, but in reality they don't even scratch the surface. You can light up a city. You can even light up a runway. But you cannot light up epic mountains that were formed by geological forces over millions of years. You can try but you will fail. To be quite honest, you can't even try.

Wisps of powder blow diagonally across the vague asphalt road. A snowplough turns in the distance. There is no need to indicate, it is the only thing on the road and it resembles an oversized lunar research vehicle. It approaches the diesel pumps of Circle K and then heads off past the school towards the incinerating power station.

High in the mountains, the piste basher, the plough's spiritual cousin, grooms red runs, driving between chairlift support posts, making the powder even and uniform, organising nature to suit our own absurd leisure requirements.

Two cappuccinos in the café at Willy's. My companions are pensioners. I like pensioners. They tend not to be too loud and they talk at a reasonable pace. They're here for an early shop, and for the hot, well-priced coffee, but they're *really* here for a glimpse of community life. At the top of the world, the end of the map, through the eye of the needle that is Esseberg tunnel, you cling to whatever marginal humanity you can find. You may not have a lover to caress you or a child to soothe when they wake from a dream, but you can always rely on your fellow shoppers.

I work for two hours on stories for Lena. She still needs me to feed her the articles that fill the *Posten*. I won't let her down because I am a diligent little monster, but also because she took me in after Noora died, just like she did after Mum died, and she let me be. No expectations or unsolicited advice. She fed me stews and spicy soups, leaving them at my door when I couldn't make it out, and she protected a space within which I could grieve. Lena has never been a mother but she has the most beautiful, genuine instinct for it.

I owe her everything.

Researching the body recovered in the snow – now identified as twenty-three-year-old Björn Akerman from

Angland outside Åre – I learn several pertinent facts. The time of death has been narrowed down to a two hour window between 8 a.m. and 10 a.m. The official reports mention the word *lividity*. This makes me think of the bible, of *Leviticus*. A morbid connection of my own making. Lividity is in fact the skin colour change that takes place after a heart ceases to beat. The report also mentions core body temperature, and the fact that blood toxicology reports have not yet been released. This is potentially important because there is a rumour that the victim was an alcoholic. Cause of death is listed as strangulation.

Strangulation.

The very thought of it.

Because, the thing is, you cannot strangle yourself. You can hang yourself, sure. You can self-asphyxiate in a dozen creative ways, but strangulation, to me, implies human hands tight around your neck, finger muscles digging deep into your windpipe, restricting air, cutting off oxygenated blood arriving to your brain. It implies hands-on murder.

Now we know for sure what has thus far been whispers and conjecture.

There is a killer here in Ice Town.

17

If this happened in Gavrik I would bother Thord for information. Fingerprints and fibre analysis. I would ask if they have any idea of hand size from any finger indentation marks. If that hand size might match to Peter Hedberg. But here, in a town dominated by steep-sided mountains and one of the deepest lakes in Jämtland, the police don't know me and I have zero leverage.

The important thing is to quickly establish a web of contacts and confidents, of informers and gossip-merchants. Lena calls them *leaky buckets*. It is my job to pull on all the loose threads and weave a story. And, in doing so, help in any way I can, hold the police to account when necessary, and attempt to find justice of one sort or another for the victims and their families.

Easier said than done.

Homesickness strikes me like a lightning bolt on a clear day. I stop and, facing a wall, scroll through photos on my phone. Tammy and me down by the reservoir. One of us both 'enjoying' a mosquito-infested picnic on the northernmost edge of Utgard forest last summer. Voluntarily. I don't know who I am anymore. And then there is one with Noora by my side. Tam on the other side. It steals my breath. We thought we would have years together. We assumed that was a given. And now I am here all on my own.

Something catches my eye.

A red Saab similar to my editor's slows as it passes Mrs Wikström's building up the street. I set off. Are they tabloid doorsteppers? Photographers? I speed up, careful not to slip on ice patches, and the red car moves away with a skid. A woman watches them drive off. She wears a fur hat with its own tail and she is walking a black cat on a leash.

'They didn't seem like they were locals,' I say, gesturing up the street.

The woman with the cat stares at me for a long time. 'Are *you* local?'

'Not really. But my grandmother was from up here. A little further north in fact. Sami.'

She stares at me again. She has no compunction about staring right into my face. I have to move away.

'Be careful out and about in Esseberg,' she says. 'Events are afoot.'

'What do you mean?'

'Come back from the curb, Potemkin,' she says to the cat, her voice soft, almost coquettish, when directed to him. 'Potemkin doesn't do well with strangers, do you Potemkin.'

Potemkin, a sinewy feline, brushes up against my shin.

'Lovely cat,' I say.

'Not mine. I'm walking her for Mrs Wikström.' She stares at me for my reaction.

'That's kind.'

'Having trouble, she is.'

'I know.'

'Her boy is missing out in the hills.'

I nod.

'To think all this is going on right before Santa Lucia. The whole town turns out for it. We usually fill the church to the rear pews. A celebration of light, and all this happened. It's a confounded mess.'

'I hope they find Peter soon,' I say.

She stares at me, narrowing her eyes.

'I hope he's okay.'

The lady with the cat steps closer and utters, 'Some people thought he might turn out to be a school shooter. You hear about them on the news, don't you? Quiet boys who seem a little off. Outsiders. Video-game addicts. Well, we have enough firearms in this part of the world, enough hunting rifles. You hear about them surfing the internet for years about fertiliser bombs, and then it's never too much of a surprise when they do the unthinkable.'

'Sometimes a weird kid is just a weird kid. I know I was.'

'*Sometimes* isn't good enough,' she says.

I think about that.

'All this as we approach the Santa Lucia celebration,' she says again. 'Deacon Sahlin and Choirmaster Lind must be beside themselves. How do you comfort a town when the inhabitants are grieving and terrified at the same time?'

'I don't know.'

'Potemkin, don't eat that.'

She pulls the poor cat sharply by the leash and the cat hisses at her.

'Don't mind her,' says the lady. 'She's not comfortable around new people.'

'Does Mrs Wikström need anything from Willy's? I'm going there.'

'Does she need anything from *Willy's*?' says the lady with an expression that suggests I asked if she might want crack or perhaps crystal meth? 'No, she does not. We pull together in this building. Residents association.'

She steps inside and I walk back towards the main part of town: the chairlift station and the church with its community hall annex, and my Trade Descriptions Act breach of a B&B.

Three police cars race by me from the direction of the tunnel.

I am tempted to go climb in my Hilux and follow.

That would take too long. I set off running down the street, hoping my boots have enough grip to avoid face-planting into ploughed slush. After three minutes I am totally out of breath. The police cars have no lights flashing, no sirens. I follow them to the roundabout and on to the school, and then I have to pause, panting, my palms on my knees.

They stand in a group talking as I catch up.

I walk straight to the chief, holding myself as I go.

'Chief. Tuva Moodyson.' I try to slow my breathing. 'I might be able to help . . .'

She turns and walks away to the gymnasium building we had the press conference in. She doesn't say anything. She doesn't even acknowledge me.

The other cops smirk and follow her.

One is left behind. He turns to join them.

'I heard the Sami parliament is going to discuss the murder of Björn Akerman,' I say, desperate for a reaction.

'No comment.'

He's blonde and young. A dimple on his chin and one on each cheek. He'd be handsome if his lips weren't so thin. They look mean. Out of kilter with the rest of his face.

'I can help you, you know,' I say.

He frowns.

'People talk to me in a way they would never even consider talking to you.'

'I doubt that.'

'You're wrong. They see a young deaf woman wearing fleece-lined ICA Maxi jeans. There's no threat there. No authority. They open up to me. They see you with your height and your multi-tool and your gun and they close up like a clamshell. Not everyone, of course. The deacon will talk with you. The headmaster. But the other people, the ones in the shadows, the people that actually *know* things, they will open up to me in a way you can't imagine.'

'Who are you?'

'I'm Tuva Moodyson.'

He shrugs.

'Give me ten more seconds . . .' I gesticulate for him to offer me his name.

'Carlsson.'

'Ten more seconds, Carlsson. We can help each other. All above board. You want to impress your ice-queen chief, right? I see it; you all want to impress her. And I want to help victims of crime because I have an almost suicidal sense of justice. The world shit on me ten times over, and to balance that out I do everything I can to help people like you catch bad guys. Fair?'

He narrows his eyes and I notice that one is green and one brown.

'I'm not going anywhere. Tell your colleagues that. I am not a fairweather reporter from some elegant neighbourhood in Stockholm or Uppsala. I live in a no-name town just as miserable as this one, only ten times the size. You have mountains and a tunnel; we have forests you can't imagine. I will stay here as long as I need to. I want to make that clear. I am here for the long haul because Peter is missing and the gossip whores are painting his name with a black brush. They are judging him. Unfortunately for them, he is my community. I will offer him the benefit of the doubt until proven otherwise. I will offer Peter that and I will fight his corner.'

'Very bold. Did you rehearse all this?'

'You listen to me now, Carlsson.' I am sweaty and I am angry. 'If you or one of your colleagues find him in some gloomy warehouse or apartment you remember he cannot hear a word you say. Remember that, damn it. He can't hear you warn him or tell him to raise his hands. Please remember what I am telling you. Remember my voice. He cannot hear your commands to kneel on the floor or drop whatever he is holding. So take my words with you. Look at me, Carlsson. He can't hear you. Do not shoot that boy.'

18

Two more cars pull up and park by the swings near the
football goal. Four men, two of them in plain clothes, step
out. They walk towards Carlsson and he stiffens and nods
his head. They nod back.

'Detectives?' I ask.

'I have to go,' says Carlsson.

'I noticed you sign before. You know sign language?'

'My grandfather was deaf. He died when I was a teenager. I used to know it pretty well but I'm rusty now.'

'Give me something on this case, would you?'

'*Give* you something?'

'Teamwork.'

He smiles. 'You're not on my team. And besides, it's
not one case. They're separate.'

He starts to walk away.

'Listen, I'm here to help. Give me something and I'll
leave you alone.' I smile my best smile. 'At least for a day
or two.'

He shakes his head, like he's already chastising himself
for what he is about to say. The regret has already planted
roots. 'It'll be made public in ten minutes anyway.' He
wipes snowflakes from his eyelashes with a gloved hand.
His eyes are weary. 'Another person's gone missing,

Tuva. She was due to start her day's work at the kindergarten on Olavsplats at 7 a.m. and never arrived.'

'Damn.'

'Most likely she's fine, and it's unrelated, but we're bringing in extra manpower from Östersund. Just in case.'

Just in case.

'Is there someone hiding out in these mountains? Someone who has perhaps killed more than once?'

'Lower your damn voice,' he says, looking around. 'She's missing is all. Don't sign her death warrant yet. We're doing everything we can to find her.'

He walks away towards the school-gym double doors and he does not look back.

I return to my B&B and part of me, a significant part, is tempted to jump into my truck and drive far away. Leave via the tunnel I arrived through. Maybe I shouldn't have spoken my thoughts out loud to Carlsson.

Past Circle K, past a veterinary clinic, past a tattoo parlour with a black Christmas tree in the window complete with a devil on the top and red pentagram baubles.

Light pours over the mountaintops and the town warms a little. Pale and soft-focus; the red timber buildings suddenly appear more welcoming, and the festive lights in windows twinkle and blink. There is no wind. Ice Town is a place that seemingly changes its skin from hour to hour, day to day.

The business model of my paper, the *Gavrik Posten*, is pretty much the opposite of the national press. Many of them have turned to clickbait, social media, endless notifications and catchy soundbites. I am relieved to tell you that local, community journalism hasn't headed in that direction to the same extent, at least not in Gavrik. Lena has sent out questionnaires and surveys with copies and she even convinced Lars to stand outside on Storrgatten with a clipboard asking passers-by questions about their preferences. You cannot imagine a more passive man. He literally stood there, on the spot, all day. He didn't stop people or engage with them in any way. He was more like a statue than a canvasser. I respect him for it, I really do. But despite Lars's lame efforts we gleaned that locals want more of the same. They prefer longer-form pieces on important matters, and they want their news as viewed through a local lens. This is why I'm not rushing to tweet that another resident of Ice Town has gone missing. Instead I will take my time and write a story people want to read.

There are mounds of shovelled snow to my left. I don't mean shovelled by shopkeepers and café owners, I mean pushed by a snowplough or mechanical digger with a flashing orange light. Stunted white peaks to mirror the mountains.

'You heard?' says a man across the road. He's wearing ski goggles and a hat so I can't see his face apart from his mouth.

I wrinkle up my face.

He removes his mask.

It's Johan, the podcast host piste-basher. 'You heard about Jenni?'

'Kindergarten worker?'

'Jenni Karlsson. Only a few years younger than me. My parents would buy meat rabbits from her family.

They were decent rabbits. Good for breeding and eating.'

I can't help scowling

'And she was a nice person.'

I soften my expression. 'I'm sorry.'

'I've recorded and broadcast over a thousand episodes investigating true crimes from all over Europe, all over the world. Some of them really affected me, especially offences relating to kids or anything twisted. You know the kind of thing I mean. But this feels totally different. Like, this is not supposed to happen in our *own* town, you know?'

'I know.'

'You don't know. You're not from here.'

An older man with a walking frame asks Johan a question so he turns away from me to answer. I can't read his lips anymore and I can't hear either one of them.

I stand like a lemon at the main intersection of town, two minutes' walk away from the church and community centre. There are spruce branches laid outside the entrance again, and candles flanking it.

My phone vibrates in my pocket. Thanks to developers and accessibility activists, if the phone was on my bedside table or desk it would also flash its torch to show someone is calling. That's progress.

'Lena,' I say, smiling. 'How are you?'

'I'm worried about you.'

'I'm a lost cause,' I say. 'Worry about someone else.'

'I'm serious. Another person missing. A young woman?'

'I'm looking into it.'

'Listen, Tuva. Don't roll your eyes. I know you're a frontline journalist and you have your national award and all the online trolls and admirers that go along with it, but nobody will think less of you if you sit this particular one out.'

'No chance.'

'Or maybe investigate the story, but base yourself in Åre like a sensible person. I've skied there with my cousin. It's stunning.'

I look around at pedestrians with concerned expressions, mothers holding their children closer to their chests than they might have done a week ago. I feel the oppression, the frigid air weighing down on this ignored community, the wall of sheer cliffs around us.

'I'm fine here, honestly. I'm being careful.'

'Thord was asking after you.'

'Tell him to mind his own fucking business.'

'I'll forget you said that.'

'I have a murder case to dig into. That, and a missing deaf teenager who nobody here seemed to like very much. And, now, a missing kindergarten assistant. There's something very dark here, Lena. I can feel it.'

'I was afraid you'd say that.'

Johan turns back around. He's gesturing to me he needs to go.

'Lena, I'll call you back.'

Johan says, 'See you around, Tuva.'

'Best guess. Who the hell is doing this? Who has the potential, the bottle, to make people go missing in Esseberg?' I ask him.

'The *potential?*'

I nod.

'If you're talking about Ingvar, about the conviction, then think again. It's not him.'

I was not talking about Ingvar, I was talking about Peter. And I had no idea of Ingvar's prior conviction.

'You don't know it isn't Ingvar,' I say.

He exhales and the air fogs between us. 'I'm telling you, it's not him, Tuva. Look elsewhere. Ingvar's served his time. Twenty-five years he'll never get back. If there's one thing my pod has taught me, it's that people can change no matter how abhorrent their past actions. Ingvar is good at maintaining the lifts and living a quiet life. I'm telling you, he is a changed man.'

19

I don't work from my bedside desk because cabin fever is well and truly setting in. An overheated room next to a solarium behind a hair salon is not somewhere you want to sleep all night and then work from all day. I drive around in my Hilux until it is warm enough, gathering my thoughts, and then I park in Circle K well away from the pumps.

I search for Esseberg residents named *Ingvar*. There are seven. Four of them are children because there is a bizarre trend these days in Sweden to give kids old-fash-ioned names like Bengt and Margareta and . . . Ingvar.

Three left. For the first two I find their LinkedIn profiles and social-media links. Then their home addresses and phone numbers. The third is rather different.

Ingvar Persson, 56.

Convicted murderer.

Johan wasn't exaggerating.

No Wikipedia profile but there are blog posts and arti-cles written about his life, and the crime he committed when he was twenty-two years old. One person on Twitter, today, suggests that he may have struck again. That is the only recent reference I can find. Somewhat surprisingly, there are numerous articles and papers from the past decade, in the years since he's been released. I dig deeper. After a while I need to switch my engine on again to warm up. Disapproving glances from one man in a gilet, but what can you expect from a man who makes that kind of sartorial choice?

Ingvar Persson completed his undergraduate studies in criminology and law while under lock and key at Kumla high-security prison. He later went on to complete a master's degree in criminal psychology. Before he was released on parole he wrote several published papers on the long-term behavioural impacts of Foetal Alcohol Syndrome, and a retrospective analysis of the 1961 Bobo Doll Experiment. He also began work on his book *Unlocking a Dangerous Mind*. The book was later completed after he was released, and was published by a now defunct independent press in Umeå two years later. He has no web page or social-media presence whatsoever. I research his crime. There are scant details online but I discover he was convicted of beating to death a neighbour in his apartment building. There are reports of a brick being used. The victim was a forty-seven-year-old man of Finnish heritage. The judge in the case noted the ferocity and brutality of the attack, and the fact that the victim was a widower father to his three surviving children.

The gas station scene is bleak. I pause reading because I need a moment for all this to sink in. *Three … surviving … children.*

I sit gazing out of my snow-splattered windscreen. Drivers arrive in their SUVs and estates and fill up with petrol. They go inside, collars raised, hats on tight, and they emerge with a hot dog or a protein bar, and then they cocoon themselves as quickly as possible once again inside their private vehicle. Life this far north, *Alaska north*, is a process of moving from one heated space to another as quickly as possible. It is more extreme than Gavrik. Up here, we are all surviving on life support whether we know it or not.

A fuel-delivery truck arrives so I start my engine and pull away so not to block its path. The wind gusts and my dash shows it is one degree above freezing. A heatwave, relatively speaking.

I drive around, but in a town this puny you start going round in circles pretty fast, wipers brushing away powder, pedestrians staring at you like you've lost your mind as you pass them for the fourth time in less than an hour.

There are cops moving door-to-door, buzzing, knocking, enquiring, taking notes. There will be pressure from above, from bosses, mid-year appraisals coming up, people desperate for promotions or to hang on to the position they have. Pressure to find two missing people and one killer. There is palpable stress in this cursed valley.

I decide that the best way for me to gain the trust of locals is to add value. I understand missing-persons' investigations. Ever since that horrific summer at Snake River, my best friend taken, I have known how to organise. I make a rough list – search-party logistics, outside help, leaflets, posters, Facebook-group organisation, TikTok – and email it to the public email linked to the church group community centre. It's the deacon's wife, I'm fairly confident of that. She emails me back five minutes later asking if I would be prepared to run something on TikTok because she has never used it. I agree. I don't tell her that I have never used it either.

I park behind the church; they have an enormous car park, ever hopeful for converts, and walk round.

A tap on my shoulder.

I spin round half expecting to find Ingvar standing there with a rough brick in his hand.

'I didn't mean to shout,' says the Chief of Police.

I didn't hear anything.

'Hello, Chief.'

'Can we have a quick talk?'

Her demeanour is still stern, professional, senior, but her tone has softened. She walks to the coffee house that forms part of a tattoo parlour – I think the tattooist works in the basement – and I try to keep up with her. She's much taller than me so it is not easy. I look like a child trailing her mother.

She opens the door for me and it bleeps.

We ask for two black coffees, and then we sit in the window staring at the church over the road, and the towering peaks behind it.

'I received a call this morning,' she says, still staring straight ahead. She looks tired.

I blow on my coffee and look over at her. 'Oh?'

'Chief Björn Andersson of Gavrik Police.'

Oh, shit.

'He tracked me down,' she says. 'Knew my old boss over at Falun PD back in the eighties. He was very brief. But he told me you were above board, trustworthy in his eyes, and that you were an adult.'

'An *adult*? I'm thirty years old.'

'He meant you're mature. Level-headed.'

My head's never been close to level.

'Okay.'

'It's possible you could be of use to us. There will be national press here soon, more TV types. And I want to try to control the information flow as much as that is possible these days, to protect the integrity of the case. My team's primary job is to find these two people.'

'And to catch a killer.'

She sips her coffee. No sugar. No blowing it.

God bless Chief Björn. Years ago he would never have considered doing this for me. I was a pest in his eyes. But our shared grief for Noora, living through those dreadful months, the funeral, the memorial service, affected him more than I ever expected. Sometimes the hardest rocks turn out to be porous.

Two uniformed officers run past the café then double back. The chief stands up. They burst in through the door, breathless.

'Chief. You need to see this.'

20

The chief doesn't say anything to me or even look at me; she stands up and walks straight out of the door. I rush outside, slip, fall on my backside, watch the police car drive away, then run awkwardly to my Hilux. Sweating, I drive east towards the one roundabout in town. I drive past the school and I can see them in the distance. In the movies I would have a radio capable of scanning emergency service frequencies but this ain't the movies. I need to keep them in sight so I speed up, my hands gripping the wheel tight, and after a while we approach the colossal power station. It has a razorwire-topped boundary fence and a horizontal security barrier that rises and falls. The police keep driving and I start to wonder if people go missing in this town and never turn up because there's a state-of-the-art incinerator capable of burning organic matter at far higher temperatures than even crematoria operate at.

All that smoke rising high from the chimneys and away over the mountaintops.

All that DNA-free ash.

I pull myself together and swing a right. In the distance, perhaps three kilometres away, on a snowy hill notable for the absence of pine trees, I see four or five figures: black ants standing upright against dazzling snow.

The police car stops.

Brake lights.

I park and approach.

Five police. Two civilians being questioned by a uniformed officer I identify as Carlsson.

I walk closer.

The police quickly cordon off an area. The air is tight and humid, like it might sleet at any moment, and the slopes around feel unsteady all of a sudden, a dozen catastrophic avalanches waiting for a catalyst.

I take three more steps.

Breeze cools the skin on the back of my neck.

Five metres from me on the other side of where police tape *should* be.

Down in the snow: a face.

As if tucked up cosily in a perfectly made bed. White mattress and duvet. Fresh white sheets. A woman's face: her cheeks frosted.

I should grab my camera, thrust forward, push the boundaries, take advantage of this opportunity, but I do not. She has thick eyebrows like Noora had. Her eyes are closed. Flakes on her lashes and her brows.

'Back, please. Get back now. Police only.'

Carlsson walks to me, his hands out, and I retreat. I notice his belt. His gun, cuffs, baton.

'Who is she?' I ask.

'Move back,' he says again. 'Well back. Everyone move back.'

Everyone? It is only me. The other two are already walking back to their Volkswagen, the shock setting in. Are they the people who found her?

'I'm a reporter and I am staying back. Was she strangled?'

He scoffs at that and tells me, 'Move back. Let us work.'

I retreat further and he goes back to the others, to the frozen body in the snow, and then I skirt the scene and take my photos. At this angle, with her face thirty centimetres down in the snow, the images on my screen don't show her. Just the faces looking down. The woman trying to set out crime-scene tape to form a perimeter when there are clearly no physical features to attach the tape to. She takes four sticks from her police truck and stabs them into the earth. The sticks don't stay vertical, though. They fall because they cannot penetrate this hard, frozen ground. One collapses completely. The tape is undignified considering the horrors it has been used to contain, to control.

The skies darken.

A town in distress.

The police follow crime-scene protocols to the letter. Nobody enters or leaves the immediate scene unnecessarily. They do their best to stay within their own bootprints. A crowd of three gathers on the far side. The potential avalanches hold on, paused, clinging on to whatever minimal friction is afforded them in these sunlit hours. But I can feel it. That potential energy. Thousands of tonnes of frozen water ready to release. This crime scene of one victim could rapidly turn into something far worse.

A K9 unit arrives.

Then the podcaster, Johan, approaches strapped into his cross-country skis. He is wearing a fur hat. Looks like a rabbit.

'What's going on?' he asks.

'They've found another body.'

'What?'

'It's a woman. It could be the missing woman from the kindergarten, I don't know.'

'This is out of hand.' He rubs his hands up and down his neck. 'They have to do something.'

'They're doing it.'

'They have to do much more.'

We watch together as they erect a grey tent over the immediate area.

'This isn't normal,' he says, shaking his head. 'Not here.'

I don't say anything.

Astrid, the journalist from Norrköping, arrives in her station wagon.

'I heard they found her,' she says. 'Tuva, how did you get here so fast?'

'Me? I followed the chief.'

She eyes me suspiciously.

'I don't get tip-offs,' I say. 'It's a small town. Stay close to the police vehicles and you'll see what they're all up to. They found her in the snow.'

'Are they sure she's dead? She asks.

'I only caught a glimpse,' I say, showing her the screen on my camera. 'Looks like she's been there a while.'

I wonder to myself whether the victim's organs can be used for transplant. They are cold. Preserved. They might still be salvageable. Then I curse myself for thinking such a thing.

'Have they arrested Peter Hedberg yet?'

'Don't jump to conclusions,' I say. 'We don't know . . .'

I am interrupted by a flurry of shouting further up the slope. Two police officers begin to run, one with his hand on his gun, and a K9 specialist dog strains on his leash. I move in that direction. I jog past the dead woman in the snow and the police who are now down on their knees working. I start to run through deep powder, my legs tiring, my heart racing, and both Johan and Astrid overtake me. They sprint and the police yell a code back to their colleagues. One stands up, his gloves covered in wet snow, and commands us to stay back. His cheeks are red from the cold and his colleague is digging frantically with his bare hands.

Horrifically, *another* face: frozen, white, burnt by frost.

Down in the snow.

A man's face.

21

They scramble to check that his airways are clear, that he can breathe, but it is soon patently clear this man will never breathe again. A helicopter from Östersund hospital arrives overhead, hovers, then flies to the west.

While one officer, a woman with red hair under her hat, checks again for a pulse, her colleague, arms open, insists we move back.

They enlarge the cordon.

Officials in uniform, panicking.

Too much, even for them.

It is not easy to maintain the integrity of a crime scene in true wilderness. There are no buildings, no lockable doors or gates. There are no walls to keep prying eyes away. No roads to close. There is only whiteness, a vast rolling hellscape of it, and the pervading sense that whatever has come before is nothing compared to what still awaits us.

Astrid is on the phone to her editor, moving stories around on the front page of their paper, while Johan vlogs for his Instagram account. I do not like his tone. The excited nature of his voice, like he can already quantify the click-through rate to his podcast via the link in his bio, he can already estimate the boost to his subscriber count and the identity of key new sponsors attracted by improved metrics.

I drive towards the church. I am not religious and I have never been religious. Dad was a casual protestant, I think, until an elk collided with his Volvo and killed him a week after my fourteenth birthday. Mum was a committed atheist to her dying breath. So why am I drawn to these places of worship, and specifically, now, to this church? For answers? Or because, like everyone else, I'm desperate for sanctuary, for evidence of goodness?

Two more bodies. Three, now, in total. Was the second body Peter Hedberg? Part of me wants it to be because then he wouldn't be the killer. Or perhaps he would. Perhaps he did the unthinkable, twice, and then took the lonely decision to step into nothingness. I am experienced enough to know that I am *way* out of my depth, and that the same goes for this whole damn town, for local police and residents alike. The only possible exception, and I hope I am right about this, is Chief Skoglund.

Multiple victims in shallow graves. Under snow. Stiff and lifeless, their still-open eyes weighed down by accumulating flakes. As a child I had a Lego man I used to put to bed each night in a matchbox, closing it until only his eyes and the tip of his head were visible. I thought he looked safe in there but now I feel claustrophobic just thinking about it. These bodies looked strikingly similar under the snow.

If Peter is still on the loose, if he is responsible, then what could have driven him to this? He was bullied, or taunted at least. Excluded. But what was the tipping point for a series of acts this heinous?

I stop at the traffic lights and glance into the windows of a small red cottage with white trim. A domestic scene. Ordered. Christmas candle-esque lights in the windows and a tree by the window, its resinous needles pushed right up against cold glass. The pulsing light of a TV inside. And upstairs: a child's bedroom. Books stacked on the window sill. A star, lit with a bulb, and a cardboard angel stuck to the glass with tape. My heart sinks. I yearn for a moment with little Dan, my neighbour's son. Someone beeps behind me and I notice the green light and accelerate hard, my studded tyres biting and propelling me forward. I would give anything for a casual chat with Dan tonight. I'd babysit and we'd have meatballs and macaroni, and a glass of milk each. I would ask him about Super Mario and Sonic, and we would rank our favourite Christmas movies. His is *Home Alone* but he says *The Snowman* makes him feel more 'Christmassy'. Mine is *Die Hard,* but he will have to wait a few years for us to watch that one together. He judges this to be unfair.

The skies darken again and the slopes all around us seem to steepen, to lean in.

In the far distance, at the end of this long, straight road, I notice an absence of light. The mouth of the tunnel leading away from this settlement, away from danger. I am tempted, once again, to keep on driving until I am safely on the far side. I suspect many long-term residents feel the same way.

I park, for the second time today, behind the church.

Up the mountain, beside the Grand Hotel Pinnacle, there is an intense orange glow. Smoke. Some kind of bonfire up on the summit. Eric or perhaps Karin Bates the caretaker-cum-chef-cum-waitress burning God-knows-what in an oil drum or pit fire. I gaze up at it, my neck straining, and it shines like a second sun.

I lock my Hilux and walk around.

No one on the streets. The word will be out by now. I have lived through something similar to this before. Parents sitting their children down after class to explain how they will pick them up directly from the school gates for the next few days, no buses or walking with friends. Couples will be checking their locks and alarms. Grandmothers will call their progeny later tonight to urge them to stay home and skip hockey practice this one time. This wintry air does not carry the scent of death; rather it exudes the unmistakable tang of fear.

Before I venture inside I sit down on one of the painted benches outside the timber church. The ecclesiastical blue and gold clock sits over my head, fifteen metres above me. Another tragic accident waiting to happen.

Locals are leaving.

Peter Hedberg might be a triple murderer. He might still be walking among us.

'Tuva!' yells a voice from across the street.

Astrid.

'What's happened?' I ask. 'Tell me.'

She arrives out of breath, her hair in front of her eyes. 'What is going on here?'

'What do you mean?'

She drags her hair back. 'Two more bodies.'

'I know.'

'It's the kindergarten teacher. Positive ID. Photos already circulating but I wouldn't look if I were you. One of the police officers knew her pretty well, so I'm told, and she had a distinctive tattoo.' She takes a deep breath. 'The other body is a quiet local guy who lived alone in one of the flat-roof buildings behind Circle K. Small place like this, people get ID'd quickly, although nothing's been confirmed by the police yet. Dead guy had a long scar someplace on his chin. Worked part-time writing a newsletter for a chain of ski hardware stores.'

'What else? Cause of death?'

'They haven't said.'

'What have they said?'

'Reinforcements coming in from Östersund.' She takes a deep breath. 'Word is they're hunting down Peter.'

'Hunting him *down*?'

'That's what someone told me.'

I shake my head.

'Listen, Tuva.' She looks borderline hysterical. 'You ever think, maybe, you know, it's now too risky for us to stay here? I mean, the B&B has no security whatsoever. Anyone can walk in the solarium and get through to us, there's no reception or anything. My editor thinks I should stay in Åre or Duved.'

'My editor suggested the exact same thing.'

She sits down next to me and nods enthusiastically. 'There's a massive queue of cars and trucks ready to leave through the tunnel in the next time slot. Johan told me the cars are stuffed with duvets and food. People are fleeing. They're not prepared to stay.'

'You go if you want,' I say. 'I'm staying right here.'

'I don't think you should stay. I don't think either of us should.'

'You ever watch the news on TV when a war kicks off?'

She frowns. 'Of course.'

'Those reporters. Women like you and me in Iran or Syria or Nigeria. They have the same role as us. They are terrified. But they do their jobs.'

'Come on, it's not the same.'

'It is exactly the same. Those journalists in blue helmets and plate carriers are reporting on a story. A *developing* story. Nobody can guarantee their safety but they stay to bear witness for the rest of us.'

'To bear witness?'

'Because if they don't. If *we* don't. Then how will everyone else know what is happening? How will people find out the truth?'

22

The light is slipping away.

I walk up the base of the mountain a little way, staying on well-lit paths, and eventually I am rewarded with a vista of the whole town. Lights in windows. The queue of cars at the tunnel slowly shrinking as each vehicle is swallowed whole. Steam and smoke rising from various chimneys and pipes, the largest of which stands to my left: the incinerator power station.

The pistes, few as they are, are still open. It might look like late evening when floodlights are the only pinpricks of brightness rising up into the velvet-black sky, but, no, this is mid-afternoon.

I trudge over to the lifts. Three people working. Two of them in blue jackets. Eventually I locate the third.

'Ingvar Persson?'

He looks over at me and sniffs. 'I'm working.'

'Can I get some help, please?'

He frowns. 'Ask one of the others.'

I walk up to him and he withdraws a pace or two. I see that faint cross tattoo beneath the shadow of his eye.

'I heard you're a doctor,' I say.

He picks up a toolbox and walks away, so I pursue him. With a spree killer on the loose, if that is what this is, I need to get in peoples' faces and stare into their eyes. My mother always said she had a gift that ran through the maternal bloodline of our family. The Sami bloodline. She said she could look someone in the eyes and see right to the back. She would claim she could look at their soul. I'm not sure about that but it's never harmed me to ask direct questions and then wait. To appraise. Maybe it is because I have developed an ability to read body language better than the average hack, to pick up signs, to be watchful. Or maybe my mother was right after all.

'I heard you're a doctor,' I say again, louder.

'I'm not anything.'

'You have a PhD. I need your help.'

He says something but I can't understand his words from behind so I run and overtake him.

'I said I need your help.'

'And I said no.'

'That's unacceptable.'

He stops. Sets down his toolbox in the thawing snow. Looks at me with his head at an angle.

'Thank you,' I say. 'Can I buy you a coffee after your shift, please? Buy you a hot dog at Circle K at least?'

'I got food.'

'Can we talk someplace?'

'Can we *talk* someplace?'

'Yeah.'

'No, we can't.'

He looks battle scarred in these harsh lights. Hard and etched. The lines on his forehead are so deep you could hide things in there.

'Did you hear about the two bodies found today?'

He takes a pack of gum from his pocket. Removes a piece. Places it slowly on his tongue. 'You know I did. You saw me there.'

'Aren't you concerned?'

He chews the gum and looks up at the mountain.

'Three in as many days,' I say.

'I got to get back to work. Test the brakes.'

His red jacket has a transparent pocket with his ID badge. *Ingvar Persson.* Lift Chief.

'You're the chief.'

'I told you, I'm not anybody.'

'Johan says different. Tells me you're a behavioural psychologist. An expert.'

'I fix the lifts.'

'Who's doing this, Ingvar? I mean it.'

'You *mean* it?'

'What's going on?'

He puts another piece of gum on his tongue. Double gum. 'How should I know?'

'You live in this town. I thought you'd be interested.'

'I do not live in this town.'

I raise my eyebrows.

He raises his eyebrows right back at me.

'I'm not asking you about what you did in the past.'

'Good.'

'I'm asking you about the present situation.'

'The present situation? The present situation is I need to test the brakes and check oil levels. You hold me up here much longer, young woman, and we might see a cascade of falling chairlifts. You think you could live with that?'

'Who is attacking people in Esseberg?'

He bites his lip. 'Go talk to the police. Or the other TV pundits. Maybe they know.'

He starts walking away.

'What do your bosses at the Pinnacle Hotel think about all this?'

'I'm not biting.'

'The janitor up there. Receptionist. Karin. She says you have a better understanding of what's going on than anyone else in this town.'

'She should stick to making soup.'

'Can you please help me, Ingvar?'

He walks away four or five steps and then turns back to face me and the town over my shoulder. 'I'm an old man and I live a quiet life in a secluded place. And from you I sense trouble, young woman. So, excuse me.'

He walks away up the slope towards the next chairlift tower and then he begins to climb the steel ladder affixed to its side.

I spend three hours manically working the town. Eavesdropping in Willy's, showing the pastor's wife the amateurish TikTok account I set up for the search of Peter Hedberg, quizzing tattooists and hairdressers on if they've heard any news, because, let me tell you, if there's anyone who hears potentially valuable gossip it's tattooists and hairdressers. Something to do with trust. I find nothing concrete but the layers and strands of my web are beginning to firm up. People need to see my face three times before they'll grow accustomed to me and start lowering their barriers. It's down to me to fast track that process.

I watch a food truck set up outside Wrath. It's a *Cevapi* truck and the menu is an eclectic mix of Balkan and Greek delicacies. A guy I've seen driving a snowplough chats with the owner of the truck wearing full camo. I'm not exactly sure what Cevapi is but I make a mental note to return later for my dinner.

Three phone calls with my hearing aid synced to my phone via Bluetooth, all following up on leads and potential interviews with people who know, or knew, Peter, and then an email arrives from Lars.

A link.

No small talk or pleasantries, whatsoever.

Police bulletin pertaining to the bodies found in Esseberg.

I know what this is. Usually, when the police have strong leads, they play their cards close to their chest. But when the stakes are this high – an active killer at large, multiple victims – they're forced to release more information than they would ordinarily prefer in an attempt to jog someone's memory or bring in a reluctant witness.

The bulletin contains two key pieces of information gleaned from recent autopsies.

Firstly, each victim was strangled. That is confirmed. By examining the bruising and soft-tissue damage it has been determined that a rope or belt was used, and that the perpetrator is mostly likely someone with significant upper-body strength.

Secondly, residues of capsicum was found in the nasal mucosa, or nose mucous membrane, of each victim. Likewise with the mucous layer of the eyes. Capsicum of this concentration is indicative of defensive pepper spray.

This high-concentration pepper spray is legal in many countries but it is not legal in Sweden.

I can't help imagining those brutal final breaths. Stinging eyes and a band tight around your throat. Strangulation so fierce you can't fight back or scream for help. And the knowledge that even if you could scream, there will be nobody around to hear you.

23

I drive against the flow of traffic, past the pension-admin offices, each identical square triple-glazed window lit with an identical electronic Christmas candle, and on towards the town's only high school. My Hilux dash tells me the world is cooling once again. It thawed for long enough to give up its secrets, to reveal two new corpses, and now it is returning to baseline.

Flurries of light snow captured by streetlights.

A Renault minivan with its bonnet open, jumper cables hanging down in the gritty, slush-like frigid entrails.

I drive on and I am numb. Less afraid than I have any right to be. This is the most high-risk story I have ever covered, objectively speaking, and yet I am numb to it. Perhaps it is because I have witnessed death up close. I have watched the last breath taken, the last moment lived. I held Noora's hand tight in mine and I witnessed that watershed. I felt it, and there was no dread.

When I arrive into the school grounds one uniformed officer directs us away from the main car park, away from the haunted-looking parents in Gore-Tex outerwear collecting their innocent children, each one clad in a bright ski jacket with reflective strips, because, you know, safety first.

I lock my Hilux and it feels every kind of wrong to be here attending a press conference about a potential spree killer, a potential *deaf* spree killer, while children still play football and chase each other within shouting distance of the microphones and press-pass lanyards. Before I enter the standalone gymnasium building I turn and watch them through clouds of my own breath. They play on, oblivious. Screeching and laughing, taunting one another like children have done for millennia. But, here, the little ones have to play in the dark. This is the norm at this latitude. They play through blackness and murk, in temperatures considered lethal in most corners of the world, and they squeal with delight at each kick and whispered joke. The next generation of Ice Town. I expect many will eventually leave. I watch their rosy faces and I can detect distinct pecking orders within each group. Spectrums of self-confidence and boldness. A microcosm of humanity: goodness, surrounded by chaos and terror.

'Tuva,' says Carlsson as I approach. He's a typical Nordic man so it is difficult to distinguish flirting from indifference. In this case it's probably something halfway between.

People whisper while we wait for Chief Skoglund. Hushed tones. Reporters all around me check their phones and open their laptops. There are three with cameras at the back of the room and I nod to a tabloid guy from Stockholm and another from Gothenburg, and then I take my place. I cannot partake in their snippets of gossip and hearsay. Not with so many speaking, at low volume, in a room with poor acoustics. A woman taps my shoulder and I turn around. It's a respected Dalarna journalist I met during the Rose Farm survivalist-community story. I smile and then I notice Astrid, the reporter with the station wagon, seated in the back row. She's typing a message on her phone. She looks up to face the front, so I turn, and Chief Skoglund and two others are standing at the lectern.

'Everyone, a warm welcome. I'm very grateful to you all for travelling, some of you from across the country, to attend. Let me reintroduce Per Gustavsson, Investigator-in-Charge, and introduce Elina Olin, Senior Forensic Pathologist at Östersunds Kommun. I will make a short statement and then we'll take as many questions as practical.'

You could hear a pin drop in here. I couldn't, but you could.

'Tragically, the Åre police department have now recovered a total of three bodies, all with similar injuries. The first has been identified as Björn Akerman. Now I can confirm that Jenni Karlsson, a thirty-one-year-old kindergarten assistant from Esseberg was discovered adjacent to the Esseberg-Ekeby power station by local skiers.' Skoglund tells us time of discovery, and grid reference coordinates. 'Subsequently, Åre police also discovered the body of Max Wallström, a local writer and copy editor, in the same approximate location. As I am sure you can understand we are dedicating all the resources and manpower at our discretion to find the perpetrator as soon as possible and bring them to justice.'

Hands go up all around the room.

'We'll take questions in a moment. But now I'd like to pass over to Elina so she can update you on the forensic results. My thanks go to Professor Bakir and his team at the national forensic centre at Linköping for expediting procedures. We are all working hard to find whoever did this to Björn, Jenni, and Max. Elina, please.'

We watch them swap places. I make a note of Elina's full name and job title, and then I look up. She is nervous. Attractive. Fifty-five or perhaps sixty. Grey hair and green eyes. The kind of clear, glowing skin I won't be sporting when I'm her age. I don't sport it now.

'Thank you, Chief Skoglund. I'd like to brief you all on several forensic aspects relating to this case. I believe you have received the basic facts already. Firstly, it has been concluded that all three victims died from strangulation, specifically from ligature injuries. We don't know what form of ligature, but most likely a belt or tie or similar. Materials analysis is ongoing. Evidence of bilateral sternocleidomastoid muscle haemorrhage has been noted, along with hypoxic brain injury; both to be expected with strangulation. We believe all three victims were killed in the locations where they were discovered. They were not moved or tampered with post-mortem. I can also confirm that residues of *capsaicin*, a chemical irritant and neurotoxin, was present on all three bodies. This compound is present in pepper spray as used by law enforcement. The compound has been analysed and found to be approximately two per cent concentration, a formula not available to civilians. It is the combination of strangulation and pepper spray that contributed to the red, swollen eyes of all three victims.' She looks at the chief for a moment, then back to us. 'We can also disclose that we discovered semen on the outer clothes of Jenni Karlsson, although there are no indications that any physical sexual assault took place. We are working hard to expedite our serological analysis. My thoughts, and the thoughts of my team, go out to all the families affected.'

It strikes me as strange she brought up the semen stain if there was no sexual assault. Could it have been a fetishistic killing? I've read about sexual sadism. I wish I hadn't. This fact must be significant otherwise she wouldn't have mentioned it.

The chief replaces her.

'Again, as I'm sure you all understand, there may be some questions we are unable to answer at this time but owing to the seriousness of these circumstances we will do our best. Does anyone have a question?'

Arms shoot up into the air. *Everyone* has a question today.

She points to a man in the front row, a guy with a bald head and thick black-rim glasses. I think he's the senior reporter from the *Östersunds Posten*.

He clears his throat and then asks, 'Is Peter Hedberg the prime suspect in this spree killing?'

Flashbulbs erupt all around the room.

24

Chief Skoglund makes a concerted effort to appear unruffled. She says she'd recommend we don't jump to conclusions prematurely, and she says terms like 'spree killings' can be misleading and unhelpful. She does not, however, say a word about whether Peter Hedberg is indeed the prime suspect but she does reiterate that their working hypothesis is that the crimes are linked and it is likely they were committed by the same perpetrator.

Spree killing. The term feels out of kilter, somehow. I associate the word *spree* with shopping: a high-speed dash around a mall, not mass homicide in the mountains.

I can already predict some of the pieces those sitting to my left and right will publish beneath their bylines and their bio photos. There will be a box giving diction-ary definitions of 'spree killer' and 'serial killer'. The former is a person who murders in a contained period of time. The latter is someone who develops a pattern of behaviour, and whose crimes can be spread over many years with large gaps of time in between. The former tends not to take souvenirs from victims. The latter often will.

I raise my hand again but the chief points to a man behind me.

He asks about the semen sample, how fresh it was, and on what item of clothing it was discovered on. The chief says she can't comment on those details at this stage.

'Okay, well if you can't talk to us about that, what reassurances can you give this community that the Ice Town killer won't strike again?'

More flashbulbs. And just like that, a nickname is born. Maybe. They tend to evolve through iterations. The chief straightens her back and says, 'We've bolstered our team with specialists from Östersund and the further afield. We have brought in the behavioural-crime task force. This show of manpower is almost unprecedented outside of major urban centres. We are also in the process of establishing a temporary police station outpost in Esseberg, located in a vacant portion of the Vårdcentral surgery. At least one officer will be based in the town until the perpetrator is brought into custody. I want to give thanks to Doctor Zhang and his colleagues for making the space available to us at such short notice.'

'One constable working from a pharmacist's storeroom won't save this town,' says a broad woman in front of me. She goes on, 'There's a monster on this side of the tunnel. How many more residents need to die before Peter Hedberg is caught?'

I look into the chief's eyes and I judge she wants to speak out about how everyone in Sweden is innocent until proven guilty, and how the rule of law is a central pillar to any civilised society, and how the media should take some responsibility when casting shade on any one individual because the rabid vigilante 'justice' that can result must be avoided at all costs. But she is wise and experienced so she bites her tongue for a moment and then says, 'We will not rest until we have identified and apprehended whoever did this.'

She points to me.

'A question for Elina,' I say. 'What is the behavioural-crime task force doing to help apprehend the killer? What specific methods is the task force deploying?'

Elina says, 'I can't go into detail on specific operational matters, but I can tell you what is already in the public domain. The task force works extensively to identify signatures and patterns of behaviour. The force has specialists who dredge social media for clues and identifiers. They cross-reference the biographies of each victim to find commonalities. Then, as a team, they build a profile of who might be responsible. Anything they can do to narrow down the pool of potential suspects has value. We're all on the same page here.'

'Curfew,' booms a gravelly voice from the back. A smoker, I presume. 'The deacon mentioned a curfew. He said it's the only way to make people feel safe after the tunnel closes each night and there's no escape. I think he's right. What do you say? Should we close the streets after dark?'

That'd be from lunchtime, pal. Not practical.

'We're considering extra measures,' says the chief. 'Everything is on the table.'

There are further questions about whether the podcaster, Johan, has been given privileged access to police information, which they vehemently deny, and whether the school should close, which the chief says is a decision for the Kommun.

The room is tense. More tense than I have ever seen a police press conference. The reporters look restless. That is not so strange in itself. But the police themselves, the people with training and firearms, the women and men in charge, they also look nervous. I think back to what the deacon's wife told me. The parishioners being a flock of sorts.

When the sheepdogs and shepherds show fear in their eyes then the sheep have no one left to turn to for protection.

'One more question, Chief,' asks a smartly dressed man by the wall. 'It is well known in these parts that the Grand Hotel Pinnacle has given refuge to serious criminals in the past. To one convicted murderer and, years later, to an armed robber and arsonist. Have you searched the hotel and its grounds? Are you confident the suspect isn't hiding out up there far away from prying eyes, travelling down from time to time to satisfy his bloodlust?'

I make a note of what he said so I can investigate further from my room later tonight.

'We're searching everywhere for clues and leads,' says the chief. 'Nowhere is off-limits to us, not even the tunnel itself, and every local business and household we've approached has been accommodating to our search efforts.'

From that I wonder if they're searching the tunnel itself. I imagine it has service shafts and subsidiary air-ducts. A person could hide there, deep inside the mountain.

'How many more bodies will be found,' asks the same man. 'People have to live this side of the mountain through all this. You get to leave each night, back to Åre, back to safety, but the local population here don't have a choice. Answer me this: how do we know there won't be more corpses discovered when the snow thaws in spring? How do we know there aren't *dozens* out there?'

The lead investigator looks at the chief and gestures he'll take the question.

'As Chief Skoglund stated, our multiple teams are working tirelessly to bring the perpetrator to justice as swiftly as possible. The efforts underway are unprecedented, I can assure you. Now, I'd like to leave you all with one question for your readers and viewers. We are interested in talking to one particular individual seen close to the rear of the incinerator power station yesterday morning. Said individual is tall, and was seen wearing black ski clothes and black boots and a black ski mask.' Suddenly I feel hot in my coat. I'm sweating. My hearing aids are sore in my ears. 'The individual wears a size forty-five boot. I would urge anyone matching this description to come forward as soon as possible so they can be eliminated from enquiries. And if you know of this person's identity, please do get in touch with the police immediately. Don't approach them yourself. Don't speak to them or make contact in any way. Call us immediately.'

25

As I drive away I see Astrid holding a cup of takeaway coffee from Circle K while she interviews a local woman on the street. To most civilians it might look like a conversation between friends, or someone from out of town asking for directions, but I can tell it is an interview by the body language. Astrid is mirroring her interviewee's posture and stance, putting her at ease. She has her phone in her hand, no doubt using it to record audio so she can write it up accurately later. And she is nodding a lot, smiling, prompting the interviewee to keep talking.

Something in my bones tells me the previously grand hotel on the summit might hold the key to this case so I decide to make my way up the mountain again. The man's question adds to my suspicion. But being trapped in the town at the bottom of the valley is one level of isolation, and being trapped on the mountaintop, in December, with no train up or down, is quite another. A blonde blue-eyed teenager supervises as I pass through the barrier using my pass and it may as well be little Dan standing there making sure the engines and cogs are working safely. I brace myself to be scooped up by the jerky, moving chair and then I'm suddenly up in the air, weightless, and the relief is palpable.

I catch glimpses of someone in a red jacket, it could be Ingvar, as I rise up and over the lip of the first cliff.

I take a deep breath and the wind buffets me around and I grip the safety bar with both gloved hands.

Higher. Me in the middle of the chair in a vain attempt to keep it balanced.

I can sense the altitude gain and I daren't look back over my shoulder at the lights of Esseberg in case I lose balance and slip below the bar. The fall, in some places, is sixty metres or more onto jagged, inaccessible rock. Any rescue attempt would be almost impossible.

There are two skiers on the whole mountain. *Two.* A pair in blue and black respectively, and I can't help but wonder about their lives. Not all Swedish skiers are privileged. Many are simply born in or near the mountains. But people who look like this pair: mirrored sunglasses and perfect sweeping turns, skiers with narrow hips and easy, white smiles, well, I can't help thinking they've been sliding through life on a shrimp sandwich, as my old schoolteacher used to say, unencumbered by the financial, physical and emotional weights placed on the rest of us by fate, or God, or both.

Judging them that way might be grossly unfair.

Again, sue me.

I spot moose tracks below disappearing into a spinney of emaciated spruce trees. The nutrients are too sparse up here. The conditions make life possible, but not probable. You can live in a place like Esseberg but it is unlikely you will ever flourish here.

A craggy grey-black cliff to my right. I remember what Eric told me about his son perishing in this very place, and the thought makes me shudder. The loneliness of that untimely end.

Gears above my head grind and this chair rattles across another tower on its way to the summit. The chair shakes and I squeeze my thighs and my shoulders and my hands, willing it to stay stable and true.

Almost at the top.

It is easier to dismount a lift like this if you are wearing skis. I'd prefer it, and I say that as a truly awful skier who turns using the infantile snowplough method, and who will not so much as contemplate a red run. If I ski too close to a steep piste I begin to panic.

The chair positions itself over the snowy ramp and the bar raises and I stumble off.

The hotel stands resolute on its granite perch.

Heavier gusts up here. I have to bend into the wind to make it to the lobby entrance. Behind the hotel doors, in the distance, I can see the abandoned, rusty cog and pinion railway line and its single derelict platform. The Catch-22 situation is tragic, really. This hotel is stuck between a literal rock and a hard place. Without the railway it will never again function as a profitable hotel. And without the profits the owners will never repair the railway.

I step inside from the cold.

The fireplace in the centre of the lobby flares bright with the gust of air I brought in with me. It is possibly the largest fireplace I have ever seen. You could parallel park a Fiat into it. I look to my left: reception desk with brass bell, and behind the pine counter a wall of pine pigeon-holes, every single one with a key present. Never a good sign. To my right: pine boards and pine tables with candles in holders. Magazines and untouched tourist-information leaflets in a tidy arrangement. A stack of wool blankets in a large wicker basket.

'You're still here?' asks Eric, a concerned look etched onto his brow. 'I thought you'd be gone by now. Dear God, you're still here. With all this foul news.'

'It's my job.'

'You should go back to Värmland, Tuva. Make haste. This is not the time to be brave.'

'I'm doing my job, Eric.' God, I sound like a bitch sometimes. I clear my throat and then I see the opportunity for some unexpected leverage, however tenuous. 'How about I make you a deal. Let's talk. The more you can tell me about this town – background info, local characters, grudges and tensions – the quicker I can leave. Is that fair?'

'You should leave right away.'

'I won't.'

He looks wistful and smiles. 'You remind me of someone, Tuva. It's like I'm seeing her again.'

'Who?'

'Sorry, I'm becoming nostalgic in my old age. Shall we sit over there? My arthritis is playing up a little. This cold seeps deep into my bones.'

We walk to a table and the air smells of wood smoke and furniture polish. The lobby is otherwise deserted. I wonder how long they will be able to stay open for, especially considering how the recent news isn't exactly tourism-positive.

'Tell me, Tuva, do you play chess?'

'No.'

'Shame.'

'I used to, though. I used to play a lot when I was younger.'

He smiles.

'I always play as black,' I say.

'Do you, really. Well, isn't that something. I have a rather special board here if you're interested?'

I'm not here to play games but Lena taught me to pivot into whatever the interviewee is interested in, especially if it is an activity that facilitates easy conversation, something that may cause them to lower their guard.

He takes me over to a green baize card-and-backgammon table. He reaches down and carefully brings up a board, the one I spotted on my last visit. It is already set, and it is unlike anything I have ever seen before.

'That's . . . novel.'

'Look at it.'

How could I not? The table looks hand carved from oak. I can tell it's hand carved because the edges aren't exactly straight, they conform somewhat to the grain of the wood. The more I see the more uncomfortable I become. The white squares are pale grey and the dark squares are mahogany brown. But it is the *pieces*.

'Unusual,' I say.

'My father bought it years ago from an artisanal craft fair down in Falun. It was created by siblings, you see. One worked on the white pieces, one on the black.'

I look at him.

'The sisters were master carpenters, I suppose, in their own way. My father said they lived deep in the woods. He said one of them was very quiet. My father gave the set to me for Christmas one year.'

Alice and Cornelia Sørlie of Utgard forest. Their reach extends all over this land.

'I've never seen pieces like these,' he says. 'Before or since. People don't carve intricately like this anymore. Too many man hours.'

'I think I might know the sisters who carved this board.'

'No,' he says, smiling. 'I doubt they're alive anymore, Tuva. They were old when my father bought it from them.'

'I may be wrong,' I say, holding up a pawn to the window light. Inspecting its gaping mouth and sewn-shut eyes. It's exposed ribs: likely shrew or vole bones. The intricate lichen attached to its face like a lace bridal veil. 'But I recognise their work.'

'How extraordinary.'

I feign ignorance. Or innocence. 'What are the pieces made out of?'

'The black pieces are charred moose antler. My father would jest how the bases of the white pieces are likely human bone. They're not, I'm sure they're not, but I think the carpenter sisters told father as much to impress him.'

I place the pawn back down.

'There was a police press conference earlier about the two new bodies. A journalist said your hotel has been used in the past to hide criminals. Is that true?'

'Yes, quite true.'

His honesty makes me take a moment.

'Go on.'

'I wish my father were still here to explain himself to you. He was much better with words than I am. You see, he and mother felt a tremendous debt to the community. Our hotel flourished, attracted the great and the good from Stockholm and Oslo, was talked about in the high-society circles of Östermalm and Torekov, and even London and Paris. Father loved running the place. He was an excellent skier and climber. So, because of his good fortune, being able to live up here even though he was an outsider, he felt an obligation for public service. He worked with the Kommun on various projects and he funded the small library down in the town. But he also felt a strong Christian compulsion to help those whom society deemed undeserving, and offer them a second chance. So, yes, those rumours are quite true. He once gave shelter to a convicted arsonist who happened to hold up a bank in Umeå. When released from jail, Father allowed him to work for board and lodgings, and a fair wage. And then, when Ingvar Persson left prison after serving a life sentence, Father, in the last years of his life, was the only man in the town willing to give him a chance. Of course, there were certain safeguards put in place. Ingvar was a self-confessed killer after all. He had a lengthy probation period, and he wasn't permitted inside the hotel for the first few years of employment. My father granted him a life interest in a small, isolated plot of land above the town. He built a modest cabin there and that's where he still lives to this day.'

I focus on Eric's words but my eyes keep glancing down to the bizarre rooks and bishops in front of me. The equine heads of the knights have sharpened incisors and black jewels for eyes. Each bishop sports acorn breasts and holds a thorn dagger down by her side. The queens are naked, as are the well-endowed kings. The level of anatomical detail would make a sailor blush. The battlements of each rook are entwined with knots of poison ivy and adorned with the decayed heads of their enemies: most likely juvenile frog skulls.

'Have police questioned Ingvar Persson?'

'Oh, I expect he will be assisting them with their enquiries.'

'So, he's a suspect?'

'No, I mean he's probably helping them with profiling. They call upon his services in certain instances. The authorities once used him to befriend a child killer in prison, you see. I am told Ingvar managed, within a day or two, to ascertain the whereabouts of the killer's last victim, a four-year-old boy, in Västra Götaland. That afforded the child's parents some closure, I expect. They were able to bury their boy in accordance with the traditions of their church.'

'But, he killed.' I say. 'Do you think Ingvar might be capable of killing again?'

'All I can tell you is when my son died on the black cliff, Ingvar was the only man willing and able to ski to him through that blizzard storm. I couldn't even make it there myself. You have no idea how that feels, to be unable to help your own child in their hour of need due to, I don't know, cowardice? Incompetence?'

He looks away.

I don't know what to say to him. 'Thank you for talking with me.'

'What kind of music do you like, Tuva?'

I frown. 'Me? Oh, I don't know. All types.'

'Such as.'

'I listen to a lot of Johnny Cash.'

He looks at me and his mouth falls open a little. He closes it.

'I want you to leave this town,' he says.

'I'll leave when the killer is caught. Have you seen Peter Hedberg in the past day or two?'

'I don't really know him.'

'Has your partner been questioned by the police?'

'Don't be ridiculous.'

'Has Khalyla been questioned yet?'

'*Yet?* I think this conversation is over.'

'Have we met before?' I ask, because it feels like we have met. I get a familiar vibe from this hotelier. 'I worked in Malmö for a short time. Did our paths cross in Malmö, Eric?'

He gives me a strange look but doesn't say anything.

'Malmö?' I say again. 'A few years back? Did we talk?'

'It's unlikely,' he says, smiling. 'Now, are your skis and boots outside under the awnings or in the kit room?'

'My *skis?*'

'The lift is closed, Tuva. It is closed for essential maintenance. They didn't tell you that on the way up? They should have let you know. You didn't see the signs? The only options available to you now are to borrow skis and make your way down, or else stay the night up here with us at the hotel.'

26

I stare at him. 'You're not being serious? This is a joke, right?'

'This is a *hotel*, Tuva. Once voted the finest hotel in all of Jämtland. It wouldn't be the worst thing to stay a night here at the Pinnacle. After all, I've lived here most of my life save for a few memorable years in Stockholm. Would you care to see a room?'

I squeeze my eyes together and try not to look flustered. 'No. Thank you. I have to go back down to the town. I have interviews to conduct. Police to talk with. I can't be stuck up here.'

'Then I suppose you'd like to borrow boots and skis. Come with me to the kit room.'

I follow him along a long, dimly lit corridor with thin grey rug, and on through a rickety door.

This is why I should live in a big city with a subway system and Uber drivers.

'Down here is Karin's domain, really,' he says. 'You should see her tools and how she maintains them. She keeps this place going.'

'How so?'

'I wasn't blessed with dexterity, Tuva. Can hardly use a hammer and nail, to be honest with you. Karin keeps an old building like this watertight. Makes sure the snow stays outside. She is a marvel.'

The room has a long, oak table with various waxes and bottles of polish. There are skis stacked neatly: modern fibreglass skis and old narrow wooden skis with leather bindings. A rack of brightly coloured ski boots and poles of various lengths and types.

'You're not a snowboarder type are you?' asks Eric.

'No.'

'Thank goodness. How tall are you? One-seventy?'

'Something like that.'

He hands me a set of skis.

'Boot size?'

'Forty-one.'

A figure passes by the glass doors to outside.

'Who was that?' I ask.

'What?'

'Someone walked by.'

He shrugs. 'This is a hotel, Tuva. I know it may not feel quite like one but I assure you some people choose to come here.'

'Of course.'

'Let's see,' he says, and then he hands me a pair of boots with newspapers scrunched inside of them. I glance up at the wall, at the straps and bindings and wrenches. 'They might be a little cold and damp but they are the best we have. You can leave them down at the ski shop tomorrow, or whenever suits you.' He looks dejected. 'It's not like we have much demand for rental kit up here these days.'

'There's no other option?' I say. 'I'd pay gas money if someone could drive me down on a snowmobile?'

'We don't have one up here,' he says. 'What with the avalanche risk and the fact that most of the mountain is protected.'

'Protected?'

'Ancient Sami lands, you see. There are strict rules. Every man's right to roam still exists here, of course; it's a constitutional right everywhere, but that right does not extend to motorized vehicles. Skis are the only way down when the lift is out of action. Let me find you a good helmet.'

I squirm. 'That's okay. I ski like an uptight tortoise, super-cautious. I never pick up enough speed to make it dangerous. And the helmets interfere with my hearing aids. I don't like them.'

'I insist you wear a helmet, Tuva.'

You can insist all you like, mate.

'Thanks, but no. Like I said I'll head down extremely slowly. I'm not a strong skier.'

'All the more reason to wear a helmet. Listen, if you refuse to wear one I can't lend you the skis. I'm sorry. I have a duty of care as the proprietor of the Pinnacle. If you won't wear a helmet you'll need to stay here until the morning.'

I feel like a fifteen-year-old again. Except, when I was fifteen, Mum was in a depressed, sick, vacant state; unaware of what I was doing most of the time. And Dad was cold in the ground.

'Fine,' I say, sternly.

He smiles and hands over a helmet. It's a little large, which is a good thing, but I don't tell him that. 'Snug,' I say.

'As it should be.'

I pull on the rigid, uncomfortable ski boots as he unlocks a set of double doors and cold air rushes in to meet us. We move outside and I place the skis down on the powder. I press my heels down and feel the skis click into the bindings. He hands me my poles.

'There's only one blue slope so be very careful you stick to it. And try not to take too long down. The fogs are rising up the mountainside. The breath of the lake, you know.'

'Thanks for lending me these.'

'Always stick to the marked pistes. Do not take short cuts or deviate from the groomed runs in any way. Stay to the right. Watch out for patches of black ice.'

'Bye, Eric.'

He checks my helmet one more time. He's a little too close. 'Ski safe, Tuva.'

I push off with my poles. The powder is fresh and deep and I am quite at ease gliding away slowly from the hotel towards the top of the unmoving lift. The floodlights bathe the slopes in a pale, ghoulish light, and the town twinkles far below.

A blue run, clearly signposted. I have tackled these before. It won't be pretty but I will manage. Lena would tell me to keep my wits about me. Tam would say *break a leg* because she's Tam. Noora might have kissed me through my helmet. It strikes me that we never had the chance to ski together. Neither of us particularly liked skiing, but it seems unfair we never had the chance.

Tentative, shaky turns.

Nothing elegant or fast. But effective snowplough beginner turns. I stick to my sedentary, low-speed technique and make my way down the blue slope. It is broad and even and there is a light mist: murk encroaching.

After ten minutes I'm sweating through my shirt and my shins are hurting. I'm not built for this shit. But I am making progress. Someone on a parallel slope skis down at five times my speed. A black blur. I keep traversing my piste; the fine vertical lines from Johan's basher is evidence of its lack of skiers. I have to push with my poles and angle my skis to make it up an incline and then I ski through dead trees and a thick cloud of frozen fog rises up to greet me. I look back and I cannot see the hotel through the snow-laden pines. I gaze down and I can no longer see the town. The fog thickens up around me like a sauce. I am panting and I feel trapped inside this damn. unwanted helmet. I ski but I can't see the snow in front of me. Confounded mountain. I stop. A crack in the treeline to my side. A branch giving way under the weight of the snow. It looks shallow. Steady. I bite down hard on the inside of my lip and set off.

If I go slowly I can't get into too much trouble. Sure, it might take me all night to make it down alive but I *will* make it down alive. This fog, though. It's like being stuck deep underwater. I can no longer tell my left from right.

I intensify my snowplough technique to brake, and tip over a ledge I never saw coming, and now I'm travelling too fast. *Way* too fast. Accelerating. Out of control, the wind making my eyes water. I squeeze with my thighs and my calves and come to an abrupt stop in deep snow but I am hanging on for dear life.

Panting.

I glance up. Nothing. Not one feature to take comfort from. The fog is dimly lit so I know I'm not too far from the lift system but I have no idea what piste I am on. Is this still the blue? It must be. It's blue, a steep section, but still blue. Deep breaths, but my guts are tangled. They know the truth before I do. I angle my skis to carve deeper, to ski down with the brakes on full, my legs tensed. I turn to face the angle of the mountain, and then, losing whatever control I had, I plummet.

The rush of icy wind against my face.

Feedback in my hearing aids. Squealing and crackling. No idea what's coming. Like skiing into thick smoke.

I scream like a child and brace myself and somehow come to a halt on the edge of the piste. I'm safe but this slope is too much for me: it is more like a wall or a cliff. The angle is completely un-skiable, even in good conditions.

I can't go up and I can't go down.

I am trapped.

27

I'm not even sure I'm on a marked piste anymore. It looks like a piste, the little I can see, but the surface is uneven. Fresh snowfall, and in places the run is too narrow; more of a chute or a rockface than a recreational ski slope.

I stab both poles deep into the snow and hang on like an inept rock climber. The wind gusts. I have a strong urge to check my phone, for reassurance as much as anything, but I can't risk letting go of my borrowed poles. After what seems like ten minutes I make the decision to proceed down the slope, but to take it literally one metre at a time. *Slow is fast and fast is slow*, as Dad used to say. God, I miss him right now.

It strikes me how absurdly dangerous skiing on mountains can be. I took a wrong turn in the fog. *One mistake.* I went left instead of right and missed a piste sign by perhaps ten metres. And now I am sliding down a near-vertical cliff face, my left boot high above my right, desperately trying to keep control, my legs shaking from exertion. One slip, one false move, and I will hurtle down this slope to my certain death.

My muscles burn and my back is drenched with sweat, now freezing to my skin as night approaches, but I am hanging on.

A shuffle, and I come to a stuttering halt. A short, terri-fying slide. Another shuffle, snow accumulating beneath the leading edge of my downhill ski. So little control of my own destiny. Nature, dominating. I am exhausted. How much further to go at this rate? An hour? Six hours?

My chest compresses tight as I think of Peter up here with me. He was an ice hockey star. He skied and snow-boarded, and, perhaps, he killed. I imagine meeting him on this misty precipice. I would stand no chance. It would be laughable. A child on an inflatable with a bloodthirsty great white circling underneath, biding his time.

I slide a metre or two and hit sheet ice. My legs lock tight to maintain some modicum of stability, but one of my skis slips and I cannot recover it.

The speed is appalling.

I bump and slide, falling, pushing back up, regaining some balance, and then I plunge and roll. If the powder wasn't so deep I would be unconscious by now. One ski detaches and I lose it to the freezing fog. I could cry and give up. Instead I stay perched on the cliff, clinging to the steepness with my fingernails, ice blasting my cheeks, and I do not quit.

I will not.

I shuffle along on my backside. Half a metre at a time. *How do you eat an elephant?* My mother used to say. Clearly, she'd never tried. I do not locate my lost ski. It might be two kilometres downhill by now.

The light intensifies. My hip hurts and I must have bruised half my back. I shuffle and cling and I am creep-ing closer to one of the steel columns supporting the chairlift cables.

I don't know how quickly I will succumb to frostbite out here. My skin already feels red. *Frostnip*, the precursor to genuine frostbite, is damage to the outer layer of the skin, cells penetrated by ice. I feel the surface layer of my cheeks beginning to break down and perish.

There is nothing to look at.

Nothing to see.

I cannot spot the town or the power station or the church. Above, I still cannot see the hotel. I can't even find the chairlift, but I can sense I am edging closer. One ski missing. A pathetic urban creature sliding down an icy rock-face with nobody waiting for me at the bottom. What if I never return to the B&B? Locals have family members to search for them. Neighbours and colleagues to grieve.

I settle into a rhythm. Slow and steady. If I spread my boots and keep alert I can limit the risk of falling. Slow. Cautious. Thank goodness Eric insisted I wore a helmet.

The only light on the piste is artificial. Floodlights are common in Scandinavia when daylight hours are short. The resorts are only viable with lit pistes and perhaps that is one reason there is a colossal trash-burning power station in this town.

The fog clears a little and the slope shifts from cliff to perhaps a double black diamond run. Impossibly steep but not life-threatening.

I move a little faster, still shuffling.

And then a crack echoes across the mountain.

A boom.

I flatten myself to the snow. Some instinct. One side of my face submerged in freezing powder.

Everything goes dark.

28

I want to scream into the darkness but I stay silent.

The lights might come back on.

They won't, though. A floodlight hit by a bullet will not miraculously repair itself. Someone saw me here, or *knew* I was coming down. It is cleaner to kill my light source than kill me directly. Same end result with significantly less risk.

I'm not sure if I am being paranoid or reckless. Am I ten per cent of the way down this infernal mountain or fifty per cent down? My senses are being stolen from me, one by one. And at this temperature, my hearing aid batteries might not last much longer.

I drop my right leg down and scoot lower, clinging to this icy cliff face, and, honestly, I could weep. I can't see how steep it is below me. I can't see anything. In the distance there are vague glows of warmth from nearby floodlights, but through this haze they appear distant. One step at a time. How do you eat an elephant? Fucking elephants. I would rather eat two of them than navigate this mountainside in the dark.

I'd check my phone but that would necessitate removing a ski pole from the snow and dangling even more precariously than I am already doing.

There are no more gunshots. It only took one bullet to knock out the floodlight. A hunter in a hide with a quality optic, resting his barrel on his rucksack, squeezing the trigger, matching it up with his breathing. There are dozens of such hunters in this town.

I keep going.

My skin is breaking down. Ice crystals burn and then they stop burning. A bad sign. The phenomenon my own mother warned me of each winter. *Always keep your hat on* she'd say. *If you can't feel your cheeks anymore, if you can't feel the cold, run back home as fast as you can.* This is what it is like to be raised in winters that can, and do, maim indiscriminately.

After all this scooting and sliding, my body begins to fail me. My hands are too frozen to be useful, and my shoulders and hips burn from exertion. I do not cry. I keep going.

The ground flattens and I can see more now. The fog has lifted a little, and I'm approaching the next floodlight.

Smoke.

The delicious scent of wood smoke hanging in cold air. I perk up. A sign of civilisation. An aroma we have been drawn too since the dawn of time. Am I back in the town already? Moving closer to the church? The ground flattens and I still don't trust it but I move faster.

A light in a window? Thank god. I slide and then I can walk again. Hallelujah. I walk clumsily, using my sticks to keep me from collapsing.

A shack. Rough sawn timber and a corrugated steel roof. It could be a supply hut or a maintenance building.

The light from the window shines down and affords me a proper view of the place.

I am safe.

Finally.

A pile of logs neatly stacked against the wall of the hut. Two solar panels on one awning. The wind blows snowflakes diagonally across the scene and then I notice it down in the snow.

At first, a singular drop.

Then a cluster.

My mouth falls open as I track the trail of blood, each warm drop deep under the fresh powder, each vertical channel edged in red.

I stare at the trail.

There is no way back.

I will skirt the building, and then, even though I'm limping, I will run for my life. That will work. No, I'll hide. Which is right?

Movement in the upstairs window.

I glance up but I am frozen in place.

Backlit in the snowy window. A face in silhouette, and a scarlet red ski jacket.

29

I make a dash for the treeline as I emerge from the side of what I now know is Ingvar Persson's house. His dogs bark and growl, and their chains tense as they surge towards me, their eyes bulging, their muscles tense.

'Are you lost?' asks Ingvar.

I keep on running for the trees but my progress is laughably slow. The snow is too deep here and I am too tired.

'I said are you lost?'

I slip and fall.

He approaches, each footstep a slow crunch.

Red jacket, red hat.

'Don't!' I say. 'How do I get to the town?'

'The town?'

I scowl.

'No, you need to come inside my house, young woman.'

'No.'

'You need to warm up.'

The dogs keep barking. They were all living outside in the snow, chains attached to poles attached to their collars.

'How much further to town?' I say, my teeth chattering.

'Five kilometres as the crow flies, more or less.'

'Is there a snowmobile? Or a taxi?'

'A *taxi?*'

'People are expecting me. I have an appointment with the police chief. They will come looking.'

He steps closer. His face reddens as he bends over me. 'What are you doing in my backyard?'

I pull back. 'The lift is down.'

He frowns. Pitches his head to one side as if studying me. 'I know it is. Routine. You'll need to ski down. Where are your skis?'

'Up there somewhere. Fucking mountain.'

He looks up the slope, then back to me. He does not offer me his hand.

'I will lend you my old skis. Come inside, get warm.'

'I'm fine out here.'

He takes a deep breath. Looks at me, then sighs. 'Your cheeks are turning white. You are not fine. You have no respect for the mountains and you don't know what you are doing out here. People like you need rescuing and then people like me have to risk our own necks to find you. Come inside now.'

'Have you seen a man out on the slopes? A man with a rifle?'

'Plenty. Hunting is permitted this time of year.'

'Someone shot at a light.'

'A light?'

'Shot the bulb?'

'And why would they do that?'

I shiver and shrug. 'To make sure I wouldn't make it down in one piece.'

'You city types think you're so important. Nobody shot a lightbulb. I'll get my old skis.'

'I can't ski down.'

He blows air through his chapped lips. 'I will take you down with my dogs. One condition. You come inside and drink some hot soup or coffee. You need to warm yourself.'

The thought of a hot mug in my hands buoys me. But it could be a trap. And I don't entirely trust my mind after this ordeal.

'Hot soup *outside*,' I say. 'Then we go.'

'Who do you think you are?'

'Hot soup *outside*,' I say again, firmly. 'Please.'

He mumbles something under his breath about entitled city people and walks off to his cabin. I drag my broken body over to the dogs and wait for him. Through the window I catch a glimpse of his kitchen. A dark wood table with one chair. That strikes me as unusual. Most people would have a spare for visitors. I have four chairs in my kitchen. There is a wood-burning stove with blackened kettle. Elaborate cuckoo clock affixed to the wall. An array of different ropes, already knotted, hanging from sharp meat hooks.

The window opens.

He sticks out his arm.

The mug of soup steams diagonally into the cold evening air and I accept it.

'Goulash,' he says.

'*Tack*,' I say.

The mug has a hand-carved wooden spoon in it. The hot, meaty liquid burns my lips but I devour it. Sweet gems of carrot that melt as soon as they reach my tongue. Soft, spiced potatoes. A background flavour of smoked paprika. My body revives, and my spirit follows soon after. I watch Ingvar take a bucket to each of his four dogs, and, using a long-handled ladle made from pine, he pours what looks like bloody elk entrails into their food bowls. Ah, that's what I saw before in the snow. Natural, high-energy dog food served by a rehabilitated mountain man.

I finish the soup and hold the mug tight, sapping every degree of warmth from it.

Ingvar tethers his over-excited dogs to a sled. He hands me a huge fur coat and I have fever-dream flashbacks to the witch in Narnia: a bedtime story my father read to me as a girl.

'I'm okay, thanks. No fur.'

'You're not okay. Put it on your knees if you don't wear it, I don't care. But take it.'

I take it.

'Someone was out there on the slopes earlier. It felt like they were tracking me. Stalking me through the trees.'

'It can feel that way in nature. You might have had wolf eyes on you. They watch us all.'

He rides on the back of the sled, one boot on each steel rail, and I take the only seat. The dogs strain at their chains and the lead dog, Duke, pulls the hardest. Ingvar mutters something about how dogs are safest in bad weather. They have a sense of the snow, for the ice patches, for the cliff edges.

I am warm beneath the heavy fur.

Did someone try to do me harm on the slopes? Or is my mind becoming increasingly unreliable and paranoid?

My eyelids are heavy.

He is at my back.

The dogs power us towards the town and I start to make out the power station silhouette in the distance on the far edge of Esseberg, smoke billowing from its one towering chimney.

My belly full, I am almost hypnotized by the movement of the sled through and over the powder. I am warm and sleepy from the motion.

And then I remember, abruptly, with the suddenness of waking from a nightmare, sitting bolt upright in the dead of night, that the man mere centimetres from my head is a convicted murderer.

30

A bump as the dogs cross an icy ridge and join a sign-posted trail, a groomed route for local cross-country skiers. In an instant, I am more at ease, which is preposterous as these are exactly the kinds of trails each of the three victims have been discovered on or near. I cannot help it. Gliding past picnic tables and laminated route maps, the town growing as we speed towards it, my muscles give up their tension as adrenaline drains from my system.

Past the power station and the high school. I can see the church steeple with its old clock, and the brutalist concrete pension-admin offices, and Willy's with its illuminated sign, and then, in the far distance, the gaping 'O' of the tunnel.

Ingvar commands his lead dog to slow.

The dog comes to a halt.

'We cannot run my dogs in town. This is as far as I take you.'

I stand up and my legs are unsteady. I fold the fur coat and thank Ingvar. Maybe he *has* paid his debt to society. Served his time. Maybe I need to reassess my prejudices no matter how reasonable they seem to be. Maybe I need to grow into a better person. I thank him again.

The Lutheran church bells ring out to deserted gritted streets. People are hunkering down at home or else they have fled to friends and relatives for the weekend. Who could blame them?

I stagger along a freshly shovelled pavement and almost fall into the Golden Paradise B&B. The sunbeds are unoccupied. Each booth has an open door and they look like upturned caskets from some dystopian version of the future. The word *casket* brings back traumatic memories from Rose Farm again. Memories I work hard to bury, if you will excuse the pun.

I walk through to my room and as I fumble with my key Astrid emerges from her room.

'See you, Tuva.'

'Night.'

She pauses and looks at me. 'Are you all right? You look bloody awful.'

'I'm a shit skier. What can I say?'

'Sorry?'

'Doesn't matter.'

'Are you drinking enough water? Are you sleeping?'

She stares at me a little too intensely, a little too closely. I try to escape into my room. I need rest. 'I'm fine.'

'Wait,' she says, placing her hand in the way of my closing door. 'I'm going out for some Cevapi. Join me?'

'No, thanks. I'm exhausted. And I need to write up some work.'

She looks at her watch. 'Not going to happen. You need a break; I can see it in your posture. Come out with me for an hour. Forty minutes. Clear your head.'

I sigh.

'If you don't come I'll call your editor and tell him you need a break. You'd do the same for me.'

I'm not sure I would, actually. And my editor is a *she*.

I remember the sight of the food truck. 'What is *Cevapi* anyway?'

'Only the most delicious food this side of the tunnel. Guy comes every Friday and Saturday with his van, so I'm told. He's been coming for years.'

I can hardly keep my eyes open. But I am also famished hungry despite the mug of meat soup. 'How far is it?'

'Near Willy's. Five minutes away, max. You coming?'

I want to tell her about the shot I felt and heard on the mountain. The lightbulb going out. But the more I think about it, the more I suspect the bulb simply blew. Perhaps my imagination got the better of me.

'Let me change out of these ski boots, then I'll be with you. Give me two minutes.'

She goes back to her room.

When I sit on my bed and heave off the rigid technicolour boots Eric leant me I start to sob. Years ago I would have pulled myself together but I am a little wiser now. I let it happen. And then I actually feel better for it. Noora told me not to get in my own way when I feel something. I wish I could see her one last time to thank her for that and for a thousand other things.

I knock on Astrid's door.

Room 1.

She opens it and says, 'Have you been crying?'

'Jesus. Are the walls that thin? My hearing's not good enough to notice.'

'No, no. I can see it in your eyes. You okay?'

'I'm fucking starving.'

She smiles and we set off. Three minutes later we are standing in a short queue for the navy-blue Cevapi food truck. The menu options are limited, which, according to Tammy, is a positive sign. Never eat from a food truck with seventy-five menu options. She also told me: avoid discount sushi at all costs, and don't trust a kitchen if you don't like how they present their customer toilets. Smart woman, is Tam.

'What are you having?' asks Astrid.

'I don't know. I'm too tired to read. What are you having?'

'Cevapi with *kajmak*, onions and *somun* flatbread. Mine's the vegetarian version. Food of the Gods. I'm buying.'

'No, I can't let you do that.'

'You get the next one.'

She's friendly but she's not flirting. She's attractive but she's not my type. And anyway, it's too soon. It might always be too soon. That part of myself has been switched off ever since Noora slipped away.

We order. I take a Coke with mine and Astrid orders sparkling water with lemon. We sit on the white wooden bench outside the church eating steaming bread rolls filled with small, skinless sausages, hers made from cabbage or something, mine beautifully spiced, savoury juice dripping down my fingers.

'Nylon fibres,' she says.

'Excuse me?'

She finishes her mouthful. 'The fibres found on the necks of the two latest victims are nylon. Black synthetic material. Police are trying to source the type of belt, if that's possible, maybe even the manufacturer, and ascertain which local stores stock it.'

'Who told you? You have someone on the inside?'

'It's on the news, Tuva. Where have you been all day?'

I shake my head and take a large bite from my Cevapi.

She's right. I haven't checked anything. I glance at my phone. The one message that catches my attention is an email from Eric. He's checking if I got home okay. The crack of that bullet replays inside my head. The lights going out as I clung to the granite cliff.

I type my reply. *Yes, thanks. But I lost a ski. I will pay for it in full if you let me know the value.*

I send the email. Later I will tell police what happened on the mountain today. My *interpretation* of what happened.

And then I notice another message from earlier today. It is a reply to one of a dozen emails I sent earlier to old friends, acquaintances and summer work colleagues of Peter Hedberg. This message is from Alfred Persson, a contemporary who moved to Åre after high school. I found him through a social-media post: a screenshot of a YouTube video of the two of them playing Dungeons & Dragons.

Alfred's message reads, 'We need to talk.'

31

I wake from a restless sleep to my phone vibrating and the torch flashing. I didn't have any claustrophobia nightmares, a recent speciality of mine, but I did wake once in the early hours from a dream where I was hanging onto icicles dusted with loose snow, desperately scrambling for a better hold, as the mountain slowly and silently steepened to vertical, threatening to toss me back to the town I was scrambling away from.

Maybe I should work in ICA Maxi on the checkout or help out at the Hive self-storage place back in Visberg. Luka Kodro might give me a job at his pizza grill. At what point do you change course? Lars did it. He was the full-time reporter at the *Gavrik Posten* for years and then he told Lena, out of the blue, that he wanted to go part-time, to focus on his succulents and his puzzles, to write his extremely long memoir, and I must say I respect him for it.

A question pops into my mind. A series of questions, in fact. Firstly, why did the police mention the semen stain they found on Jenni Karlsson's clothes? Was that an error of judgement, because such a stain may have no connection whatsoever to the crime or perpetrator, or was that an indicator that it *does* have relevance? Secondly, how long does forensic work on such a sample take? I check this. Initial discovery can be made with a UV light, but the next stage is an AP or Acid Phosphatase test to detect an enzyme secreted by the prostate gland. There are other confirmatory tests such as the p30/PSA RSID test and the Christmas-tree stain. But none of these would identify the specific individual responsible. Apparently, downstream applications are required to develop a DNA profile from the semen sample. Honestly, I am in awe of forensic experts.

Breakfast consists of two cups of coffee and a cardamom bun the size of a small rotisserie chicken. More like medium size. I walk out through the solarium, one vertical sunbed occupied, someone inside toasting themselves to perfection, alien blue light leaking from the gaps. The air outside is crisp. A woman cross-country skis from Willy's, her backpack stuffed to the brim, and her terrier follows behind with an expression of *what is this shit. You think I enjoy this? You consider this some kind of treat? Leave me at home next time, human.*

A town of a thousand. Perhaps a hundred fewer after the recent exodus. The perpetrator is still walking freely among us as far as we know. The thing is: even if you are scared, how do you leave if this place is your home? If you're an HR manager at the pensions office you still need to go in most days. If you drive a forklift at the garbage-burning power station you can't just call in and say it is too dangerous to work. For most people, the truth is you still need to turn up. In practice, for most people, you cannot leave even if you want to.

I scrape my Hilux. The temperature has dropped and the ice crust on my lights and windscreen takes an age to remove. A man I vaguely recognise from the church hall passes by with his face pointing down, eyes on the ground. Is it the snowplough driver? Or the deacon in civilian clothes? I haven't managed to meet him yet, only his wife. Why does he look down at the ground like that? Because he doesn't want to fall or because he doesn't want to become the next target?

The lit roads are empty and the mountain vista is still invisible to the naked eye. We breakfast in the dark and we eat dinner in the dark. We wake up in the dark and we go to sleep in the dark. Such is life, as Ned Kelly said just before he was executed. The only lights I can see outside the town limits are the Grand Hotel Pinnacle, so high it appears like some celestial body, a white dwarf, perhaps; and the roving piste-basher that Johan is driving straight up a red slope, an anchor chain attached to a lift tower to prevent a catastrophic fall.

I shudder just thinking about it.

The tunnel has a system. You come through to the town on the hour. Until then, you need to wait behind a barrier and red light. And when you want to leave town, you do so at half past. Right now it's twenty-five past.

My engine idles. I need to check my oil levels one of these days because Dad told me never to completely rely on the electronic sensors and warning signs. Of course, he was talking about cars fifteen years ago, but still.

Green light.

But then the light changes to red. The truck in front slams on his brakes and I do the same, my seatbelt biting into my chest. The sign says the tunnel has closed for the day. I start sweating as the words scroll across. It says there has been an incident. Am I stuck here now? For how long? I scratch my wrists: some imagined itch. The lights inside the tunnel switch off, one after the next. I may as well be facing a sheer cliff. One of the cars in front manoeuvres and drives back to town and I switch down my heating because I am struggling to breathe. It's closed?

Someone ahead of me beeps their horn.

The screen glitches.

The light turns green.

They must have resorted something. Switch it off and switch it on again.

I drive slowly, part of a confused convoy, and the mouth of this tunnel swallows me whole. From darkness, to light, ironically. The walls of the tunnel change from smooth concrete to craggy, wet rock, and I begin to sense the full weight of this vast mountain bearing down upon us. A form of wormhole. I notice smaller, narrower auxiliary tunnels and holes I missed last time. This thing is so deep underground I cannot contextualise it, so I switch on music to help me avoid the thought. Willie Nelson, one of Dad's favourites. Mum couldn't stand him. She liked classical music, piano concertos, and then, after Dad died, I never witnessed her listen to music ever again.

After seven minutes I emerge and it feels fucking wonderful. I have left that locked-in town, and the new vista that presents itself to me is divine. Wide open space. In the distance, a stretch of highway I can thunder along all the way to Åre. Lakes and forest on the periphery.

Normality, relatively speaking.

I use the half-hour drive to bring together whatever pieces of this grizzly puzzle I have collected so far. Three

victims, all apparently unrelated. No bodies found yesterday, thank goodness. But, on the flip side, still no suspect
in custody. Peter, whom some assume is a suspect,
perhaps the only one, is still missing. Is he missing or is
he at large?

Åre. The scenic mountains behind it: gentler slopes
than Esseberg, less foreboding. More reds and blues in
the mix. Nursery slopes with cartoon characters and
conveyer belt lifts. The town itself is welcoming, somehow. There is no metaphorical door to slam shut behind
you, I suppose. No sense of being trapped. Rather, Åre
has a Max Burger restaurant, a Peak Performance
store, and a creperie. There is something reassuring
about chain stores. A committee of sensible grown-ups
has studied this town and deemed it suitable for their
goods and services. The same, alas, cannot be said for
Esseberg.

I park as close as I can to the Lilla Krog coffee house
and bakery and I cannot help but smile. I shouldn't. I'm
here to interview a teenager about his potentially murder-
ous, or dead, or both, friend. This is *not* a good day. Far
from it. But I see their lights and the Christmas décor
and their array of baked pastries and I can't help but feel
relief. Call me a basic bitch if you like. I've been called
worse.

As soon as I step inside the busy café I identify him.
Poor guy. Alone. He is wearing a denim jacket and plaid
shirt and he looks like he hasn't slept for a week.

'Alfred?'

He nods nervously and gestures for me to sit down.

'Thanks for talking to me,' I say.

'I don't know if I can or should. I don't know anything anymore.'

I sense his skittish energy. He might be about to bail on the interview; I've had that happen before. I slow this down.

'I'm starving and cold. Need caffeine. What would you like?'

He is sat gripping a bottle of water in his hand. He has already peeled off the label.

'I'm good.'

I show him my credit card. 'Business expenses. We need to make the most of it and I hear the pastry situation here is strong. Come on. What can I get you?'

'Cappuccino,' he says.

I turn to head to the counter.

'And . . . a chocolate muffin.'

I smile and order and bring them back to Alfred. He watches me as I pour sugar into my coffee and stir.

'I don't know what to tell you. I've never done this before.'

'That's okay,' I say, resolving to delay bringing out the Dictaphone so I don't scare him into silence. 'We can just talk. No stress, okay. Do you live nearby?'

'On the edge of Åre.'

'Nice town.'

He sips his cappuccino.

'It's a lot busier here than in Esseberg,' I say.

'You can't compare.'

'You went to school there, right? What was it like?'

He tears up his water bottle label into small pieces. 'It was all right. I wasn't one of the cool guys. In a big city maybe you can blend in, or keep out of their way, hide in plain sight, but in Esseberg if you're not one of the cool guys it's over.'

I frown.

'Everyone knows what you are. All the girls know.'

I nod.

'You can't change your reputation. They all know your story. It's set in stone.'

'Yeah,' I say.

'Pete was almost one of them, you know. He was almost popular because he was so good at hockey. He was the highest scorer when we were thirteen. Even though he was deaf he was really well liked.'

'And then?'

He shrugs. 'And then sometimes life sucks.'

'Too fucking right.'

He frowns at me.

'What happened, Alfred?'

'To Pete? Sounds small now. He went up a division. Played for the under 18s, the team the scouts look at each season. He was talking about going professional. But, for some reason, that group was hostile. The other players made fun of him. At first he thought it was like hazing, you know, an initiation. But then it got worse. I remember watching him shrink. He was this confident guy when we were younger. Had plenty of friends. And then he lost it all.'

'But you were still his friend.'

'Yeah, but he quit hockey and he had no dreams left. His gran had sold her car to buy his gear. She told him it was because she didn't feel safe driving in the dark anymore, but he knew she was being nice. And then his world fell apart.' He shakes his head. 'Pete's gone.'

'I'm sorry he's missing.'

'You need a dream if you live in a small town like Esseberg. You need something to cling to.'

'I get what you mean.'

'If that dream dies it's tough to recover. He used to talk about leaving in a blaze of glory or something like that. Making his mark. He was angry about what happened to him and I think he was right to be angry.'

'Do you think he's here in Åre now? Have you heard from him?'

He shakes his head.

'Do you think he's involved in any way with the murders?'

Alfred bites his lip. He hasn't touched his muffin.

'Maybe he's just gone away. He likes music, the metal bands. Sometimes I wake up and think he's gone off to form a band someplace. Caught a ferry to Finland, maybe. But that's not like him. Pete wouldn't just go. Not without telling his gran. She was like his mum, you see.'

I decide to leave the Dictaphone in my bag. I'll write up my notes as soon as this is over.

'What shoe size is Peter?'

He recoils. 'You think he did it, don't you? Just because he wears a size forty-five doesn't mean he did it. I wear a forty-five as well, you want to arrest me?'

Damn.

Now I know Peter wears a size 45.

'Where could he be, Alfred? Do you know of any hiding places he had when he was younger? An abandoned cabin someplace?'

He shakes his head.

And then something clicks. I see his eyes widen.

'What is it? What's on your mind?'

'Nothing.'

'Come on, Alfred. We need to find him.'

A long pause. 'We used to explore the tunnel sometimes. Years ago. It's bigger than people think, you know. There are smaller passageways.'

'And?'

He looks around the room. 'Pete liked a woman back when he worked at Willy's. They were mates. People said he was stalking her, because she's fit and he's, you know, deaf.'

'Deaf means your ears don't work. It's nothing to do with attractiveness.'

'Yeah, I know that, but the other lads don't. Anyway she and him used to go up to the hotel, the Pinnacle, when she was starting out trying to get brand deals and stuff, build her following. He'd take videos and pictures of her at the old railway station. The locked-up one. Racy photos.'

'Why did they do that?'

He sighs and ignores my question. 'I didn't think he'd ever do something like this.'

I don't say a word.

'But now I'm not so sure.'

32

I spend three hours in central Åre researching open source intelligence aka local true-crime blogs and Facebook groups I've joined in the past days. I write a series of lists. They usually help. Lists of people I want to interview, in order of priority. Lists of locations I haven't yet visited, and that I need to photograph. And then lists of theories and unresolved threads. Peripheral locals I am suspicious of. People who haven't looked me directly in the eye for one reason or another.

The one link that tenuously connects them all, as much as it hurts to admit it, is Peter Hedberg.

I search my emails for the message from Eric Lindgren, only to discover he has left me a new one. I reply requesting a chat with Khalyla. Asking if he could set it up either at the hotel or down in the town. He replies ten minutes later, with some lame message I wasn't expecting from him, suggesting I speak directly with him, saying last time it was a pleasure and he would like to see me again. I am surprised. Sure, he stares at me a little too long, looks at me a little too closely, but I never expected this from Eric. My instincts are usually good. They have to be in my line of work.

I buy a postcard from a kiosk. It is horrendously over-priced but I buy it anyway.

Lunch is a Max burger with fries and a Coke. No ice. Too much ice around here as it is. Before I leave town, something I am reluctant to do for a dozen different reasons, one of them being my survival instinct, I order a takeaway coffee for the journey. I ask for a tall white coffee and they ask if I would like liquorice and ginger-bread in that. Liquorice and *gingerbread*? Maybe Ice Town is safer after all.

The skies are bright and clear on the way back to the tunnel.

No fresh snow.

My dash reads five below.

I call Tammy with my phone connected to my hear-ing aid, and I have butterflies waiting for the call to connect.

'Tuva Moody, thirty under thirty. How's the north pole?'

'Unsafe.'

'I fucking heard. You're not still in that tunnel town are you?'

I slow down for a snowplough turning off.

'Tuva?'

'Sorry. Yeah, I'm heading back there now.'

'Three bodies?'

'Yep.'

'Walk in the light. Stay away from assholes and creeps. Keep your locks locked.'

'Thanks, Mum.'

'I'm serious.'

'I know you are. You okay? How's business?'

'Fair. That cold snap wasn't ideal. Customers too frozen to venture out. They'd rather drive through McDonald's when it's that chilly.'

'You're doing okay, though?'

'Course I am.'

I sigh.

'You eating?' She asks.

'Of course I'm fucking eating. Am I *eating*? I just devoured a Max burger and fries. Have you ever known me *not* to eat?'

She laughs.

'The weird thing is, Tam. This case. Some TV stations are calling him the Ice Town Killer or the Pepper Spray Killer. It's the first time I've had doubts in the back of my mind. Like, this one story might be too big for me. You know?'

'Too big?'

'That I'll struggle. To do justice to all the families. It's so fast moving.'

'Thirty under thirty,' she says again. 'If you can't, nobody can.'

'Bullshit.'

'I'm serious. You're the best I've ever seen when it comes to sticking your pointy little nose in. They even gave you a bloody award saying so. Take it one day at a time, okay? But don't put yourself in harm's way. I can't live in Shitsville without you, Moody. Got it?'

'Got it.'

'Listen, I've got to go. I'm outside the wholesaler and I need supplies for tonight. Call me anytime you like.'

'I will.'

I drive on and the tunnel is open as it's just past the hour. I enter the shadows. I asked a man in Wrath the other night if it is colder in the centre of the tunnel than in Ice Town and he explained it is the opposite. It is like a microclimate under so much rock. He said it was a pretty constant temperature all year round.

On my passenger seat is the postcard I bought in Åre for little Dan. It's split into four quadrants, each one displaying a different view of the mountains. I will send it tonight or tomorrow.

I emerge from the tunnel and the light seems much more dim on this side. A faded bowl valley. A deep, infected gash in the surface of our world.

I park outside the Vårdcentral surgery. There are three police cars here. And one more unmarked, judging by all the gear inside.

I go in.

Carlsson's on his own working at a computer.

'Carlsson.'

He looks up at me. His eyes, different colours, are beautiful. But he is tired. Cracked lips. He looks like he needs a good homecooked meal. Join the club, pal.

'Has the chief told you?'

'Told me what?'

'You don't know?'

'What don't I know?'

'I can't.'

I sigh. 'Where is she?'

He chews his lip.

'Where is she, Carlsson?'

'She's at the hospital.'

Oh, no. 'What happened to her? Is she okay?'

He shakes his head. 'There was another attack on the mountain, Tuva. But this time the victim survived.'

33

Carlsson refuses to give me any further details about the surviving victim. So I jump into my Hilux and race back towards the tunnel I just drove through.

It takes me over an hour to reach Östersund, despite breaking the speed limit the whole way. If I were still working in London I would have no chance of finding a victim when the police refuse to disclose which hospital they have been taken to, as there are dozens of potential options. Not so in Jämtland. There is only one major hospital in the entire region – a region the size of 50,000 square kilometres, a region the size of Slovakia or Costa Rica – and I am entering its gritted, salted car park right now.

Stacks of snow banked up at the extreme edges of the vast hospital lot. The white lines delineating each parking space are invisible beneath the crust of ice and slush. We park as best we can this time of year. Another loosening of standards. We let our hair go unwashed to avoid the morning chill. We are tolerant of hat-hair and dry, red cheeks. Standards adjust because, fundamentally, in the dark months, we are vulnerable. We live with a pervasive and inescapable sense of danger. The cold can kill you, the roads can kill you, the carbon monoxide from a fireplace can kill you. I am not alone in feeling closer to the grave this time of year.

I don't pay for parking. No time. I don't make eye contact with the receptionists or orderlies, I just walk in. It is a relatively small building. I make my way to the Emergency Department. There are few people in the waiting area. I walk through into the ER proper and a dashing male nurse intercepts me.

'You need to check in at reception, and wait,' he says. 'Back there.'

'They told me to come straight through. It's my best friend.'

'I'm sorry,' he says. 'You have to talk to reception first.'

I give him my best *just let me in, I'll be no bother* face but he stands resolute. From the waiting area I make frantic calls to Lars to ask him to dig for details. Is the perp in custody? What condition is the victim in? Did the victim raise the alarm while on the mountain? Have they identified their attacker? He starts work. Lars isn't fast but he is extraordinarily conscientious and thorough.

I monitor the newsfeeds and local social-media groups for comments. There are rumours Peter Hedberg has been arrested and there are also rumours the surviving victim was sexually assaulted. I hope to God this marks the end of this frenzy.

A man comes in bleeding from his neck, an apparent accident at a construction site, and he is taken through to the ER. Minutes later someone comes through with a mop and bucket on wheels, and removes the blood drops marking the man's route. We cannot abide it. A civilised country has no blood on the floor of reception. Not one drop. On the other side of the door is open flesh, exposed, the corporeal body broken and vulnerable. Yet on this side, the waiting side, our bodies are intact and we maintain hope and cleanliness. The membrane separating these two hemispheres is permeable. I know this only too well.

No updates from Lars.

I step outside to see if I can find any parked police cars from Åre but I cannot. Perhaps she arrived in an ambulance? Or a helicopter?

Rumours online that the victim is Katia Hallgren of Esseberg, a senior administrative assistant at the Pensions Office. Thirty-eight years old. I search for more details, for Facebook photos and Instagram Reels. She is a slight woman who wears fashionable large-rimmed glasses. Former amateur gymnast and figure skater. She has two children. There is a post, a recent post, on her Instagram feed, where she shares a photo of her once-estranged mother at what I assume to be a birthday party. They are both wearing green paper hats, and she writes a caption telling her 78 followers to *hold your parents close and to tell them you love them.*

Suddenly I am very tired. Of this pulsating trauma, this demon hurting local innocents, but also of life itself. I have seen too much. Watching Noora die erased my own fear of death. But that fear has been replaced by a low-level dread of life. An acceptance, a brutal acceptance, of the meanness and randomness of our existence.

A police officer walks past.

'Excuse me,' I call out.

He turns to face me, a puzzled expression on his face.

'Katia Hallgren?' I ask.

'Are you a relative?'

I almost lie but I can't quite bring myself to do it. It would be crossing a line.

'Neighbour.'

Not technically a lie. We both reside, at least for this week, in the same desperate town.

'I can only talk to relatives. I'm sorry.'

'Is she . . . is she going to be okay?' I ask.

He steps closer to me. Scratches his beard. 'She's going to live.'

He walks away.

I let out a long, stale breath. This is excellent news. It lifts me. Because she bloody well deserves to live, to thrive, to see her friends again, to be a mother to her children; and because I sense, for the first time in days, that nature is reverting to form. Good will once again vanquish evil. But mainly, on a practical level, I am relieved she will be able to tell her story, to share her account with police, to describe the beast who attacked her. Scars, tattoos, height, build, dialect, identifying features. This perpetrator is making mistakes. He is greedy or out of control. And so this day, with any luck, will mark the beginning of his downfall.

★

Back in Esseberg I pass by a man pushing a stone, possibly a gravestone, on top of a sturdy wooden sledge. He wrestles with it and curses as it gets caught on grit, and then he keeps on pushing.

I park outside the tattoo parlour slash café. Outside I find Johan talking to a pair of young women. He doesn't have his camera with him this time.

'Have you heard the latest?' he says, turning his back on the women.

'What?'

'The survivor.'

I nod.

'I knew her a little. She used to date a friend of mine from college. They went out for six months.'

I usher him away from the women, towards the peace and quiet of the church car park. We stand beneath an overhanging section of tiled roof.

'What do you know about her?'

He sticks out his bottom lip. 'Katia? Nice woman. Almost forty.'

'Do you know what condition she's in? Police told me it wasn't life threatening.'

'I haven't seen her,' he says, leaning against a wall. 'She's covered in pepper spray, I know that much. Sore eyes and so on. She's probably in shock.'

'Has she given an ID of the perp?'

'Not exactly.'

Damn it.

'All I know is what Constable Vedin told me. He found her. She was screaming, rubbing her eyes, running down the mountain. He heard her and brought her safely into town.'

'What did he say?'

'She was hollering. Said someone had sprayed acid in her face. She'd lived in London and Berlin, you see, for quite a few years. She was more streetwise than most Ice Town residents. Thought it was an acid attack.'

'But it was pepper spray, right?'

'I don't know, Tuva. I have less access than you and the other *trad* newspaper reporters, remember? But I do understand procedure. She'll be in the hospital with doctors and police. She'll be standing, if she's able, on a large sheet of paper. They will carefully undress her. Any fibres or hair that fall will be collected, together with her clothes, on the paper. It will all be carefully bagged and tagged. Doctors will treat her injuries. They will take samples. Saliva, skin cells, swabs, material from under her fingernails. They will photograph her injuries. It is a harrowing process for a victim. I had a woman on the pod last year, a survivor, and she talked through these procedures, and the aftercare and therapy, in minute detail. I think that episode helped a lot of people.'

I find his account, fairly, or unfairly, uncomfortable. It's because men like him don't really know. They *think* they do. They listen to podcasts like his, and they watch interviews with victims and experts. They can empathise to a certain extent, many of them can. But they will never know quite what it feels like, from a horrendously young age, to be vulnerable to attack. In polite society we feel safe enough in a well-lit room with witnesses all around. A certain veil of civility is maintained. We can manage. But then, after office drinks, walking back home down a side street we prefer to avoid, it is like we are thrown back ten thousand years. Darkness and shadows. Johan, despite all the first-hand accounts of crime he has studied and documented, will never fully comprehend the risk we take each day just by going about our business. I read a meme once about how men are afraid women will laugh at them, and women are afraid men will kill them. That thought haunts me to this day.

34

Last night is a blur.

Ever since Noora died I've been trying to look after myself, really I have. I slowed down my drinking and I even bought a few vegetables each week. I didn't eat them, they rotted in the fridge, but I bought them. When I game too much or work too hard there is a little voice inside my head telling me to slow down. It's not my voice; I'm a fool, it's *her* voice. She doesn't scold me or shout. She just tells me to ease off the gas and take a moment.

Yesterday afternoon I went to a dark place. Working in my room, I was relieved the latest victim managed to escape, of course I was. But I was also filled, and I am ashamed to admit this, with emptiness. Because this is almost over. This story. The killer will soon be apprehended. I have seen it before. They become lazy or blatant. They fail to cover their tracks, literally or figuratively, or fail to factor into their wicked calculations that there is more law enforcement out investigating them. Sometimes they become audacious. Or they stop caring, safe in the knowledge they must be caught one of these days. The fact that this time is fast approaching fills me with melancholy. I want the carnage to stop, of course I do. But then I will return to Gavrik. I will return to my desk and my apartment. And when I do she will still not be there.

Some people are good at crying, or talking, or both. I am not. Last night I worked past the point of exhaustion. I wrote up interviews and I constructed potential-suspect profiles, and then I drew a map linking all the victims and other key locations of interest. At home I would have polished off the evening with three hours of gaming. Not here. I don't have the hardware. So, instead of talking or crying, or becoming immersed in the latest version of *Final Fantasy*, I went to Wrath, alone. I spent time at the bar and then in a poorly lit booth with two couples. One of them knew Peter Hedberg from his Willy's days. Said he was a good kid. You might think I would have felt at risk in a biker bar full of tattooed leather-clad metal fans. They are not my people. But in fact they accepted me and they made me feel completely safe.

Trying to set up a meeting with Khalyla, even over the phone, has been exceptionally frustrating. It appears she thinks she's Mariah Carey. I have been passed off to her agent and her publicist. I refuse to negotiate with one of her managers for a ten-minute chat. Sure, she has half-a-million Instagram followers and is well paid by lifestyle brands all over the world, but you would think she might also be invested in trying to bring the Pepper Spray Killer into custody.

That is what he's being called.

The nickname is sticking.

Last night at the bar, people talked as though Peter was already arrested, charged and sentenced. It is remarkable how, despite our considered philosophies and ancient institutions of justice, deep down we are still animals. We demand an eye for an eye. Swift retribution. What we want, really, instinctively, is instantaneous cleansing so we can go on with our daily lives, working for bosses we don't respect so we can earn money we don't deem sufficient to go on living in homes we're eager to sell or renovate. There is a reason people sit at work surfing realestate sites. We have to look forwards otherwise we will stop.

I open the blind.

Fresh snowfall.

The scene outside is something from a 35 mm camera where the film doesn't develop quite as it should. The exposure settings of Ice Town are off. This place is noir to its bones.

Over a nutritious breakfast of Daim ice-cream (I left the tub outside all night in nature's deep freeze by pinching a Willy's carrier bag in the window hinge) I watch several podcast episodes on Johan's YouTube channel. It isn't the largest true crime podcast in the Nordics but it is up there. The recordings – made from what looks like a cosy, Scandi guesthouse or cabin, complete with large picture window, black-and-white portrait photographs, rough pine walls and a red 'On-Air' lamp – are long. Some last over five hours. He is meticulous in his work and I am impressed. The episodes are filmed and then they are divided later into short clips. In these snippets he analyses the body language, behavioural ticks and verbal cues of his interviewees. I watch extracts from several episodes, each of which have over a hundred thousand views. One interview with a retired prison guard. Another with a falsely imprisoned man who had his rape conviction quashed due to modern DNA evidence. Finally, a conversation with a former enforcer from a Mexican cartel. This video is different from the others in that the interviewee is in the dark and his voice is disguised.

The ice-cream soothes my hangover and it helps settle my stomach.

I noticed last night that Astrid, the reporter from Norrköping, snores like a horse. Thin walls is an under-statement. Not a delicate horse, either, but a horse bred to pull a wagon or heavy canal boat. It wasn't an issue for me. I removed my hearing aids to recharge the batteries and order was restored.

My priority today is to interview the survivor. She lives in this town and, according to a brief police statement, she has suffered no life-threatening injuries, so I am hoping she'll return from Östersund today. I have seen on the news how Åre police have stationed an officer, a man I recognise from the presser in the school gym, outside the family residence. According to my phone, that house is a four-minute walk from my B&B. I am conflicted about meeting with her so soon after the attack. She doesn't need me pressing her for details, she needs counselling and support from her loved ones. Not only because of the trauma of the incident, although that must have been atrocious, but because of any possible survivor guilt. She must be wondering why she lived and the other three victims did not. She must be pondering the empty space left in those families, and how she is still able to live her life.

I pull on my base layer, then my mid-layer, then my ski clothes. The weather app tells me it is nineteen below zero.

My phone buzzes in my hand and I notice a message pop up on the screen.

I pull off my hat.

Overheating already.

The message is from Lena.

Peter Hedberg has been found.

35

He's been found?

I call Lena immediately. She doesn't pick up.

I run through the solarium into the street. Everything looks absurdly normal. An older lady makes her way slowly along the slippery pavement, elasticated metal spikes stretched over her boots.

I call Lena again but this time her phone is busy.

I reply to her – *Is he dead or alive?*

The wind stings my cheeks as I stand staring at my phone. No reply.

My eyes start to water.

I look around the town at the power station, the almost-flat roofline of the school, the old church clock, the illuminated Willy's sign, the cuboidal pension offices, the tunnel queue in the distance.

I scan Twitter. Nothing yet. I look at various apps for breaking news. No mention. How come Lena knows before I do? I open the Facebook group for the church.

Our prayers are with the family of Peter Hedberg. May he rest in peace.

I can't catch my breath. He's dead? My God. Perhaps he killed himself. Or else the police found him and they shot him. He couldn't hear their commands.

A message emerges below the announcement on Facebook.

'I'll pray for the victims. One of them was my cousin. As for Peter Hedberg, he can rot in hell.'

Incoming call from Lena.

'He's dead?' I say. 'How did you find out?'

'Old contact. Listen. Four kilometres east of Esseberg town centre. Past the road to the power station. I'll send you the GPS coordinates now. Go.'

I pull myself together and start the Hilux. My heart is beating hard against my ribs which makes no sense as he is dead now and this is all over. Finished. I should have experienced more of this nervous energy when he was still on the loose, when the whole community was at risk, but part of me mourns this one particular killer, assuming he did indeed do this. Because Peter could have been me, and vice versa. If I had reached him a week ago, before all this began, perhaps I could have connected with him and lives would have been saved. If culpable, I condemn his actions, of course I do, but I also mourn him.

Radio on the whole way. Lena has a lot of old contacts. In law enforcement, the civil service, the judiciary, major newspapers. She has her own web and she protects it and looks after it.

Breaking news of a man's body found near a salt bin east of Esseberg. Police request citizens not to visit the scene as they will not be granted access to the area.

A salt bin? Not inside. The very thought of it gives me chills.

I put my foot down.

Salt is used for preserving meat. Stop it. Don't think those thoughts, Tuva.

There are already seven vehicles here when I arrive.

I run towards the cluster of heavy coats in the distance. The snow is deep and the surface has a hardened crust so I fall through every few steps.

They have not erected a tent over the cadaver. Perhaps because they know there isn't any precipitation forecast today. Or, perhaps, because the local police department may have, somewhat understandably, run out of crime-scene tents.

They have placed screens around the body. Ten metres or so from the salt bin. Men and women in white suits, barely visible against the snow, work meticulously. Uniformed officers guard the scene. I approach Carlsson, a bruise on his cheek, and ask if it is Peter Hedberg.

'Step back, please.'

'Is it Peter?'

He sets his jaw. 'Step back now.'

I stand with the others. We watch as a man in the distance climbs a pile of boulders and, once he is a kilometre or so away, start to photograph the scene from above using a telephoto lens. I think he might have an angle sufficient to see over the privacy screens. And he will have the entirety of Ice Town in the background, too. It is the kind of photograph – well lit on a day like this – that will be bought by every major newspaper in the land.

I scan a few degrees to the west and look higher up the mountain. I see the shack, barely visible behind thick snow-laden pine trees. A man with his sled dogs. Red jacket. It can only be Ingvar.

Two women carry a stretcher with a body bag and place it gently into the back of an ambulance.

'Fucking murderer!' yells a woman to my right, causing me to jump a little. She's pointing at the body bag. 'Scum!'

I back off from her.

More people arrive. A man I recognise from the church, I think he's a volunteer there but his real job is driving a snowplough at night, and then the Viking-esque poet-bouncer from Wrath.

He nods to me.

I nod back.

'Did himself in,' says the bouncer, his voice a deep drawl.

'You know that for sure?'

'Hung himself.'

'Out here?'

'First-aid tourniquet found tight around his neck. I know the neighbour of the woman who found him, used to come to the club most weeks. Tourniquet round his neck with the windless tucked in. He took his own life.'

'Windless?'

He looks down at me. This bouncer must be as tall as a door.

'On a CAT tourniquet, a proper one, the kind police and military use, the kind I was trained on when I was in the army, you tighten the nylon belt round an injured limb, as high up as possible, and then once it's fixed in place you rotate a windless, like a rigid stick, and that tightens it even more. Leverage of ten to one, or might even be twenty, I can't remember. So you can cut off

197

circulation in the event of a severe bleed. I learned all about it during military service. The importance of not bleeding out, of damage control before seeking higher medical care. On a limb you still have plenty of time, hours, probably, before the tissue dies. Peter was found out here with one round his neck. He couldn't live with himself, I expect. Came up here and ended it all.'

36

I spend a total of three hours interviewing everyone who will talk to me. I speak to the cousin of the first victim but she is so angry and heartbroken I will be unable to quote most of what she says, and afterwards I feel guilty for carrying on the conversation as long as I did. When someone is as vulnerable as that, in pain, in shock, they can open up and divulge things they later wish they hadn't. I speak to a painter and decorator who skis the route once or twice a week in preparation for the 90km *Vasaloppet* race. He is composed but also haunted by the fact he might have slid directly over Peter's frozen face before it was discovered. I try to reassure him that it would be unlikely. But I can tell by the look in his eye he is not convinced. He says he won't be able to ski there again. He also says police were talking about digging at other sites, excavating compacted snow. Other sites? I push him for more information but he has none. Then I talk to five others and although I am asking pertinent questions and recording everything on my Dictaphone, at times my concentration lapses. I start imagining Peter's final minutes, placing that tourniquet around his own neck, tightening it, securing it, waiting for the oxygen loss to force him to black out. I think about how lonely and desperate and guilty he felt. How his own grandmother was just a few kilometres away worried sick about him. I think about his childhood, being excluded from conversations and jokes and games. Kids mumbling things and him asking them to repeat and them saying: *it doesn't matter, it's not important.* Nothing excuses killing people in cold blood, if that is indeed what he did. But I still feel for him.

Most of what I discover by interviewing locals is rumours and gossip. Nothing actionable or useable in a court of law. But I do not operate in those clean worlds. I work in the real world, the shadowy, grimy place where storytelling clashes with facts. Hearsay and gossip, while they never make it directly into my work, still inform the mood and themes of my long-form articles. Rumours he was found dead and cold with a can of Czech-made pepper spray in his pocket. Rumours he had an old photograph of Khalyla, the influencer from the Pinnacle, in his jacket pocket. Rumours that he'd recently had arguments, vocal and public arguments, with both the church deacon *and* Eric Lindgren. And, finally, rumours Peter had been spending time with Ingvar over the past months, up at the isolated cabin I stumbled upon, and that he was keen to explore a potential career in psychology or criminology. From these conversations I manage to crystallise the web of connections that make this town what it is. I gain a sense of the social mitochondria connecting each family and neighbour.

The wind is gusting.

I turn up at the temporary police base in the Vårdcentral surgery and there are two officers in place but neither one of them will speak to me. I ask them if there will be a presser or a statement and they continue to blank me. So I call Carlsson instead and he puts the phone down. This is the problem reporting from a town that is not your home patch. Over the years I have built up layers of sources, gossips, grasses, frustrated council members, and genuine friends in the local community. Way out here, I have nothing of the sort.

I drive to Peter's grandma's apartment but she's not in. I don't know why I came. I guess I understand, on some level, how most people avoid you when you are grieving. Like it's contagious. After Noora died everyone except Lena and Tammy held back. If they spotted me in ICA Maxi they wouldn't know what to say. They deviated to another aisle. And then, one Saturday, I received a delivery of flowers to my apartment. They were spring flowers: grape hyacinths and narcissi. Nothing showy. But they were Noora's favourites. She used to wait for them to bloom on Lovers Walk, the small park built on an escarpment outside my building's balcony. The flowers were from Chief Björn and his wife.

My thoughts turn to Chief Skoglund of Åre police. I call her office number and ask to be put through to her. She is not available. I email her.

There has been no press conference called. I walk to the church and it hits me that this sanctified place at the centre of Ice Town will now revert to form. It has been a meeting place and organisation centre for the missing-persons' searches for some time now. All that will end. It will now once again be a place for reflection, mourning, and the celebration of lost lives. Graves will be dug when it is warm enough to do so. Services will be held. And, in time, this town, like every other town like it, will find a way to heal and move on.

Astrid and one other reporter, a pale, insipid man from Stockholm, approach.

'No presser,' says the other reporter.

'I heard maybe tomorrow,' I say.

'They just want it over now,' says Astrid. 'That's what the old choirmaster told me. They want for all of us to go back to where we came from and for them to rebuild their lives in peace. He wasn't being vicious. He said when reporters come all the way out here they know they're in trouble.'

'You leaving?' I ask.

'Tomorrow,' says Astrid. 'My editor wants me back in the Norrköping office. Colleague goes on maternity leave soon so they need me. You?'

'Tomorrow or the next day,' I say. 'Loose ends to wrap up.'

'That'll take months,' says the mousey reporter from Stockholm. 'I've never seen a case like this with no clear motive and no discernible connection between victims.'

I think about mentioning how someone can just snap. Anyone can. How that's how Noora ended up like she did. How maybe if you are deaf and you live up here and you're excluded by your peers, how all that can build and build. I am not excusing it, but I can, on some level, understand it. Instead, I say nothing.

When I return to my room a message comes through from Chief Skoglund. It says she is too busy to talk. It also says she could be free at 7:30 p.m. for fifteen minutes. She says she has rented a bungalow for the week in Esseberg to save driving to and fro through the tunnel. She says we can talk over pizza.

37

I drive to the furthest reaches of Esseberg, to the suburbs on the outskirts of town. Takes all of six minutes.

What do you bring a police chief who invites you over for frozen pizza? There is no *Systembolaget* in this town so I can't buy wine or liquor. There isn't a florist either. And this is why, next to me on the passenger seat along with an empty pack of wine gums and my windscreen scraper and my spare hat, is a paper bag of crisp green apples.

I pull into number 320.

Picket fence, shovelled path, post box at the end of the short drive, an ornamental well in the garden.

I knock on the door.

She opens it almost immediately and she looks exhausted. Tired eyes, a fine cut on her lip, unwashed hair. She is wearing a grey fleece and jeans.

'Come in,' she says.

I hand her the apples and she smiles.

'Thank you. I need the vitamins.'

The house is bare and empty. It has that sterile Airbnb feel. Generic IKEA artwork in cheap frames. Not a single photograph. No mess, either. Just her uniform on a wire hanger dangling from a cupboard door. Her carry-on luggage bag lies open on the floor in the bedroom. Some kind of trauma kit open: shears, gauze and latex gloves accessible. A case of Red Bull sits on the kitchen table.

'You live like me,' I say.

'I don't live like this normally, Tuva.'

I do.

'I need to be back at base in forty-five minutes. Should be enough time for pizza. We have a pepperoni and Hawaiian in the oven. Your choice, I don't care which.'

'Mind if I take the pepperoni? I'm not keen on fruity pizza.'

She nods. 'That's fine. And just so we're clear, any conversation here tonight is strictly off the record. You cannot quote me. That understood?'

'Understood.'

'Okay, then. Red Bull or water?'

I point to the water and she pours me a glass.

'Is it true Peter was found with a tourniquet around his neck? Was that self-inflicted? Is he solely responsible for the other murders?'

'You don't ease into it, do you, Tuva.'

'My dad taught me that when playing chess the best form of defence is attack.' I think of Eric. I don't want to think of Eric, I want to think of Dad. 'He taught me not to hold back.'

'This isn't chess and you're not defending.'

It is always chess. Every single time. And I am defending the victims and their families.

'Is there DNA linking Peter to the other murders?'

'Tuva, I'm sorry. I can't go into operational details. That's not why I invited you here.'

'So why did you invite me?'

She checks on the pizzas through the oven door. 'To break bread with you. Share a quick meal.'

I frown.

'Did Chief Björn ask you to do this?'

'No,' she says. 'Nothing like that. It's just that I heard about your partner, Noora Ali, through the police grapevine. I'm so very sorry for your loss, Tuva. I heard you helped care for her.'

'Of course I helped care for her.'

'I know a little about how that can be. For me it wasn't so traumatic, I must admit. It was my mother and she was sick. This was years ago. I cared for her when I was working through the academy and starting out. I was her night carer for a long time. I had help but I looked after her as much as I could. She was a strong Sami woman.'

I don't know what to say. I almost say sorry and I almost say I considered caring for my mother but she never wanted me to and she went into a hospice before I could help her in that way. Instead I say nothing for a long time.

'You did that at the same time as being a cop?'

She scratches her head and shrugs. 'You did it at the same time as working as a reporter. We find a way, don't we? At least for a while.'

'I guess we do.'

'My mother, rest her soul, was the last generation to be seriously discriminated against. We Sami are still not accepted by many. We're still misunderstood. Some people still think we are less evolved or less civilised than other Swedes. But her generation and the ones that went before her had it so much worse. She was one of the girls forced to leave to study in cruel boarding schools.' She rubs the bridge of her nose and sips her Red Bull. 'Some of her friends were forcibly sterilised by the state. It was utterly horrific.'

I consider telling her how, even though it is very different, the deaf community also feel discriminated against. How mainstream schooling can be difficult, and how deaf schools can also be difficult. But I swallow it down.

The oven timer flashes zero.

She brings two slightly burnt pizzas over together with a carving knife.

'Sorry, I don't have a pizza cutter here. Just a rental. I have one back home.'

'What would you say if I told you someone might have shot at a chairlift light, possibly to cause me to lose my sense of direction on the slopes after dark.'

'Did someone shoot out a light?'

'I'm not sure.'

'Gunfire isn't that unusual at this time of year. Hunting quotas are there to be filled. But if you think something unlawful occurred I'd suggest you visit the station and file a report.'

'Right.'

'The officers will take you seriously. If you're concerned don't think twice about it.'

I tear my pizza apart with my bare hands, the cheese stretching as I do it. The burn feels good.

'Are you going back home tomorrow?' I ask.

'I don't know yet. The investigation is only just getting started.'

'What do you mean?'

She blows and then takes a bite of her ham and pine-apple pizza. 'I mean the news might move on now, your gang might migrate to the next big story, but a viable case needs to be constructed so justice can be done and the victims' families can finally understand and deal with what happened to their loved ones. And, crucially, *why*.'

'What do you think happened? No case specifics. Just your thoughts.'

She looks at me suspiciously.

I eat.

She swallows and takes a sip from her can. 'There is still much to unpack and investigate. The behavioural-crime task force have their theories. I'm not one for hypotheticals, but they have uncovered some interesting links and patterns.'

I stay quiet.

'The victims were all under forty. They all shopped at Willy's. And they all had relatives or close friends who played in the top-level hockey teams.'

I nod for her to go on.

'Peter wore a size forty-five boot,' she says. 'But so far the print patterns at the other crime scenes don't match Peter's known footwear.'

'What does that mean?'

She picks up a piece of pineapple with her fingers. 'Could mean we still need to find the right boots. Alternatively, it could mean we still need to find the right killer.'

38

Chief Skoglund suggests we take coffee in the living room. I doubt she has even stepped foot in there yet. We walk through with two mugs of instant and she opens the wide patio door to breathe in some fresh air.

'You smoke, Tuva?'

'Weed?'

She bursts out laughing. 'Well, I was asking about cigarettes.'

'Only when I drink.'

She nods to herself and chuckles again. Then she stands on the narrow edge of timber decking outside which isn't covered with snow. She lights up.

'You sure?' she asks.

I nod and sip my Nescafé.

'The young man you had coffee with in Åre. Alfred. What did you think?'

I frown. 'Normal kid. Is he a suspect?'

She sighs. 'Everyone's a suspect at this stage.'

'Alfred?'

'We have CCTV of him in Esseberg recently, emerging from the tunnel on foot. He claims he hasn't been in Esseberg recently. Anything you can share?'

'I never got a vibe from him.'

She stares at me. 'Okay.'

'Do you have family near here?' I ask.

She blows smoke from her nose. 'Not really. I have some up north. They still work with reindeers. My southern family think they are old fashioned and stubborn. They're right about that. My family in the mountains think the southern relatives are soft and, because they don't work with reindeer anymore, they are not true Sami. I guess I'm stuck halfway in between.'

'I've heard people say that. The *not real Sami* thing.'

She takes a drag. 'It is nonsense, that part. If you're Sami you're Sami. That holds true whether you work in a gas station or you are out lassoing reindeer every week wearing *Gakti* and sleeping in a *lavvu*. But it is complicated. I grew up believing in God and the church because my mother was so desperate to be Swedish and fit in. She forbade us to eat with our hands like she did growing up. She forbade us to say anything in Sami, even though she still gossiped in her old language with her friends right until her death. It is not a black and white thing.'

I zip up my sweater.

'You want me to close the door?' she asks.

'No, it's okay.'

'My father's people are from Alaska. I was born there, you believe that? I was born on the other side of the world.'

'Inuit?' I ask.

She smiles. 'People always ask that. Inuit-Sami. One hundred per cent indigenous. No, he wasn't Inuit. He was a steelworker from Detroit who moved up to work in the oil fields and met my mother when she was on a two-year work placement through the consulate. They fell in love and eventually they moved here.'

'You have an American passport?'

'I used to have one. Made travelling over there a whole lot simpler. But I haven't renewed it for a long time. I am a small-town girl at heart and travelling never did much for me.'

I nod and sip my coffee.

'You haven't asked if I'm married or have kids or anything?' she says.

I frown at her.

'People usually ask.'

'None of my business.'

'That doesn't normally hold you back, Tuva.' She smiles and I see smoke curl out in front of her lips and hang in the cold, unmoving air.

'You married?' I ask.

'Single. No dependents.'

'Snap,' I say.

'But for the Grace of God go I,' she says.

'What do you mean by that?' I say, moving closer to her.

'I don't know. I am sleep deprived and high on caffeine and nicotine. Just that I've seen a lot. Out here in the mountains there is not much separation between you and whatever evil happens to be out there. In a big city the darkness is spread over many police zones or precincts. Everyone deals with their own portion. Here, this whole kommun, an area the size of a small country, it all falls on my shoulders.'

'You're able to resolve problems, though,' I say. 'That's a kind of power. I merely write about what you manage to achieve. You bring resolution and that's worth something.'

She bends down and stubs out her cigarette in the snow. I see two more deep-frozen butts down there already.

'Nothing's ever resolved,' she says, still crouching down. Then she says something I can't hear.

'Sorry?' I say. 'I didn't catch that.'

She stands up and looks directly at me. 'There is no resolution, Tuva. Not really. We tick boxes and make arrests. We take people to court, to prison. But there is no neat tying up of loose ends. There is only those same ends, frayed, flapping in the breeze. Families crushed. Generational mistakes repeated like clockwork. Educations ruined and chances erased. The impact of these killings will echo in this marginal town for a hundred more years. Four unnecessary deaths. The children that might have been born who will now never exist, and the wonderful changes those children might have made. Instead we have heartache, and loss of faith. I am no longer looking for things to be solved or resolved. I am aiming for persistence because that is all we really have. Endurance. The radical acceptance of a raw deal.'

I have to look away.

'I'm sorry,' she says. 'Long fucking week.'

'It's okay.'

'Nice to have you here. To have company.'

I bite my lip. 'Have you been up to the Pinnacle? Eric and Khalyla? They're friendly up there. You could take an hour break from the town and breathe some fresh air, relax.'

'I have been there briefly,' she says.

She drains her coffee in one long motion.

Her phone rings on the sideboard.

She picks it up and turns away from me. I struggle to hear what she's saying. I catch snippets. 'Is that confirmed?' Incomprehensible mumbling and then, 'Do you have an address?' A pause. 'On my way.'

'What is it?' I ask.

She slams the patio door closed. 'I can't say.'

'Chief, please.'

She grabs her keys and coat and ushers me outside. She locks up and runs off to her car.

'Chief.'

'Not now.'

'Chief. Let me help. Give me something.'

She looks back, shaking her head. 'Forensic results on the semen sample. Ninety-nine per cent sure it is not Peter's.'

'And?' I say.

'We have an ID.'

39

'So, who was it?' I ask. 'Peter's innocent? Can I come with you?'

She checks her gun and says, 'No, you can't come with me.'

'I'll follow.'

Her radio crackles. She looks into my eyes and says, 'You will not follow. We're talking about a potential multiple-murder suspect. Come find me tomorrow.'

She races off in her dark grey Volvo. No flashing lights or sirens.

The neighbourhood is silence once more. Snow-topped mailboxes and bushes. Kids asleep safe in their beds. The vague, crackling blue light of TVs in upstairs *allrum* living rooms all around as people escape the reality of this crime-ridden town by watching fictional equivalents so they can feel secure for an hour or two.

I am paralysed by indecision. Every fibre in my being tells me to drive right after her, to pursue the story, to record it as journalists have done, in one shape or another, since the dawn of the modern world. But I respect her. Not because of her rank and position. *Despite* all that. I might evolve into a civilian version of her in twenty years.

That destiny may be unavoidable and because of that truth I listen to her commands.

A gunshot in the distance wakes me from my standing dream and I jump into my Hilux and speed away.

In a place this size you can find the activity in minutes. I drive literally three blocks before I notice the lights. I pull up a few houses away. There is a cluster of police cars with their headlights pointed at one two-storey dark red house. Police officers have their guns drawn, an extremely rare occurrence in Sweden. Through a loud-speaker on one of the cars they tell the man in the door-way to place his hands on his head. They tell him to step forward slowly. Keep coming. No sudden moves. They tell him to walk down the steps and stand on the drive-way. Two police officers holster their 9 mm pistols and approach cautiously. They tell him to keep his hands where they can see them, and to stay calm. The officers handcuff him and calmly lead him away to a car. There is no scuffle or resistance. Four officers enter the house, guns drawn, torches lighting up each room. One of the officers in the car shouts, 'Suspect still at large. We have the older brother.' I know there isn't a tactical SWAT team or *Piketen* within range. The closest RRTF unit is in Stockholm. In a town like this they have to make do with what they have, and usually what they have is Tasers and standard-issue pistols and handcuffs. And what assail-ants may have is shotguns and rifles with sufficient cali-bre to bring down a half-tonne moose at five hundred metres. The difference is not comforting.

Two officers emerge from the suburban house. They announce it to be clear. A police van arrives and a two-man dog team steps out. They enter the house. A German Shepherd and a Belgian Malinois. The dogs are kept on leashes. I see in the doorway one dog being offered a jacket to sniff. The canine becomes instantly more alert, but he does not growl or bark. The man is led out into the garden by the dog. Officers all around perk up.

'He left hours ago,' yells the handcuffed brother. 'Said he was going to Åre.'

The dog sniffs the ground, the air. Then it barks and scratches at a path through snow-topped bushes, its nose to the ground. I have to move to get a better look. The chief is talking into the radio on her lapel. One of the Volvos moves to light up a dark corner of the garden with its headlights.

Both dogs bark as they reach a woodshed. I photograph everything. I record a video clip of them breaching the flimsy shed door. Moments later I hear a man's screams as he's bitten by one of the dogs. The handler struggles to remove the dog from the man's calf. The man has long hair and a biker jacket. Something over his face and hands. Paint, maybe.

Neighbours stand on their porches. Some peer out from the perceived safety of their living-room windows.

The dishevelled, bearded man with a dark mullet hair-style is dragged handcuffed towards the cluster of police vehicles. He is cursing and shrieking about suing the police department. His T-shirt has a polar bear motif design. He says he needs a doctor. He says he is losing blood.

The chief walks straight to him. I move position to behind a tree. I can't hear too well from here with all this commotion but the scene is lit so brightly I can read her lips plain as day.

'Philip Wallin, you are under arrest.'

40

I sleep well for the first time in weeks. The knowledge that someone has been arrested, is in the process of being questioned and possibly charged, affords me some modicum of reassurance. I am not sure it does the same for Peter Hedberg's grandmother and relatives of the other victims.

Wallin was, in fact, arrested on a possibly unrelated firearms charge. I wonder how many probing questions it will take from detectives for that to be boosted up to murder? Is he accused of *all* the killings? He must be. The prosecution process can be hard to fathom from the outside. I guess they have probable cause for whatever firearms charge he is accused of, but need time to make the more serious charges stick.

I talk to a connection in the *Åklamgarmyndigheten* prosecution authority, someone who owes me a favour and has a stronger sense of justice than professional discretion, and deduce that Wallin is in fact suspected of all the killings, and that as he has no employment or regular routine it is possible he could have been present at each one of the attack sites. My contact doesn't have any colour on the possibility that the Jenni Karlsson attack was sexually motivated, but does say the forensic serology results link Wallin directly to the stain, and also that local police aren't aware the two knew one another before the date of the incident.

After a shower and nutritious breakfast of five milk-chocolate digestives and two strong coffees, I set out into the world. If I were local, today would mark the beginning of a whole series of fresh stories. I would be covering the burials and services, and then the lead-up to the trial. But I am not local. Last night I agreed with Lena I'd head back to Gavrik tomorrow. Forty-eight hours to tie up loose ends before driving south to write the big story. The authorities need to work on the case but also look into lessons learned, and how they can apprehend a killer more quickly in such an isolated community. My job is different. I need to write about these heinous crimes in such a way as to focus on the victims and the ripples that emanate from the actions of the perpetrator, rather than the perpetrator himself. It is vital, in crimes of this nature, not to glamorize the killer. Because that temptation is strong. We're all human. We each have an inherent fascination with serial killers, but the story isn't for him. Philip Wallin, assuming he is responsible, is a pathetic figure in all this: a college dropout apprehended in a tool shed. Instead, I will be writing thorough pieces on the young hockey star, the kindergarten assistant, the man who wrote a successful newsletter, and the woman who worked in the pensions office.

Two people in the solarium broiling themselves between carcinogenic lamps. Business is picking up. I guess that is what happens when a danger is removed from the streets.

I want to check in with the chief, and also with Peter Hedberg's grandmother. For the story, but also just to make sure she has food. And I want to, in the most gentle way possible, interview the partners and neighbours of the other three victims. First I have a hard-won appointment with Khalyla up at the hotel. I am keen to hear more about Peter from her perspective.

I scheduled the meeting at 10 a.m. on purpose because I refuse to be left up at that hotel, or worse, somewhere on the mountain, as night creeps in. Never again. Khalyla, through her manager, gave me a twenty-minute slot and that works fine with me. This is going to be a busy day.

The ski lift behind the church car park squeaks and creaks. I take out my lift pass, scan it and go through the barrier. Ingvar, the lift operator, is wearing his red jacket. He might look relieved that the spotlight has moved away from him, or perhaps that is me projecting what I *think* he is feeling. I smile weakly when I see him and he looks down at his shin-high boots.

The fresh, cold air is a tonic as the chair lifts up and glides higher up the mountain. There is something mighty therapeutic about leaving Ice Town behind.

The parents of Esseberg may rest easier in their beds now Philip Wallin is in custody. We have no motive or backstory yet, no murder charges, but I now know that Wallin has a criminal record as long as my arm, albeit for relatively minor crimes such as theft and bar fights. The main thing is, police can now find answers. And yet, absurdly, again, this all feels rather anticlimactic. Reminds me too much of Noora's death. How still and quiet and normal the world seemed after she passed. It made me want to scream at strangers. *Don't you know she's gone? Don't you realise?* The incongruity of it all. When I'd drive all night, staring blankly at the star-speckled sky, at the brake lights of haulage trucks, I'd be tempted to swerve straight into the central reservation or an oncoming lorry. But I was never nearly brave enough.

The chairlift rattles as it passes over a support post, and I see Johan's snow basher far below, the lid to its engine open, Johan checking cables with another man dressed in black.

I switched to pouring vodka down my neck. Rum is my drink of choice, gold rum with a mixer, usually a Coke, but after she died I switched to vodka. It seemed more fitting. Back then I didn't even stop when the shakes came; when my hands would tremble so hard after waking I couldn't insert my hearing aids. I did not stop. Until my neighbour told me one day that if I carried on like this she wouldn't let me see little Dan anymore. She was right. And that moment was the beginning of my recovery.

A trio of skiers make smooth turns below me. I watch them through my dangling boots as they carve and jump. One of them deviates from the piste altogether and skis through dense trees before joining the other pair.

The hotel looms on the summit like a warning. That steep roofline, the multiple chimneys, one smoking, the giant outdoor chess set covered in snow. It is sumptuous and derelict at the same time; grand yet somehow undersized.

I search for news on my phone. They are going deep into Philip Wallin's history. A keen ice-hockey player and winner of the golden puck two years in a row as a teenager. He studied population studies at Umeå University before dropping out after two years. There is one photo being shared on social media, credited to *Aftonbladet*, showing Philip and Peter together on the ice four years ago, and another team photo with their faces circled. If responsible, what caused Philip Wallin to kill four people? What sent him over the edge? I watch interviews with neighbours, some of whom describe Philip as a model neighbour and others who say he has a troubled past and wasn't liked by some of the local women. One even goes on to say Philip had run-ins with a local biker gang over dealing prescription painkillers on their patch but then she realises she's said too much so clams up. Once an interviewee does that it is all but impossible to get them back.

A plane flies high in the pale sky leaving contrails. I fly myself, up over an icy waterfall, some liquid water still flowing beneath solid ice, and the contrails fade and dissipate. There is no direct sun here, not at this time of year. Any light we receive is fractured and weak; any warmth fleeting.

I glean from a local Facebook group that Philip's older brother, Krister, the man I saw last night handcuffed at his front door, is still being questioned.

I brace myself for the top of the lift.

The bar unlocks and I raise it.

Khalyla is here waiting for me wearing a fur-trimmed white jacket and fur-trimmed boots. She is smiling and she has her head at an unnatural angle for good lighting as if she is expecting me to photograph her.

I dismount in my typical ungainly fashion and walk over.

My phone beeps.

A message from Lena.

Philip Wallin, prime suspect, has been rushed to Östersund hospital following a seizure. He is said to be in critical condition.

41

Khalyla steps closer to greet me but I am thrown by the news. A seizure? I shake her hand and smile but I'm wondering if he suffered from an underlying condition and if police had knowledge of that fact. Could he have been beaten? My first reaction is: no, not in Sweden. But that is an immature response. Normalcy bias. Of course it can happen anywhere in the world. And, in a small town like Esseberg, in a wild, isolated region like Jämtland, everyone is connected to everyone else. You don't have six degrees of separation here. Three if you're lucky. Perhaps one of the guards is related to a victim. That should have been screened, but in reality, in an overstretched police department where resources are scarce, these things can be missed. Or *dismissed*. Worse, even: this could have been set up. The prisons in Sweden are famously comfortable and humane. It is possible a victim's relative used their sway with the Wolverines, or directly within the police, to make sure this case never even makes it to court.

'Tuva?' says Khalyla. 'Are you okay? You were miles away.'

'Forgive me,' I say. 'It's been one hell of a week.'

She smiles awkwardly and leads me into the now-familiar lobby. Pine everywhere. The fire is crackling and there are four tables occupied. It almost looks like a normal hotel. Karin is behind reception working at a computer. She nods her welcome. The carved-troll chess set sits unused in the corner, the black king on its side, defeated.

'I've set up a meeting room,' she says.

I follow her and she takes me into a narrow room with a large picture window at the far end overlooking the valley below. Conference table with eight chairs. Tea and coffee making facilities.

'I've been interviewed many times,' she says, sitting down. 'Though mainly for fashion magazines and sites. Sorry this took so long to set up. Please, fire away.'

I place down my Dictaphone and switch it on.

She stares at it.

'How long have you lived in Esseberg?'

'All my life.'

'How old are you, if you don't mind me asking.'

She smiles. 'Thirties.'

My guess would be thirty-nine and eleven months. But she looks beautiful with it.

'And can you tell me about your work?'

She frowns for a split second and then says, 'I try not to think of it as *work*. I was an early adopter of Instagram and I am blessed with a stunning location up here on the mountain. I document my life, I guess. Share the vast, ancient mountains with the world.'

'How do you do that?'

'Reels, stories, videos, posts. I have a YouTube channel. TikTok. Facebook. People send me their products some-times. Yoga outfits, sunglasses, hats, bags. They like the way I incorporate their branding into my aesthetic. Down by the river in the summer months with the wildflowers. In the snow before Christmas, wearing a cashmere sweater from a French couture house. I manage the look of my content, and I make sure the brands I work with, my sponsors, match my vision.'

What a lot of horseshit.

Forgive me.

'Your *vision?*'

'Grounded living. Meditation. Good karma.'

'I see. And they pay you for a photo?'

'It is more than a photo. A lot of work goes into each and every piece of content. Brands pay to gain access to my audience because my audience have grown to trust me.'

'Smart. How much do they pay for a picture?'

'That varies a lot.'

'Like, a hundred kronor? A thousand?'

She smiles. 'It varies. I'm fortunate. I make a very good living.'

I nod. 'Some people down in the town think Eric is some kind of sugar daddy. Keeps you in the life you have become accustomed to. I can see that's not accurate.'

She takes a deep breath. 'How astute of you.'

I backtrack a little. 'Did you ever think of leaving town? I could see you living in LA or Milan.'

'My USP is the mountain backdrop.'

'*USP?*'

'Unique Selling Point. This landscape is my aesthetic.'

'It sounds more like you keep Eric.'

'I help him with the upkeep of the hotel during this difficult period.'

'Oh, you do? You back him?'

'The hotel is an institution. I'm an investor, of sorts. A patron. I want him to bring the railway back up here, and I want him to celebrate the centenary in style. It is extremely important to the family.'

'How many members of the family are there?'

'Just Eric.'

'Right. Can you tell me a little about Peter Hedberg? I understand you used to work with him.'

She stands up and pours herself a glass of water. She looks at me.

'Coffee, please.'

She pours me a cup.

'I never worked *with* him but we both worked for the same employer back in the day. Feels like a lifetime ago. I didn't know him well but we were both outsiders here. We lived in this town our whole lives, but because of his deafness and my skin colour, we were never fully accepted. It's very sad what happened.'

'What did happen?'

She hesitates. Like she thinks I'm trying to trip her up. 'Four people died.'

Might be five, if Philip Wallin succumbs to his seizure. 'But *why* do you think this happened? You've lived here for thirty-plus years. What would drive a local to kill?'

'God knows I've thought about it,' she says. 'Throttling someone. The claustrophobia of this place. The tiny gene pool.' She shudders. 'Can you imagine growing up locked in that tight valley down there?' She takes a few steps and stands by the window. 'Less than a thousand people. Everyone in everyone else's business. I think half the town's been on the verge of a killing spree for decades.'

'Really?'

She sips her water. 'Tensions grow over time. Conflicts brew and fester. Neighbours fall out but they stay neighbours because it's practically impossible to sell your home here. The town was difficult to live in when the mountain was full of winter sports enthusiasts for half the year. Now it's almost impossible. I can manage on top of the mountain but I would go out of my mind if I still lived down there with the others.'

'Did you know a guy Peter's age called Alfred? One of Peter's friends?'

She shakes her head.

'Did you ever suspect Philip Wallin of being dangerous?'

'People fear the bogeyman. Some faceless monster. But the ones you need to watch out for are the quiet, normal folk who live right around the corner. The ones you pass every day. Anyone can snap, Tuva.'

'You must be relieved he's been caught.'

She wrinkles up her perfect nose.

I raise my eyebrows.

'I'm not entirely convinced Philip was working alone.'

I don't say anything. The tactic fails. I utter, 'Go on.'

'The two corpses found in roughly the same place, near the power station, in the shadow of Ingvar's cabin. Can you imagine how difficult it would be to kill two full-grown adults one after the other. I'm not sure Philip has it in him.'

'You knew him?'

'Not well. But I know he was a heavy smoker. Lots of health problems.'

'Does Philip have any friends or associates you're suspicious of?'

She shrugs. 'My family are from the Philippines. My grandmother used to tell me a story. She used to say you have to watch your back. You can't even trust people in authority. She'd tell me over and over about Juan Severino Mallari. Have you heard of him?'

I shake my head. 'He lived here?'

'No, he lived where my family comes from in the 1800s. A man of the church. Juan was a Catholic parish priest. A man of God. He did what Deacon Sahlin does each week in Esseberg. He looked after his flock. Baptisms, marriages and funerals. Choir rehearsals. Guidance. Confession.'

I shrug.

'He also killed fifty-seven of his parishioners.'

42

The atmosphere in the room changes.

'What are you saying, Khalyla?'

'Nothing. I'm telling you about Juan Severino Mallari. Do you know why he killed all those people?'

I shake my head and the meeting room is cold.

'Because he thought his own mother was cursed. Despite being a man of God, of the cloth, an ordained priest, he believed his own mother was cursed and he needed to kill in order to save her. These are the men who walk this earth.'

I take a moment and then I say, 'Statistically, there are extremely few of them.'

She lifts her chin as if preparing to pose for a photo and then she says, 'There are more than we think. You can keep your statistics. How many hangings, overdoses, slit wrists and shootings do you think are falsely attributed to suicide or an accident each year?'

I wasn't expecting that. 'Very few.'

She juts out her jaw even more. 'Statistics are inherently flawed because *we* compile them and *we* are inherently flawed. Sometimes the police and medical examiners attribute a death to suicide because they are not sure either way, or they're overworked, or they don't get paid enough, or they're short-staffed, or the victim was a junkie or a sex worker or a migrant. You don't think that happens?'

I start to answer but she jumps in first. 'It happens every damn day. Consciously or unconsciously in border-line cases. Because some local politician or gang leader wanted it or because an innocent error was made in the chain of evidence.'

'You seem to know a lot about all this.'

'Yeah, well, if you were ethnically Filipino living up here in the north pole with everyone suspicious of you ever since you wore a training bra, maybe you'd know a lot about it, too. The police are fallible.'

'I'm not arguing with you.'

She looks down at the Dictaphone. 'Turn the tape off.'

'You sure?'

'Turn it off.'

I do as she asks.

'I don't get to speak to anyone my own age, Tuva. I'm so busy maintaining my image and building content for clients I never have time for a real conversation. I'm sorry this turned heavy so fast.'

'It's okay.'

'Eric and me. It's not what you think. We dated for a long time. I love him with all my heart. He's a sweetheart. But we're not together like you think we are. Not anymore.'

I nod. 'I think I'd get lonely up here.'

She tips back her head. 'You have no idea.' She drops her chin again to face me. 'Sorry. I'm just agreeing with you. It's healthy for me to talk to an outsider. I'm just sorry for *you*, that's all.'

'For me? What do you mean?'

'This place, is what I mean. You see the tunnel and the quaint Lutheran church and the virgin snow. But underneath it all, once you scratch the surface, this place is riddled with corruption. Between biker gangs selling prescription meds, and local politicians receiving backhanders and hunting trips, and sex workers caught in the middle. This whole valley is rotten to its core.'

A knock at the door.

I flinch.

Eric pushes his head through and says, apologetically, 'Anyone need refreshments? Food? Karin is in the kitchen.'

We both shake our heads.

Eric gesticulates to Khalyla. He opens his eyes wide. I look at her. She shakes her head slightly. These adjustments in posture may not be apparent to some but I am programmed to notice. Body language fills in gaps when I'm lip-reading, because, unfortunately, there are usually lots of gaps.

Khalyla says, 'My time's up, Tuva. I have a reel to film. Thanks for the chat.'

'I'll send you the piece I write on the hotel and the potential for investors. I'll mail it to you when it's ready.'

She smiles politely and leaves.

Eric takes her place. Behind him is the snowy valley and the distant mountain ridges. His eyes are red like he's been crying or cutting onions.

'It's good to see you again.'

'You, too,' I say. 'Glad the lift is working today.'

232

'Yes,' he says, but he holds eye contact a little too long and I feel uncomfortable.

I move away.

'Tell me about your childhood,' he says. 'School. What sports did you play? What subjects did you enjoy?'

'Eric, I need to get back to the town.'

He moves closer. 'What's your favourite food, Tuva?'

'I'm going to leave now.'

He reaches out his hand and almost touches mine.

'Tuva?'

'I'm going.'

'Tuva,' he says again, his eyes watery.

'Eric, I'm not—'

He cuts me off. 'Tuva, please. I never knew.'

I wait for him to speak.

'What are you talking about?' I say.

He blinks three or four times. 'I don't know quite how to say this, Tuva.'

'Say what?'

'It all fits. I'm . . . Tuva, I'm your father.'

43

I contemplate a wisecrack retort but Eric wipes his eyes with his hands and I stop myself.

What is happening?

'I'm sorry,' I say, deeply uncomfortable. 'You're . . . mistaken. My dad was Jakob Moodyson. He was killed in a car accident when I was fourteen.'

He takes a handkerchief from his pocket.

'And I know he will always be your father,' says Eric. 'He raised you. I will never take his place.'

A sinking feeling inside my chest. A heavy weight.

'He was my dad. It's not complicated.'

Eric stands up and walks to the window. 'It is rather complicated. And I am so, so sorry I haven't been part of your life. I wish I had been able to—'

'Hold on,' I say. 'Stop. You've made a mistake.' I stand up now as well. 'Maybe you have a daughter out there somewhere, I'm not doubting that. But I am not her.'

He turns. I can't see the details of his face as he is back-lit by the window light. 'I lived in Stockholm in the early 1990s, you see. Södermalm. I studied, and then, when I was working at the Grand Hotel, training as a junior manager, I met your dear mother.'

'You met Mum?'

'I wasn't expecting anything to happen but I fell in love with your mother, Tuva. It was wrong. I felt terribly guilty and so did she.'

'When she was married to my dad? You had an affair?

I can't picture it. Cannot imagine them together. I can't see it. Nope. Mum slept with this man? She betrayed Dad? I don't believe it.

'We were only together very briefly. Your parents were separated at the time.'

'You're mistaken. They never separated.'

'It was a short separation. A trial. Your mother left me and she went back to your father. She was much stronger than I was.'

'First of all,' I say, rubbing my temples. 'I don't think my mother would do a thing like that, and she is not around to defend herself from the accusation. Secondly, if they were only apart for a short while who's to say my father isn't my father? How dare you make this claim.' My voice trembles. 'How dare you.'

He walks slowly towards me until he comes to a stop underneath a ceiling light.

'Look at the shape of my eyelids, Tuva. Look closely at my teeth.' He smiles in an exaggerated manner. 'The first time I saw you I felt something. It sounds ridiculous, but I sensed a connection.'

'Well, I certainly didn't.'

He does have my downward sloping eyelids. And, sure, we both have long incisors. So what? Plenty of people share those traits.

'Honestly, I think I should go now,' I say, hot in my sweater. 'I have work to do.'

235

'He raised you,' says Eric. 'I am never going to ask you to call me Dad. Nothing of the sort. He was a parent in your life. I merely want a chance to get to know you, that is all.'

'I'm going.'

'You can talk to Ebbe if you like.'

'Who the hell is *Ebbe*?'

'Ebbe Svensson. She lived above your mother's apartment on Bondegatan. *Your* apartment. She was a mutual friend. That is how I met Ingrid.'

I'm sweating from my forehead now. Claustrophobic as if the walls of this room are slowly moving in closer, pinning me in.

I do remember Mrs Svensson. She used to have coffee with Mum sometimes. They used to play chequers.

'They played chequers?'

He smiles. 'Back then they played backgammon in your kitchen. I played chess there with her one time in fact. The little table by the window that wouldn't open.'

'Fuck. You knew Mum?'

'For a short while. I was very lucky to know her, Tuva. And she loved your dad very much. She would tell me about how clever he was, how focused.'

I am tumbling from one emotion to the next and I'm struggling to hold them all back. Panic, exhilaration, curiosity, disgust, confusion.

'I need the bathroom.'

'Of course.'

I run outside and lock myself in a cubicle and the room spins. How did this happen? In Esseberg of all places? I ask myself what Tammy would do in these circumstances.

If in doubt, do what Tam would do. So I splash water on my face and take a deep breath and go back in to face him.

'I am going to keep an open mind until, if and when I decide to go ahead, we do a DNA test or something,' I say, desperate to take back control and not quite succeeding. 'I'm not saying anything else until then and I think that's fair.'

'Of course.'

His reasonableness irritates me. Is this man my *other* father? All the missed father's days. The Christmases I have spent alone since Mum died. The way I learned to drive with nobody to practise with.

'You had a son?' I ask, my voice small.

'Oscar. Dear Oscar. He died on the mountain.'

'No more children out there in the world? No more affairs?'

He shakes his head. 'I met Oscar's mother shortly after moving back here from Stockholm. I know this is going to take you a long time to figure out, Tuva. It is the same for me. All those lost years, missed memories. But I ask of you only one thing: that you will keep an open mind, like you said. Let us think about doing that test you mentioned. No pressure from me after we get the results. No pressure at all either way. I am eager to know you a little, that's all.' He smiles a sad, pursed smile. 'I am not sure I can mourn the loss of another child.'

44

I am usually the one in control when I conduct an interview. Dictaphone out on the table. A specific tempo of questioning I have honed over the years: starting slowly, gently, then moving in to ask the more difficult questions. But I do not feel in control of anything today. The biggest story of my career seems remote. Down the mountain. And what I thought was my life, as pathetic as it sometimes is, might be no longer.

'I'm not . . . finding it easy to take all this in,' I say. 'I never saw Mum that way.'

'Was it wrong of me to raise this, Tuva? Perhaps a letter would have been more appropriate.'

'No. I'm glad you told me.' There's no way I'm going to call him *Dad*, no matter what any future test results show. Dad was Dad. Always will be. 'I've even written newspaper articles of similar things happening. Two stories in Gavrik alone, a town of less than ten thousand people. I never expected this to happen to me.'

'Life is messier than it appears.'

I stare at him, at the angle of his jaw, the dimple in his cheek, the shape of his teeth. I look closely at his eyes, at the lids, at his brows. And then I look away.

'Why don't I leave you alone for a while,' he says.

'No, you don't need to.'

'I will give you some space to think. Karin is making pea soup and pancakes for lunch. Shall I bring you through a bowl in twenty minutes? We could eat together if you like?'

This feels altogether too domesticated, too much like a family home. I start to freak out and overheat again. 'Can I order something from a menu?' I am terrible. An indolent child. A rude, entitled hotel guest. 'Something simple, perhaps.' I want a rum and Coke. A double. 'A cheese sandwich?'

He smiles.

'What is it?'

He shakes his head.

'What? You think that's boring. Rude. Well—'

'It is what I always order,' he utters, quietly. 'Or, rather, it is what I make for myself. One cheese sandwich coming up.'

He leaves.

Colours appear more vivid than before. I notice the knots and grain in the oak floorboards. Last time I felt like this was Noora's death. Key moments where everything else – your to-do list and your overdraft and your argument with a colleague – dissolve into nothingness.

I stand up and stretch. Then I circle the table twice before stepping in front of the picture window. It starts to snow. Sporadic flakes. This is one of those discombobulating places where it can actually snow beneath you, from the clouds hovering over the valley floor.

A sudden irrational urge to listen to the two voicemails from Mum I have saved on my phone. I haven't listened to them for over a year. They won't help. She can't tell me what happened thirty years ago. She can't explain herself or why she never told me.

The sky darkens and more snow begins to tumble out of it.

You do not think of your parents as people. I never considered my mother as a woman with desire. She was ... Mum. I viewed her through a unique lens, a narrow lens. A mother. *My* mother. I never thought deeply about her wants and needs. Her secrets.

The chairlift comes around and around, each chair as empty as the one that went before. A ski resort with no skiers. A winter-sports paradise with no winter sports. Just a local morgue filled with cadavers and a power station pumping out metallic-tasting ash.

Do I have a family now? Of course I do. Tammy and Lena and Thord and Noora's parents. Nils and Lars and Benny Björnmossen on the periphery. My version of a family.

Butterflies in my stomach.

I move forward and let my nose touch the glass and it is as if I have my face pressed to the cold window in an airplane. I need to remain calm and focused until the test results. That is if I even decide to go ahead with a test. I'm not sure. Eric might be mistaking the dates, desperate to replace his lost son.

The story down the mountain in Ice Town, perhaps one of the biggest stories of the year in the whole country, seems more distant than when I arrived here.

He walks in carrying a tray with two plates of cheese sandwiches on dark bread, and two glasses of champagne.

'Oh, no,' I say. 'I'm working, Eric. Let's not move too fast here.'

'It's only cider,' he says, apologetic. 'This one is zero alcohol. Sparkling apple juice, that's all. We are out of sparkling water, I'm afraid. Difficult to bring supplies up here with no train.'

I nod.

'Rye bread,' I say. 'So we're not related after all. I prefer sliced white.'

'Me, too,' he says. 'I call this hamster bedding, but Khalyla insists on it. She says the white stuff is made out of sugar. Keeps trying to sneak healthy seeds and vegetables into my ready meals.'

'Thanks for the early lunch,' I say, and then I bite into the sandwich.

'This is just a thought, no need to decide yet. But maybe you would like to stay at the hotel for the remainder of your stay? We have plenty of comfortable rooms and, well, we wouldn't charge you a single krona, Tuva.'

'No, I need to be down in the town. But thank you.'

A combination of awkwardness and warmth. I want to stay here with him and ask a thousand questions but I am also constantly on the verge of a panic attack.

I'm halfway through my first sandwich when someone knocks at the door.

'Yes?' says Eric.

Karin Bates opens the door a crack. 'Sorry, Mr Lindgren. You said to tell you if there was anything on the news.'

'Yes?'

She walks in and switches on the TV on the wall. She changes channel to T4.

The presenter says, 'According to officers, Mr Philip Wallin is still being held in Östersund hospital, in a secure section of the ward. Åre police have confirmed that he is no longer considered a suspect in the Esseberg murders. According to Elina Olin, Senior Forensic Pathologist, and Per Gustavsson, Investigator-in-Charge, Mr Philip Wallin had a reliable if somewhat reluctant alibi for each one of the murders. It has been posited that the DNA sample linking him directly to one of the incidents could have been the result of the sale of donor sperm. Philip Wallin's brother has revealed how Philip had donated multiple times in the past two years. It is believed that police are now in the process of determining the identity of the buyer. We will bring you updates as we receive them.'

45

I arrive back down in the town with a bump. The landing area of the chairlift is black ice and I fall as I dismount, twisting my ankle. A young man steps out from the lift office and asks, 'You all right?'

'Yes,' I say.

'Wear spikes next time. It's icy.'

Thanks for nothing.

I limp away from the lift queue, which comprises of exactly no one, and curse him under my breath. The town is breezy: light powder blowing in the wind, but there is no fresh snow falling. The ground coverage is turning grey as it absorbs particulates from car exhausts and domestic chimneys. In my experience, purity tends to be short-lived.

I have a strange feeling about Khalyla. I don't think she's implicated, at least not directly, but I suspect she may know more than she lets on.

On the way to my B&B I notice a bronze Mercedes SUV slow. Eventually it stops altogether in the middle of the road and I see its hazard lights flash.

'I want to invite you on my podcast,' says Johan, his elbow hanging out of his window.

'Thanks.' God, I'm tired. 'I'm too busy.'

'Do you know how big my podcast is?'

'Do you know how busy I am?'

He smiles. 'Okay, you're busy, I get it. But we hit number one this week. It'll be meaningful for your career. What about next week?'

'I'll be long gone.'

'What can I say that will make you change your mind? I've looked into you. The Ferryman murders, Medusa, the *Thirty Under Thirty* Award. When can I fit you in?'

'You're used to getting what you want, aren't you?'

He says, 'I'm used to people begging to be on my podcast, to be honest. Any random with a book coming out, or a new business to launch. They pretend they want to be my friend, slide into my DMs, leverage every last contact they have, desperate to appear on the show.'

'I'm not selling anything, mate.'

'Let me buy you a coffee, then. So I can convince you. No strings.'

There are three cars waiting behind his Mercedes and that's making me anxious. 'Throw in a glazed donut and we can talk.'

'Jump in,' he says.

'No,' I say, because I don't do that, especially not here. 'Circle K. I'll see you there in ten minutes.'

It is daytime. There are half a dozen witnesses. Public place. I don't feel he's a threat. But, here in Ice Town, you can never be too careful.

I return to my base and visit the bathroom. Then I roll on fresh deodorant because Eric telling me he's my long-last father apparently made me heat up for some reason. I head out.

The Circle K looks a lot like the Q8 station I frequent in Gavrik. I don't know why you develop such a strong loyalty to one specific gas station as a driver, but you do. Tam has hers, Nils has his. Lars drives a purple e-bike these days so for him it is not a concern.

I pass the pumps and snow shovels and stacks of firewood in convenient net sacks and go inside.

Two tables with four stools. One table is unoccupied. At the other is Johan: tall and kind of handsome in an unkempt way. Fringe a little too long, chin a little too pointy. He has the coffee and donuts ready on the table.

'This is *not* a date,' I say.

'Strictly business,' he says.

'I'll consider the pod request because I have some basic manners and because I have a love of gas-station baked goods.' In other words it may help me write a better story. This man knows things I do not. 'But I need you to tell me what is going on in this town first. Please.'

'You know exactly what's going on.'

'I know the surface details. Tell me what's underneath. The semen?'

'That's an odd one. I did not see that development coming.'

'I'll excuse the pun.'

He grins and bites into his donut.

'So, it wasn't Philip who killed those four people,' I say. 'He had alibis, they came forwards afterwards. But it *was* his DNA police found on Jenni Karlsson's ski trousers?'

'Like you say, he had alibis,' says Johan. 'He never really knew Jenni Karlsson, must less ejaculated on her trousers. She was a wholesome kindergarten teacher. He is, by all accounts, a low-level miscreant.'

I put my donut down because I've lost my appetite. 'What are you saying?'

'Philip sold his sperm,' he says. 'He's done it before, apparently, multiple times. I'm told he also volunteered for clinical trials overseas. Anyway, he sold each batch for two thousand kroner.'

'To a sperm bank?'

'No, Tuva, to a private buyer. There are forums, you see. Ways to meet up. You know how tired parents sell their kids' old toys through Facebook Marketplace. They meet an equally tired buyer in a McDonald's car park at lunch to sell a mostly complete Lego set for thirty per cent of what it originally cost. Cash in hand. It's like that, apparently, but with spunk.'

'In a *McDonald's*?'

'Will you join me on the podcast?'

'Did she buy it in McDonald's?'

'Not on this occasion. Transaction went down in the customer toilet of the tattoo coffee house near the church.'

I wrinkle my face, disgusted.

'What?' he says.

'In a *café*?'

'Everything I know is from one source. Reliable, in the past, but I can't corroborate their information. They say, at a precise time, the buyer left two thousand in cash in the restroom. Philip then entered, took the cash, left his deposit in a glass jar, and exited. All agreed beforehand. Then the buyer went in and took it away.'

'A woman?'

'Presumably.'

'But not necessarily.'

He frowns. 'But usually, no?'

'Any CCTV from the café? Anyone able to identify the buyer?'

'No CCTV from inside. They have one modern camera outside. Someone wearing black with a hood up. Matches the vague description from Katia Hallgren, the victim who got away.'

'Did she speak with you?' I ask.

'No. She hasn't spoken with anyone. She left town. Couldn't see much because of the pepper spray. Thought the attacker was probably wearing black. Cops couldn't even get an E-fit from her description.'

'Pepper spray will have that effect.'

'She's getting counselling.'

'Good.'

'Novel, eh? Bad guy wearing black.'

'Sounds like half this town,' I say.

'Police are cleaning up the video. Trying to see if they can spot a tattoo or a distinguishing mole.'

I frown and take a sip of coffee. 'Any theories?'

He blows air from his mouth. 'A psychopathic killer who is also trying to conceive. Or else someone bought it intending to frame Philip Wallin. They killed Karlsson, planted Wallin's DNA evidence on her outdoor thermal trousers, and hoped he'd be charged.'

'Then why did Philip hide from police if it wasn't him?'

'The pod?' he asks. 'Are you coming on?'

'Stop saying that word.'

'Well?'

'I'm considering it.'

Johan nods. 'Apparently Philip had an unregistered .308 calibre rifle and he thought the police had found out about it. So he hid in the tool shed.'

'You buy that?'

'Well, it's the truth, so, yeah. Unregistered firearm. That's what he was arrested for.'

I remember that detail. We both take a moment to drink. Someone walks in wearing large boots and a fluorescent jacket to pay for their diesel.

'They're trying to find the buyer through the website. But they're set up pretty tight to ensure anonymity. I think they'll need a warrant or something from a judge.'

'They find the buyer,' I say. 'They find the killer.'

'In theory. Jizz for justice.'

'Stop it.'

I notice a line of photographs behind the counter, behind the hot-dog machine. Sausages rotate on a grill and above them is a picture of the hotel I visited earlier today. I can't stop thinking about what Eric said. About my mother. About Dad.

Johan's phone beeps and a snowplough parks up outside causing everything to darken. Johan looks down to check his phone and then mumbles something and runs out of the gas station.

46

I run after him and yell, 'What happened?'

He jumps in his truck. I manage to reach his side just in time to wedge my boot in to prevent him from closing his door.

'What are you doing?' he asks.

There is a small cage on his passenger seat. The kind of thing you have for a hamster or guinea pig.

'You can't just run away like that. What's going on?'

His eyes darken. 'Take your leg out of my fucking truck.'

'I will when you tell me.'

He snarls. 'Police setting up some kind of perimeter on the south side of the lake. Word is they have the killer surrounded.'

I go to ask a follow-up question but he pushes me away and races off, his tyres squealing, only to get stuck moments later behind a lorry. I climb into my Hilux and tailgate Johan out of town.

My wipers do their best to scrape back the snow, and I sit shivering, trying to follow his brake lights through my frozen windscreen, through the murk beyond.

He turns off the paved street and heads down a bumpy track full of pot holes. My Hilux bumps along and then

I hit a large stone concealed by snow and the impact knocks my backpack off the rear seat. Up ahead of us all is pristine and uniform. A frozen lake: one section etched by the sharpened blades of countless skaters and hockey players, the design at once chaotic and strangely ordered.

The police are half a kilometre away but we can't drive further. The ice might not be thick enough after the recent thaw. Johan starts setting up his vlogging rig: a camera with a powerful light on a flexible Joby arm, and I track him, staying out of shot.

He was happy to talk in the gas station when it was on his terms, for his benefit, but now he ignores me completely. He just talks into his built-in windproof microphone.

The bleak future of long-form news media.

Not on my watch.

The far rear section of the lake is illuminated by head torches and the kind of lithium battery-powered LED floodlights sometimes used on construction sites in rural areas like Utgard forest. A pocket of bright light, some of it moving, in a dark, dark place.

One hour later we are banished behind a flimsy piece of crime-scene tape and we have been joined by a dozen others. People chatter about how they thought this was over. How they thought they would still be able to salvage some kind of St Lucia celebration, some kind of Christmas.

Rumours that the killer died here by suicide. Rumours they might have orchestrated suicide by cop. That would be almost unheard of in Sweden. An old man with snow in his beard says something about how the police should be sued for their inefficiency. How the culprit would have been brought down much sooner in his day.

Delicate deer tracks between us and the scene. Pin holes. The scene is screened off but it is also lit.

The policewoman guarding the area, refusing us entrance, is not in the mood for talking. I can tell she is very cold. I offer her a pocket hand warmer from my jacket and she ignores me completely.

Eventually Carlsson approaches. He greets Johan with a shallow nod and then he does the same to me and one other.

'It is important you all go home now. The temperatures are set to drop sharply tonight and we can't bring ambulances out here for you if that happens.'

'Is it the Pepper Spray Killer?' asks Johan.

'You know I can't talk about it.'

A party of four emerge from nowhere, surprising us. They are not wearing headlights. They skate, at considerable speed, across the surface of the lake towards the screened-off zone. A policeman shouts at them but they continue on. Lights are turned on them and we see each of the well-dressed quartet clearly. They shield their faces from the glare and come to a halt, their skate blades spraying fine ice-chips as they do so. It is Eric, the man who purports to be my biological father. Perhaps he is. Perhaps the truth is that simple. He is with Khalyla and Ingvar and a tall man I have seen in the church. A police officer with a muzzled dog ventures onto the ice and the dog strains at his leash. The officer almost slips but then recovers. They talk. Eventually the four skaters turn and leave, disappearing into the foggy vagueness.

The police chief arrives but I do not approach her. Journalists and police walk a fine line when it comes to information sharing. Police cannot be seen to give us too much, but if they offer too little they know the resulting rumours and misinformation can do more harm than good. The trick, as I have learned in Gavrik, is to build a professional relationship whereby when they need to give information to the press, and they only ever give the bare minimum, they offer it to me first. That is about as much as anyone can hope for.

In Cardiff or Beirut I would stay longer. I would photograph the scene from other angles and I would manoeuvre for interviews with officials and locals. But the wilderness doesn't care what I want. It is neutral to my ambition. When it threatens to reach thirty below, nature trumps any professional plans you might have made. In these conditions, in this darkness, I have no choice but to leave. Luka Kodro, the pizza grill owner from Visberg, once told me how in the winter time in Bosnia the tempo of their terrible war was shaped not by the tactics of generals and military strategists, but by the base realities of hypothermia and foot rot. You cannot fight that.

I warm myself back in my room. I enjoy a hot shower from the neck down – wet hair can kill in December – and a hot mug of tomato soup courtesy of a Willy's packet and the room kettle. Breaking news that a woman's body has been found on the edge of Esseberg lake. I let out a long, sad sigh and instinctively check the lock on my door. Then I check the window. This waking nightmare continues. I change into warmer clothes than before, two pairs of thick Scottish wool socks, the best in the world, and head back out again.

The church community centre is closed.

The coffee shop attached to the tattoo studio is closed.

There are no search parties tonight. Because of fatigue or because nobody is here to organise them or because we now understand that if you go missing in this town, with the notable exception of Katia Hallgren, you will be found dead and frozen solid under a duvet of clean snow.

In Willy's café I spot the redheaded man who wears orange clothes. I saw him before covered in red squirrels, feeding them nuts. Today he sits on his own in the corner nursing a hot chocolate and holding his trolley close to his body.

I sit down at the next table.

'I saw you with the squirrels. Beautiful creatures.'

His face lights up. 'You like them? Where are you from? You're not from here. You like squirrels?'

'They're so agile.'

'People think they're vermin. But they're really not. They're intelligent beyond our understanding. They even talk to each other. They talk to me!'

Oh, dear.

'Awful news,' I say. 'Down by the lake.'

'Terrible.'

Okay. He knows something. Or he *thinks* he knows. Perhaps a fucking squirrel told him.

'What do you think happened?' I ask.

'My niece is police,' he says. 'Mainly traffic stops. She works the drink-driving breathalyser machine. I don't drive myself.'

Probably for the best.

'She was a lovely girl.'

Oh, no. Please no. Not a kid.

'How old was the victim?'

'I'm not sure. Forties, maybe?'

I nod. 'Very sad.'

'She used to be married. To another lady.'

'What happened?'

'They got a divorce, the ladies did. Then she married a man.'

'No, I mean what happened to her tonight?'

'She got murdered.'

I look inside his trolley. One pack of bread. One pack of sliced ham. And at least three dozen bags of nuts.

'My name's Tuva.'

'I know.'

I give him a confused look.

'My name is Martin.'

'Nice to meet you, Martin.'

His expression hardens. 'Why did you come here?'

'Because I heard a deaf teenager had gone missing. Peter Hedberg. I wanted to come and see what I could do. To report on the case.'

He pulls his trolley even closer to him. 'You shouldn't be here. Did you bring all this?'

'I will be leaving soon. Do you know who could be responsible for all these deaths?

'You should go.'

'Any ideas, Martin?'

'You should leave,' he says, squeezing himself tighter into the corner, barricading himself behind the metal of his trolley. 'Go far away from this place. Don't trust the men who think they look after us all. He's done it before. I know. I hear people say things. And he will do it again.'

47

I try to press him for more details, to give me a name, but he just cowers to the point where I have to leave him be. People are starting to stare. I think they suspect I am bullying him. I smile as sweetly as I can, which isn't that sweetly, and then I walk away, out past the cigarettes and pastry stand, past the gambling booths and the town *Apoteket* pharmacy, and into the car park.

An older woman carrying her bags, shuffling as so not to slip and break a hip. A young couple arguing, their body language screaming conflict through their stern Nordic composure. They walk together but somehow their bodies are turned away from each other, twisted, repelling.

I don't suspect Martin because it would be too obvious, too clichéd. But I also know that sometimes the answer staring you in the face is the correct one.

There is only one more place to go.

I walk up a snow bank and down the other side. The road is quiet. I enter the car park of Wrath and there must be a hundred bikes parked up: black leather and gleaming chrome. Spluttering candles illuminate the entrance. Behind the building itself: the distant peaks of ancient mountains. I turn instinctively to view the opposite range, the summit with the hotel perched on top, and there is a flash of green in the sky. It is gone before my jaw has time to fall. Greedily, I focus once again on the cloudy mountaintops. More bikers arrive, their engines rumbling, the ground shaking beneath my boots, and I ignore them. Nothing compares to an aurora, not even a Harley Davidson Fat Boy or Road King. Neck bent up to the stars, I catch sight of a timeless celestial burlesque performance: shimmering ribbons of emerald light part-hidden by snow clouds.

Motive and opportunity. Does the answer to this riddle lie in this building? I have a virtual spreadsheet of potential suspects in my mind: Khalyla, Eric, Johan, Ingvar, the B&B owner, even. Karin, the police, the Wolverines: collectively or individually. Peter's hockey bullies, his old friends, his colleagues at Willy's. Nothing is sticking and that infuriates me.

I walk to the door.

'Just me.'

The bouncer moves to block my path. 'Private event.'

'Seriously? It's me. Come on.'

'Private,' he says again. 'Event.'

The scent of leather and spilt beer in the air.

I need access. To talk to locals, to probe. But in all honesty I also need a drink. 'I'll read your poetry. There, I said it. We can have coffee and discuss it.'

He doesn't speak this time he just glares at me.

I walk away.

With everywhere else closed I head back to the B&B. Tonight is one of those nights when I will throw myself into research. Booze was denied, and it is not like you can just buy it from a supermarket, not here in Sweden, so work is all I have.

No more details about the latest victim. How long can this go on?

After dredging through open-source sites and forums I stumble upon a video on Vimeo where a faceless interviewer probes the mind of our very own Ingvar Persson, the lift operator. I watch the whole thing with captions and it is fascinating.

Ingvar starts off by answering questions about his own criminal history. He has no interest in discussing this subject, that's clear by his facial expression, but he offers stunted, well-rehearsed answers. His victim was a man who had beaten up Ingvar's niece. He had beaten her once before, breaking two of her ribs. Ingvar regrets the fight. Invar didn't enjoy prison but he did learn to adapt to it, and his ongoing education was key to that adaptation. No, he has not been in contact with the family of the victim. No, he has never returned to the region he comes from. Ingvar gives a series of one-word answers to more in-depth questions about the fight itself, why he didn't stick around to offer first aid, why he didn't call an ambulance. It is clear he does not want to discuss this in granular detail.

The point at which Ingvar perks up is when he is asked about the so-called Pepper Spray Killer in Esseberg. I check the time stamp of the video. It was uploaded six hours ago. His keenness is disconcerting. His eyes brighten and he sits up straight. According to the comments underneath, this video was deleted from YouTube almost immediately. I readjust my pillows to get comfortable. The interviewer asks him what his view is of the current situation.

'We are experiencing an ultra-rare phenomenon. I hope the perpetrator will be caught before viewers have a chance to see this video. He needs to be apprehended swiftly.'

The captions are auto-generated. They are inaccurate and sadly I am all too used to this.

'You think it's a *he*.'

'Yes,' says Ingvar. 'I am quite certain.'

'But, you're not. You don't know for sure.'

Ingvar shakes his head dismissively. 'Statistically speaking most serial killers or spree killers – this perpetrator may actually fall into either category, depending on definitions used – we can't ascertain that yet—'

The interviewer interrupts him. 'What's the difference?'

'The difference? Time, mainly,' says Ingvar, his eyes alert. 'A serial killer may take long periods 'off' between murders. They may have cooling off pauses where they are fallow for years or even decades. A spree killer generally kills multiple victims in a short period of time. Usually only a matter of days, weeks or months between murders.'

'You were saying how the killer is most likely male.'

'Statistically most spree killers and serial killers are white heterosexual males with a high-school or college education. They are often married and employed. They might fit in well in society. They may even hold positions of authority or rank in their community.'

'Like a cop or a military officer?'

'Or a teacher or priest. Some have speculated that a local law-enforcement officer could be to blame. A police officer who lost control. As far as I am concerned every-one is a potential suspect.'

'What is his motive, do you think?'

'I wouldn't like to speculate as I don't have sufficient knowledge of the case.'

'Take a guess.'

'I don't guess.'

'Can you talk about their modus operandi.'

'The Pepper Spray Killer gained his nickname because he shocks his victims with a spray of capsicum at a concentration of two per cent. That is a semi-toxic formula that has proven to be highly effective against most people. It can make breathing difficult and it can temporarily blind anyone sprayed directly in the face. It also intensifies over time, with an effective disabling period of up to sixty minutes assuming no immediate access to water.'

'They spray the victim and then when they're writhing around in agony, confused and shocked, they strangle them?'

'Not strangulation exactly. The victims seem to have a ligature applied in the form of a military-grade tourni-quet. It's like a nylon belt with Velcro sections; you maybe have seen images on the news this week. Imagine the victim panicking in the snow, writhing around in confusion and pain, possibly down on the ground. The assail-ant slips the loop over his or her head in a matter of seconds and tightens. The tourniquet is designed, with great attention to detail, to be easily handled by an injured soldier, you see. You can operate it and tighten it with just one hand in case you've been shot in the arm. So the Pepper Spray Killer loops it over the victim's head and tightens. That's an extra level of shock the victim has to deal with. They are already effectively blinded, and struggling to breathe, and now they have a belt around their neck. The Pepper Spray Killer then tightens the windless, calmly, and extinguishes their life.'

I pause the video.

My pulse is racing.

I restart it. The interview says, 'Horrible way to die.'

Ingvar remains emotionless. His face is blank like he's waiting to continue with his detailed explanation.

'And all four victims were killed in this exact same way?'

Ingvar scratches the cross tattoo below his eye. 'The authorities have detailed information from the only known surviving victim, Katia Hallgren, and they have an intact tourniquet which was left in place, tight around the neck of Peter Hedberg. That suggests to me that Peter was likely the killer's first victim, or that the killer was interrupted on that occasion and had to leave the scene before he could remove the strap. Forensic specialists will be able to decide which is true once time of death has been narrowed down. It is my hypothesis that the other victim found at the same location, Jenni Karlsson, was the interrupter, so to say. Meaning our killer could have been caught that same day.'

Ingvar sounds different to the man who took me down the mountain in his dog sled. His diction is more authoritative, more eloquent.

'Why do you think he continues to kill?'

'Why did he ever begin?' says Ingvar. 'Blood lust. He has acquired a taste for it.'

'For the thrill?'

'I don't know. It is possible he kills because he wishes to dominate, to gain complete control. Killers who strangle sometimes tighten, then loosen, then re-tighten the noose so they can experience that God-like power. In a way they then have complete authority over the life and death of the individual they are dominating. They may suffer from some kind of inferiority complex, or perhaps they were never praised or supported as a child. Jealousy, jilted lovers and so on, and even career envy, can make some people do extraordinary things. It is also possible, and some would say likely, that there is a sexual element to these crimes, despite none of the victims being sexually attacked per se.'

'How so?'

I open a fresh can of Coke.

'How can I put this sensitively, some killers get off on the power dynamic. It is not the fact that they are being violent or killing another person. Rather, their particular kink may be the death throes of another human being in their care. The *spasms*. They may gain sexual gratification – as a result of an unfortunate short-circuit somewhere in the brain, perhaps – from the last gasp a person takes before their blood supply is cut off completely and their brain stem shuts down.'

The interviewer pauses to read out an advert from a sponsor and I have to mute the screen and look away. We go about our lives believing there is good in everyone. And perhaps there is. But occasionally you gain a glimpse into pure evil. An insight into a sinister world of barbarity and sadism.

I stand up and stretch.

A bad taste in my mouth.

Sulphur.

From my window I can see the mountain but I can't make out the hotel on the top. I already had a father I loved. I already had a dad.

The video continues and the interviewer asks Ingvar about behavioural profiles.

'They are of some value, but it is nothing like you see in Hollywood.' The camera pans out for the first time and I see he's wearing his red ski trousers. 'I can't, with any reliability, tell you this man's career or address or exact age, more's the pity. The only thing I will say is that he is either local, a resident of Esseberg, or else he knows the town extremely well. This man feels comfortable here. He stalks the unlit paths and cross-country ski lanes that surround the town limits, often in the dark, and then he acts with a high degree of precision and composure. It is likely he is an accomplished skier or perhaps he has access to a snowmobile to leave the scene as soon as he is done. He has not left behind any fibres or hair to my knowledge. The killer is here. I believe he is one of us.'

48

I make a spicy pot noodle and continue watching. Ingvar declines to answer half a dozen questions in a row, questions about the impact of his own crime all those years ago, and about statements made by other reformed offenders on how he was respected inside as an elder of sorts, and as such gained the trust of fellow inmates. The interview becomes more awkward. Ingvar is asked about his feelings for Johan Backman and his popular podcast.

'I am not familiar with any such podcast.'

The interviewer smiles. 'You must have heard of it, surely. It is one of the most downloaded true-crime podcasts in Europe, if not the world.'

'I live off grid with my sled dogs. When I am not repairing and maintaining the lift system in Esseberg I am chopping firewood or studying. I have no desire to listen to others talk for hours when I have so many unread papers and books on my shelves.'

'Is it true Johan invited you on to the show?'

'I think we are done here.'

'You have declined his invitation?'

Ingvar looks impatient. He stands up. 'All I know is, Johan grooms the pistes at night. He is very good at what he does. I maintain the lifts. I am good at what I do. End of conversation.'

The video terminates.

I never realised there was a rivalry between the pair. Perhaps not a rivalry, exactly, but a degree of animosity.

I scroll through dozens of related videos before finding one on Johan's channel. He has over three quarters of a million subscribers. The reaction video is a year old, and it is filmed in Johan's professional-looking podcast studio with microphones and headphones and a red 'On-Air' sign, critiquing Ingvar's analysis of an older interview where he gave pointers on the psychological markers and clues displayed by a Texan man released from prison at the age of seventy-four.

I am amazed people take so much effort to film a reaction video to a reaction video to an interview. I watch because I find this pair compelling in some way, and because I sense one or both may hold the key to our current murder case.

Ingvar explains how the childhood experiences of the released prisoner many have contributed to his predilection to murder. Ingvar goes into some depth about the killer's rejection from the school football team, and the humiliation he felt when he had to explain this to his overbearing and often absent father. At this point Johan pauses the video and speaks to the camera, critiquing Ingvar's analysis. He praises certain aspects of his commentary but he also mentions, on numerous occasions, how Ingvar's terminology and reasoning is outdated. He seems to take relish in his critique.

Before I fall to sleep I switch on the TV affixed to the wall. Regional news programme. They talk about how the Esseberg pensions office is allowing all personnel to work from home considering the circumstances. All the victims' faces are displayed on-screen in little boxes. A grid formation. Three or four seconds dedicated to their memory. Less than a second each. The news-reader goes on to detail how school attendance in Esseberg is down sharply as parents keep their children at home despite the Kommun telling them this would not be tolerated. She says there is some debate in the town about whether or not to cancel the Santa Lucia church service on December 12th. A man is inter-viewed in the street. A street less than a hundred metres from here. He says he drives a snowplough in the town. He is carrying a small dog wearing a camo-pattern coat. He says people are still out walking and cross-country skiing, trying to make the most of whatever light there is in the middle of the day, but now they're going about in pairs or groups.

They no longer walk alone.

*

I wake with an urgent compulsion to hug my Gavrik neighbour, little Dan. It feels like months since I last babysat him. Before I have even showered or eaten I text his mother to check if I can call. She replies almost instantly with a *thumbs-up* emoji.

I put in my hearing aids and clear my throat. I drink water and then I dial.

'Is it you?' he says.

'It's me. How are you, Dan?'

'I got a red robin bird in my advent calendar. It has a red chest. I wanted a Mario or a Sonic but I got a bird instead. Mamma says red birds are for Christmas.'

'They sure are. Have you written your letter to Santa yet?'

He laughs. 'I've written three already. I sent one on December first and burnt it with Mamma out in the snow. But I forgot to write about the rocket-ship Lego so I wrote a new one and I drew Santa a picture and then I said he must not use the old letter because that's a bad letter and I made a boo-boo. And I did one in school, too. I put in a Donald Duck comic.'

'Nice. I used to—'

He cuts me off. 'I like *Kalle Anka* Donald Duck comics but Mamma says I have to stop writing to Santa now because it's using too much paper and he'll get in a big muddle.'

'Your mum's right.'

'When can we watch on your TV?'

'When I'm back. I'll be back soon.'

'*Gremlins*? Or *Gremlins 2*?'

'Not yet, buddy. When you're nine.'

'Adam watched it already and he's only six.'

'It'll give you nightmares.'

'I'm not scared of anything.'

'Spiders?'

'Nope.'

'The dark?'

'Everyone's scared of the dark so that doesn't count. The dark is really scary.'

'How's ice hockey?'

'Not hockey, Tuva. *Bandy*. We play with a ball. I stopped going there now.'

'You did?'

'Mamma says the pads and the real helmet and the boots with the blade and the stick are too much money. She says I can play something else that's more fun.'

'You never know what Santa will bring you, kiddo.'

'Is it Mario?'

I laugh and I feel a thousand times better about life than I have all week. This little man is always breath of fresh air.

'I need to go now, Dan.'

'You making up a newspaper again?'

'I am.'

'You make them from trees. We learnt about it in school. Trees make paper and toilet paper as well.'

'You're right.'

'I know. Miss Andersson told us.'

'I'll talk to you soon, Dan.'

'Bye.'

He puts down the phone. There is no extended good-bye protocol with a child his age. It is always simply 'bye' and I respect him for it.

After I shower, while I'm brushing my teeth, I think about the homicidal maniac still on the loose this side of the tunnel. I thought he would be apprehended by now. And then I think about Eric. He does look like me, much more than Dad ever did. As I stare in the mirror, minty-white foam falling from my lips, I resolve to take a chance. Maybe it was talking to Dan that spurred me on. Maybe it's losing Mum and then Noora. I decide I will spend a little time with Eric Lindgren. No commitment or drama. No thought of ever calling him anything but *Eric,* not even if the tests prove his paternity, but I think it might be good for both of us if we give this a chance.

After half a day trying and failing to doorstep, in the gentlest way possible, friends, neighbours and relatives of the latest victim, I give up having gained only a couple of generic soundbite quotes, and a meeting in the diary tomorrow in the church community centre with the victim's best friend, Gemma Dahl.

I call the hotel.

'Good afternoon, Grand Hotel Pinnacle. How can I help you?'

'Yes, hello. This is Tuva Moodyson. I'd like to book a room, please.'

'Of course, Ms Moodyson. Let me just check what we have available.'

I can't hear her clicking her keyboard but I imagine that's what she is doing. Or maybe she doesn't need to because the whole hotel is empty.

'Ah, yes, I have your booking here. Four nights in the Tunnel Suite.'

'No, sorry, that's not me. I haven't made a booking yet.'

'It's all pre-paid, including breakfast and dinner. You can check in today anytime from 3 p.m. Is there anything else I can help you with?'

49

The lobby of the hotel is warm, the fire roaring and spitting, but it is largely empty. One man sits in the far corner. He has unkempt white hair and a thick white moustache. He exudes a kind of reincarnated Albert Einstein vibe as he sits reading his hardback novel by the window. I recognise him from somewhere.

Karin Bates, the janitor who is also night porter, and who also seems to be in charge of the kitchen and the reception desk much of the time, shows me to my room. She has a tactical-style first-aid kit affixed to her belt.

'It's a modest-size hotel but we have unusually long corridors,' she says, apologetically. 'You'll find some of the guestrooms and wings are locked and unheated. Some of them are roped off. We've had to switch off the water to those areas and drain the pipes.'

'But my room is heated, right?'

She laughs and taps me reassuringly on the shoulder. 'Of course. Your room is in a rather distant section of the hotel, I'm afraid, because it's the only part we've already renovated. Modern heating and pipework, relatively speaking. You will be cosy and warm, we guarantee it.'

'How many staff are here at the hotel?'

'Normally, or this winter?'

'Both.'

'Normally, six permanent full-time, including me. And then we bring in another ten or so for the busy winter season. That's when we usually have most of our bookings, although we did used to have some summer hikers come and stay, and we used to have a steady stream of corporate getaways and conferences.'

'And now?'

Karin pushes a heavy solid-wood door into another dark, cold corridor. 'You're talking to her.'

'It's just *you*?'

'We don't have many reservations because of the train, and because of some unfair reviews online. It's a real shame. Saddens me to see her in this state.'

'Her?'

'The Pinnacle. These days it's me and Eric doing most of the work. We're always up here. And then we have three girls who come in part-time. They live down in the town.'

'And Khalyla?'

She looks at me and cringes. 'No, dear.'

We keep walking. One corridor leads to the next and so on. Internal doors and uneven floors.

With some degree of pomp and circumstance she unlocks my room door with a proper key and pushes it open. 'The Tunnel Suite. Would you like me to show you how things work?

'No, I'm good. Thanks, though.'

'If you need anything just call through to reception. If nobody answers then please be patient. It may take me a while to arrive if you ask for a blanket or similar. Because of the circuitous route. I'm sure you understand.'

I smile and close the door. Then, when she's gone, I hang the *Do Not Disturb* sign on the knob outside and lock it.

The room is large and it is pure pine. It looks like a sample of forest has been dragged in from outside. Rough grain wood all over the walls and floors. All over the ceiling, even. Tongue and groove. Knots like dark eyes staring back at me from above the window and beside the desk. It is a fancier room than back at the B&B. But it lacks one convenience that I have found essential ever since my stint living and working in London.

It has no kettle.

I work for an hour on stories Lena's requested for the print. Lars asks a pretty direct question over email about when I'll be back. He reminds me that he has a holiday to Tenerife planned for December 15th for two weeks. He tells me, as if I needed a reminder, that it's been in the staff calendar since last Christmas and he needs to go because the sun helps his psoriasis. I write back and tell him not to worry. I will return before Santa Lucia.

Eric lives here. He has lived here all his life, save for that brief period in Stockholm. And so, in a very weird sense, if the test comes back positive, you could say staying here is similar to me moving back home. I laugh at the absurdity. The only home I have is the one I have created and paid for myself. A small apartment with a two-person balcony and a sweet kid living next door.

It is dark outside. The wind whistles and old snow falls from the roof in occasional flurries. Through the window, in the far distance, I can just make out headlights. Dozens of cars and trucks waiting patiently for the direction of flow inside the single-lane tunnel to reverse so they can leave Ice Town.

The room isn't cold but it makes me uneasy somehow. It is like I'm stuck out on some isolated wing of the hotel, far away from everyone else. I disconnect my phone from the charger, but either the electrics are faulty in this room or else I didn't push it in far enough because it hasn't charged. I decide to work from the lobby and select the table closest to the fire. No sockets anywhere. I move away because I'm starting to sweat. Einstein has gone but there are other guests here. Skiers and snowboarders who look far more fit and proficient than me. No sign of Eric. I guess I'm keeping an eye out for him. I might arrange a DNA test next year – swabs and cotton buds, little plastic pots with screw lids – I think private labs can process and analyse, but I am as terrified of a positive result as I am of a negative one. Perhaps I won't go through with it. What if it is positive and he turns out to be a fraudster or fantasist? The doors open from outside and the police chief walks in with another uniformed cop.

I stand up.

She says something to her colleague who then looks at me and walks through the whole lobby and out of sight. The chief approaches.

'Evening, Chief.'

'You haven't gone back south, Tuva?'

'Lots of news in your town.'

'Too much. And this isn't my town.'

'Any developments?'

'The Wolverines are out in force patrolling and walking the trails with torches and ChemLights. Between you and me they outnumber us ten to one. Just what I didn't need.'

'I mean any developments with the investigation?'

'Nothing I can talk about yet.'

'Did you question Alfred?'

'He's not our man. Alibis.'

'But he was in Esseberg?'

'I can't talk anymore on that. There's another reporter living up here with you, did you know?'

'Astrid? From Norrköping?'

'No, a young man from *Aftonbladet*. Lots of pomade in his hair.'

Slickback. 'I know him. He's okay.'

She nods, looks away, then looks back. 'Actually, Tuva. We do have one development. We'll be going public with it today so I can share it with you. You see, the perpetrator wasn't using standard pepper spray to attack the victims.'

'No?'

'It was a formulation we now know is *Bear Spray*.'

'Bear spray?'

'Illegal in Sweden, but common in the US, Canada, and several European countries. It is essentially a larger canister with more range, and often a more potent mix. It's not sold in Sweden so we want anyone with any information, anyone who has seen or heard of a friend with a bottle of this, to come forward so we can eliminate them from our enquiries.'

'Is it lethal to humans?'

'No. It's still a version of pepper spray. It'd be very unpleasant, that's all. No permanent damage. But I think, off the record, it'd be a horrific way to go. Writhing in agony from the irritants and then, without expecting it, being throttled by the neck. I struggle to imagine a more hideous end.'

50

The police leave and the hotel is quiet once again, the furniture in the lobby glowing, warm reflections lapping up the pine walls. There is something primal about a sturdy, warm building in a desolate place like this. The differential between what is outside – the wolves and bears, the cold, the unrelenting elements – and what is inside.

My belly full of rich *kalops* beef stew, I head back out to the stairs. I pull out my phone to check breaking news but I'm completely out of battery now. When I'm back in Gavrik I need to upgrade, this thing is older than my truck.

I pass two coats on hooks outside a room marked *private*. One red, one white with fur trim.

I think about what the chief told me. *Bear spray*. I always imagined you'd repel a bear with a large calibre rifle, not a can of pepper spray.

Up the stairs. I have to be careful not to take a wrong turn.

My floor. I am the only one staying up here.

The floorboards creak.

I walk through into the first long corridor, closing a heavy door behind me. The light switches on as I pass by the sensor and set off a timer. It must tick very loudly because I can hear it. The harsh light shines bright, illuminating the framed black and white photographs on the wall. A glitzy party at the hotel: guests in fur coats and white bow ties. Champagne and evening dress in the wilderness. A double-size frame with a photo of the old King arriving in the lobby, and next to it a yellowed cutting from the *Östersunds Posten* dated 1937.

I keep on walking.

A framed quote from the bible. Deuteronomy. *You will be cursed in the city and cursed in the country. Your basket and your kneading trough will be cursed. The fruit of your womb will be cursed, and the crops of your land, and the calves of your herds and the lambs of your flocks. You will be cursed when you come in and cursed when you go out. The Lord will send on you curses, confusion and rebuke in everything you put your hand to, until you are destroyed and come to sudden ruin because of the evil you have done in forsaking him.*

A door slams somewhere in the building.

Another bible quote, this one faded. Short extracts from Malachi. *And now, you priests, this warning is for you.* Then, lower on the page, *I will smear on your faces the dung from your festival sacrifices, and you will be carried off with it.*

Hardly welcoming, but I can't stop reading.

The next framed quote is from Revelation. The words are handwritten. Again, fragmented segments. *I watched as he opened the sixth seal. There was a great earthquake. The sun turned black like sackcloth made of goat hair, the whole moon turned blood red, and the stars in the sky fell to earth.* A gap, some kind of diagram, and then it goes on. *There came hail and fire mixed with blood, and it was hurled down upon the earth.*

I walk briskly to the next door but I have taken too long reading. The light on the timer goes out. I am plunged into complete darkness. On instinct I reach out for the walls, for something to hold on to, but I can't find them. This long box of a room seems to enlarge, spread out in all directions. I panic and stumble over a loose rug and now I am on my knees, a sharp pain coursing through my patella. I hold out my phone to switch on the light but then remember it is dead.

I move along, down where the wall meets the floor, my hands tracking the smooth but uneven wood surfaces. My heart is up in the back of my throat. I can't hear clearly and I cannot see.

Vibrations.

Footsteps?

What am I doing on this mountaintop? In this town, alone? It might be Eric. Coming to check on me, to make sure his daughter is okay.

I want to speak out but my voice fails me.

I move quickly to the next door. There will be a sensor there. I reach the end of the corridor, passing two rooms, their doors unusually cold to the touch, and no light emerges. I grip the door and push it open firmly. It does not budge. I heave it with my shoulder and it gives with no friction or stiffness. There is no light. I move around. Is this a power cut? It could be. The wiring in this place is likely outdated. I wave my arms around to activate the light but if anything it is even darker back here. I can't return to the staircase. I must find my own door.

Edging along the wall, I dislodge a framed photo and it crashes to the ground, smashing on impact, glass shards scattering around my feet. I let out a pathetic yelp and keep on moving. Glass crunches beneath my boots.

And then I feel it.

If you know, you know.

That prickle. That unspeakable sensation on the back of your neck or on your forearms. Fine hairs standing up. A chill. There is someone else close by in the blackness. I sense them. There is another person in this dark maze of a corridor. Watching me.

I look around desperately, squinting to focus my eyes in every direction but I see precisely nothing. There is no light to acclimatise to. I hold my arms out in front of me and there is a faint aroma in the air. Pine and old rugs, but also the light scent of peppers or tabasco. Terror grips me and I rush headfirst into the gloom, tripping and falling. I find a door, my door and I cling to it. The prickling sensation intensifies. Footsteps behind me. Louder, now. I turn my back on the darkness and insert my key.

The door does not unlock.

51

I remove the key and push it back in and try to turn it, but this is not my room or else someone has changed the locks.

A thud.

I turn around on my heels.

The corridor feels without limits again. A glimpse into outer space. A room as massive as a football stadium or barn. Where is my room? I want my own room.

I move swiftly to the next door.

My heart beats hard in my ears and my lips are so dry it is like they are cracking apart.

The scent of spice intensifies.

My nostrils burn.

The next door. I fumble with my key, my fingers shaking, and it fits. I turn it and fall into my room and slam the door shut behind me and lock it. Light on. Blessed relief. I stand bent double, panting. Then I push a chair to the door handle and wedge it underneath.

I check every corner of my room, and then the bathroom. There is nobody here.

After I charge my phone I look through the curtains at the distant town below.

Lights are on. Esseberg looks normal from here. Safe, even.

But then my attention is captured by something on the window sill outside, something that wasn't there an hour ago when I went down for dinner. I could swear it wasn't there.

I am on the third floor and there is a perfect holly sprig trembling on my window ledge.

Three bright red berries.

I use the room phone to call down to reception.

'Reception.'

'Hi, it's Tuva Moodyson in the Tunnel Suite.'

'What can I do for you?'

'Can I . . . could you . . . this is going to sound really weird.'

'What can I help you with this evening?

'Is this Karin?'

A long pause.

'Speaking.'

'Could you walk with me from my room down through to the stairs, please? Like you did before but in reverse.'

'You have something you need carrying?'

'No, no. It's just me. I don't . . . feel well. Terrible sense of direction. Could you walk with me?'

Another long pause. 'Of course. I'll be right up.'

I feel instantly more at ease. Sometimes you ponder and beat yourself up about asking a thing and then when you force yourself to do it it's no big deal after all. I'm paying for the hotel and the services they provide, whatever Eric thinks. And it is not cheap. Almost twice the price of the B&B. I never thought I would say it, but I miss that place.

A few minutes later I sense a knock at the door.

I am sweating in my cold-weather gear: long johns and moon boots. My ski jacket and pants. A thick, green wool hat Noora bought me when she completed a Crime Scene Management course in Karlstad.

There is no peephole so I say, 'Karin?'

'I'm right here.'

I remove the chair and open the door a crack.

'Are you okay?'

I nod. 'I'll be fine. Just need to go down to the town for work.'

'It's a bad night.'

Tell me about it.

'Karin?'

She looks at me.

'I found holly leaves and berries on my window ledge. Do you have any idea—'

'Damn tree rats,' she says. 'The birds and the squirrels. They leave things on my ledge most days. Vermin with offerings. Just ignore them.'

'Oh, okay. I will.'

She gestures towards the door.

I walk out cautiously, looking both ways. Then I lock the door behind me.

'You sure you're okay?'

'The light wouldn't switch on earlier,' I say. 'That's all.' I don't think she understands how terrifying the ordeal was for me. It's not her fault, it's just that darkness is a constant threat for deaf people, or at least it is for me. If I can't hear and I can't see then I can spiral out of control. I can panic. 'I want to apologise about the smashed frame. I walked into it in the dark. I want to pay for it.'

'What smashed frame?'

'The one on the corridor wall.'

'Hmm,' she says. 'That's strange. I didn't notice it.'

'I'll pay for a replacement.'

She waves that away with her hand. 'It was probably falling out the wall anyway. Whole place needs rebuilding. Don't beat yourself up about it. I have spares.'

We walk together and the corridor seems normal now. The photos. The grandfather clock by the staircase ticking loudly, loud enough for me to hear when I am next to it, its pendulum swinging back and forth. Even the bible quotes look reasonable. Except the frame *has* been repaired and is back on its nail. There is no broken glass on the floor, either.

I point to it. 'I broke that.'

She smiles. 'Must have been put back up by Eric or Khalyla. No damage.'

'It smashed.'

She frowns and guides me to the lift.

The sharp chill outside is a relief. I was starting to get agitated again walking through the lobby with that roaring fire. I had sweat running down my back.

'You want me to ask one of the others to ride the lift down with you this time, Tuva? You don't seem quite yourself.'

'No, no. I'm fine, now. But thank you.'

She takes me to the lift gates.

'No operator,' I say. 'Is it closed?'

She smiles. 'Don't worry, I can still get you on.' She uses her own lift pass to bypass the gates and lets me proceed straight up onto the icy ramp. 'Staff privileges.'

As the chair scoops me up and I push the safety bar down to my legs she says something but her words are lost to the wind. I look back but she is already walking away towards the Pinnacle.

I take a deep breath. Three more. If there is still a free room at the Golden Paradise I think I might take it. The Pinnacle can transfer my bags down in the morning. It's not just the unpredictability of the hotel and its dark corridors, it's the isolation. How quickly would police be able to reach us if there's a problem? Can the lifts be started up in the middle of the night for an emergency? I shiver just thinking about it. Perhaps Eric has clouded my already poor judgement. I check my voicemails but the reception is patchy. I hear one word in three. A message from Tammy, a long one where she tells me about some customer questioning her portion sizes. The chair passes over two towers, floodlights beaming down into the snow far below, and I listen to her tell me more about her day, her boyfriend, some ongoing problem with her building's organisation committee not permitting her to paint her door. Tam's voice is a tonic.

It is biting cold. Twenty below. Maybe colder. And the wind whistles as it passes through and over clusters of anaemic pine trees, me at canopy level. They can't receive the nutrients they need at this elevation, at these angles. This place is the polar opposite, no pun intended, of Utgard forest.

A short voice message from little Dan. I listen to it four times. Him asking if we can watch *The Goonies* or *Short Circuit* when he's old enough. He says he's seen the DVDs on my apartment shelves and he thinks he's ready because Gustav from his class has seen *Jurassic Park*. Interesting logic, kid. Nice try.

The chair rattles as we pass over another tower, the thick cable juddering over four wheels, and then it is smooth riding once again. Leaving the Pinnacle behind and moving closer to the sinister town below.

I call the B&B.

The reception is still poor but I can just about hear her voice. No luck. They have rented out my room until Wednesday next week. She says she will let me know if there are any cancellations.

I would sleep in my Hilux but it would be certain death in December. You can't sleep in your truck in this part of the world. You would never wake up again.

I start to google rentals or rooms in Åre and then the chairlift stops abruptly. The wind blows, blasting ice crystals against my right cheek, and I have to turn away from it.

The cable creaks overhead.

I check my phone and the battery shows 7%. It's the cold. Lithium batteries can drain quickly at these temperatures. Time for that upgrade. I find Lena's details in my recently called list and press call and the phone dies in my gloved hand.

It turns itself off.

Black screen against a brilliant white panorama.

My chair swings back and forth perhaps twenty metres above a steep, rocky incline, and I am completely alone. I never even had a chance to recharge my hearing aids back at the hotel; I kept them in the whole time because I couldn't bear to be separated from them. How long will the charge last out here? They are warm against my ears. They might be good for a few more hours.

The lift will start up again soon. The lights are still on and I can see the very edge of the town in the distance, the blackness of the lake and a few lights skirting its banks.

I pull my hat down tighter and tuck in my arms to retain some warmth but I am fighting a losing battle up here. The wind is the worst of it. I am being blasted by God's own air conditioner and the stale sweat on my back is freezing solid to my skin.

I hang.

The cable creaks louder.

Is the murderer taking a break? Do they have children to teach or a wife who has organised a surprise mini-break to Uppsala? Will he return to his ways or has his reign of terror ended, at least for a decade? It could be that it has intensified: more bodies, silent and motionless below snow blankets, dotted all around the town, off every trail and path. Maybe we just haven't found the others yet.

I force myself to stop thinking of such things. Not today, not after the darkness of that corridor.

I try to switch on my phone and it does switch on. A twenty-first-century lifeline. Thank all the gods. It is on.

And then it turns off again.

I place it inside my jacket pocket and move my gloved hands to protect my face from the relentless chill.

The lights connected to the ski lift turn off all at once.

I am left with nothing.

52

'Hello?' I say. And then I scream, '*Hello!*'

Nothing.

Pointless.

The chairlift hangs precariously from its twisted, steel cable. It does not move up or down the mountain as it should, but side to side. The arctic wind gusts against my cheeks, my nose, my eyelids.

They have halted the service for ten minutes because of the high winds. They always do this. But why would they switch off the floodlights? Has there been a power cut? No, the town is still glowing dimly in the distance like a knot of neglected fairy lights.

I can't see my hand in front of my face. There is no moonlight or starlight now; the snow clouds are too dense. It has been minutes. Ten minutes? It could have been an hour. I loathe not knowing what time it is.

Years ago, I interviewed a young woman in Falun hospital. Lena set up the meeting because she knew one of her college tutors. I was briefed on the basics but that did not prepare me for what I found on the ward. The nurse pulled back the thin blue curtain and there she was sat up in bed smiling. A beautiful head of thick red hair. Intelligent green eyes. Her name was Åsa and her nose, fingers and toes were all blackened like burnt charcoal.

In the weeks following, she lost them all.

Åsa told me how she had gone out drinking in Ronnie's Bar, Gavrik, with her college friends. I might have seen her in there. She told me she usually wore a heavy coat, mittens, and a hat in January, but on this particular occasion she didn't want to ruin her outfit. She told me a pulp-mill technician she liked was due to be there and she was wearing her new dress. She also told me he never turned up. She drank with her friends, played pool, and had a lovely time. She enjoyed a few cocktails too many so a friend of hers called Taxi Gavrik and a cab driver (who replaced infamous Utgard resident, Viggo Svensson, a few years back) took her home to the suburbs, to the house her parents built in the eighties. Fumbling with her key in the cold she never managed to unlock the front door. Åsa's parents found her at seven in the morning and she was frozen, unconscious, attached to the ground, and suffering from irreversible frostbite.

'Help me!' I scream, but I only manage to scare myself even more. Do they even know I'm still up here? Karin bypassed the lift scanner. I come to the sudden and horrific realisation that I could be stuck up here all night.

A noise.

I spin my head, my gloved hands still gripping the bar. I never *consciously* heard it. But my body reacted. Some visceral warning. My gut taking over. A predator somewhere in these white woods, watching me patiently from behind the treeline. These mountains are known for their Eurasian wolves. *Canis lupus lupus.* Pack hunters.

I cover as much of my face as I can with my gloves to block the wind.

They are known for their bears, too. *Ursus arctos arctos.* Some of them approach 500 kg.

Wolves can't climb well but bears can.

Bears climb very well indeed.

No. Stop it, Tuva.

I know the early signs of hypothermia. After you have been cold for a while your core temperature begins to drop and you grow sleepy and confused. Resigned to your fate.

There will be no bears.

'Hello!' I yell, panting, puffs of panicked breath clouding in front of me, hovering twenty metres above the snow and granite.

I check my phone again but it is unresponsive.

Johan might be working nearby here later on in his piste-basher. He will see me up here, surely. He will rescue me. But who is to say he's not responsible? He has a macabre fascination with true crime and criminal behaviour. He knows these mountains like no one else. And then I remember he listens to other podcasts and interviews when he is working on the slopes each night, some of them five hours long, so he won't hear my screams, and I don't know whether to laugh or cry.

Never before have I felt this vulnerable.

If I die up here and Eric is indeed my biological father then whatever divine being might be present in this universe has a perverse and twisted sense of humour. Eric losing two on the same slopes.

It strikes me that the odds of survival are growing increasingly rotten in Ice Town. One murder in a town of a thousand is bad. Five would be catastrophic.

Some vague memory of my mother's voice warning me about *frost nip* when I was a child. My memory is vague. I am so, so tired. She would not come out in the snow with me, even back then. She preferred the indoors. She would warn that if I felt pins and needles, or pain, I was to come straight inside to warm up. Have I mentioned that already?

I do feel pins and needles and pain.

I have done for years.

Noora's lullaby – a haunting song she would sing in Arabic – echoes through my muddy brain and I push it away. I must stay awake and alert.

'Hello! Can anybody hear me up here?'

The beasts can hear me. They can smell me too. Can a bear really climb a ski lift tower? Of course it fucking can. It'd be easier than a tree. And I am strapped in here like a piece of processed chicken wrapped in Styrofoam. A refrigerated snack.

The chair squeaks and one of my hearing aids beeps.

It switches off.

I cry out, 'Is there anybody out there? Anyone? You have to help me.'

Jerky for bears.

And then my chin falls to my chest and I sob. My tears freeze to my waxy cheeks. I have never felt more desperately alone. In Gavrik, I have some semblance of help, of support. I may overestimate their love and loyalty at times, convincing myself I have a true family of sorts, that I can overcome each trial with their assistance, but they are always there for me. They have my back.

And I am stuck here.

In the distance a single red firework rises noiselessly into the sky and then erupts into a thousand stars, the impact muffled by the snow. The valley glows faint red for a moment. And then I realise that might not have been a firework. Rather, it could have been a distress flare. someone pointing to the heavens in a desperate effort to receive help from outside Essseberg.

The cable creaks and I notice a vague figure far below.

'Hello!'

In the shade of a gigantic spruce tree. On the rocks. A man in grey. In black?

'Help me!'

53

'Hello?' I scream, so hard my throat hurts.

He is gone. Was it nothing? A shadow of the tree? My mind playing tricks? The dark imprint of a branch swaying in this blizzard?

I place my gloves up to my cheeks again to protect them and the lift shudders back into life and I shriek, bashing both hands back down onto the bar to steady myself.

I am panting.

The floodlights burst back on, pinpricks of yellow light marking my route like runway lights and I could weep with relief.

The town grows as I approach.

The church tower and the monolithic pensions office and the power station belching out bitter smoke.

I hop off at the bottom and my legs are weak.

'What happened?' I ask the young guy working the lifts.

'Wind,' he says. 'Gusts. No big deal.'

I need to warm up.

The closest building is the church but there is something about that place – perhaps the ivy marks still staining its timber boards like the eternal shadows of people caught in a nuclear blast – that is not at all welcoming in this light.

Three bearded men in black leather jackets and tall snow boots trudge around, their beanie hats and scarves covering all but their eyes. The men have two-way radios clipped to their lapels.

I shuffle across the road and head inside the Vårdcentral surgery. The waiting room is empty. The surgery is closed, in fact. But the lights are still on in one section of the building.

They have expanded into four treatment rooms.

'You feeling okay, Moodyson?' asks Carlsson, his head on an angle like a well-meaning Labrador.

I remember what Ingvar said in his interview about the killer possibly being someone in a position of authority.

'I'm cold.'

'Sit down a second,' he says. 'What happened to you?'

I step closer. There are files spread on desks and three laptops lie open and charging. A large map of the town has been pinned to the wall and it is filled with pins and sticky notes.

'Don't look at any of that,' he says 'Look at me.'

Am I getting close to the answer? Is that why I'm being followed and messed with because that's what it feels like.

I turn to him.

I want to tell him but I know I'll sound unhinged and that will not help our trust issues one bit.

'You want a hot coffee, Tuva? You look like death warmed up.'

I nod. I am shivering and my cheeks are burning in the dry heat.

'Chairlift got caught . . . in a storm,' I say, my teeth still chattering intermittently. 'Stuck up there . . . for a long time.'

'You need to see a nurse?'

I shake my head.

'Sure?'

I nod. 'That coffee you mentioned will sort me out.'

'Coming up.'

I was hoping he would leave to visit some staff-kitchen area so I can take a peek at the wall map and whatever other documents I can snoop on, but he takes coffee from a thermos in the corner and pours it into a disposable plastic mug.

'Milk?'

'Please.'

'We just got UHT. Shelf stable, it is.'

'I'll take it black.'

He hands it to me and I let the steam thaw out my nose. It is good but it also hurts like I don't know what.

'You should get yourself a balaclava from the ski store.'

'In this town? I'd probably be arrested.'

He smiles but he looks weary.

'What's happening with the case?'

He shrugs. 'We have a bigger team on it now. Consider it a manhunt.'

'What was it before?'

He ignores that question and says, 'Extensive door-to-door operation. We have a cyber team trawling relevant material. They're also posting on various sites, asking for information.'

'Asking? What kind of information?'

'We're asking specifically for images and footage from private CCTV systems. From domestic doorbell cameras.'

'Man in black, still?'

'Black or dark grey. Possibly dark navy. Possibly black camouflage.'

'But no more bodies.'

He shakes his head.

I take a tentative sip of coffee. It's so strong I could stand a spoon up in it and that suits me fine.

'Forensics found a hair complete with follicle,' he says. 'They're running tests.'

'What colour was the hair?'

He shakes his head. 'I can't tell you that, Moodyson.'

The church bells ring. Outside the window a steady trickle of believers walk outside wearing their down jackets and reindeer fur hats.

'Mankind's original Xanax,' says Carlsson.

'What?'

'Sorry. Are you a churchgoer?'

I shake my head again.

'I didn't mean to be disrespectful.'

'You're on safe ground with me.'

'I only meant those townsfolk . . .' He trails off, sighing. 'Two millennia of socially acceptable neural support. A better job of that support than Big Pharma could ever dream about. Addicts, every single one of them.'

'Addicts?'

'They keep coming back to their regular, trusted neighbourhood dealer. They return. Sunday school was their gateway drug. Nothing serious. But now they cannot live without a regular fix. Every seventh day they confess their sins and they are absolved. Many of them are Wolverines, that's why the congregations are larger than you'd expect. They sing and they pray to their almighty. Xanax in its purest form. Ecclesiastical pain relief for trapped souls.'

'Are you okay?'

He smiles. 'I could probably do with a few days off.'

'I know how that feels.'

A man in plain clothes enters the room and it is clear to me he's a colleague so I make my excuses and leave.

Outside, the wind has dropped and the streets are deserted save for an old woman standing outside her building.

I squint at her and then I walk over.

Peter Hedberg's grandmother.

'Are you okay?' I ask.

'No.'

'Can I help you back inside?'

'No.'

'Do you remember me?'

She looks me straight in the eye. 'Don't you dare forget about him.'

I take a moment. 'I won't.'

'I mean it. There have been other boys and girls found out on the trails since my Peter. More worthy of your time, perhaps, people with accomplishments and honours degrees. Families of their own. But don't you dare forget my Peter.'

'I give you my word. I won't. Now, please, go inside, it's freezing out here.'

'He was my only hope.'

'Don't say that.'

'My only family in this world.'

'Let me help you back inside.'

'I don't need help.' She turns and opens the door to her building. 'Put his name in print for me. His short life. Remember my Peter.'

She closes the door.

54

I walk to the Golden Paradise B&B but everything beyond the solarium is locked. Nobody answers when I ring the bell. I don't know what I expected to happen. The owner already told me it was full. But you don't ever imagine yourself in a town with no available room.

Willy's closes at 10 p.m.

I walk to Wrath and there is no private event tonight so Ulf, the poet bouncer, lets me straight in.

Three rum and Cokes later I am sat in a banquette with ripped, black leather seats, surrounded by eight bikers. Six men and two women. I shouldn't enjoy this place: the music is discombobulating and I can't follow conversations. There is a live metal band on the stage at the back and they are passable. Metallica and Anthrax classics. Their own songs receive a less than favourable reaction so they stick to what their audience know.

One biker explains to me how truckers don't like Esseberg. They would rather sleep in the truck stop at Åre even if they dropping off a trailer here. They don't like being stranded on the wrong side of a tunnel that closes each night.

I drink two more rums and then someone buys a round of vodka and salt-liquorice shots. The room smells like smoke and boot polish and ale. The barman pours vodka and then throws a bag of liquorice at the apparent leader of our motley group, a bald man called Spider, and he drops a salty lozenge in each diminutive glass. We wait for the sweets to impart some flavour and then we hammer them back and I feel the pain inside myself start to fade.

The woman to my right, Sandra, who wears a collection of perhaps fifteen silver rings in an ear so perforated it resembles a colander, asks me what I do for a living. I tell her. Away from the worst of the noise, we chat for a while about the case, about the town. I still have to lip-read and guess words because of the volume, and the liquor, but in a loud bar you probably do something similar without even realising it. She knew Jenni Karlsson, the kindergarten teacher. She says we will all be safe in Wrath and I kind of believe her. She also tells me it would usually be busier in here but five teams of three Wolverines are out patrolling the town. I ask if they are armed and she smiles and shakes her head. I ask her what the deacon would think about that and she tells me he sent them out onto the streets. I ask her about Eric and Khalyla but she doesn't know them personally. She tells me how *Ingvar the Liftie*, as she calls him, is a convicted double murderer and I don't feel much like correcting her when she's in full flow. She reckons he lives in a house with a dungeon basement and a pack of wild dogs. She says Ingvar listens to recordings of screaming babies to get him off to sleep each night.

When I visit the bathroom I contemplate vomiting so I can keep on drinking, a strategic Viking trick, but I am not that person anymore. Progress, I guess. My table of new friends attempts to lure me back but I protest and head out for fresh air.

I will sleep in the corridor outside Carlsson's makeshift surgery office if I have to. I slept, if you can call it that, for many hours in the hospital waiting rooms, on sofas and hastily arranged plastic chairs, waiting for Noora to wake up. I have developed a knack for it. My standards, low as they were, have dropped.

The cold air usually has a sobering effect but tonight it is the opposite. I stand out with the poet bouncer, Ulf Samuellson, and we get to talking about his work. He brings me a black fleece blanket with a W motif and I wrap it around myself and he asks if I want a drink for the road. I ask for a gin and juice.

The next thing I know I am in a strange room with a strange smell.

My forehead feels like it has been split open. I can't focus.

Where am I?

I am down on the floor is where I am. When I look up I see the bouncer and he is taking off his jeans.

55

I gasp and sit up straight, my head pounding. I start coughing so hard my eyes water.

The room is familiar yet unfamiliar.

My shirt is torn; a hem dangles from a corner of the garment and my head is pounding.

I need water. What happened last night? I know this hollow, burning sensation. Trying to piece together fragments of memory, booze still coursing through my blood, my hands shaking, my eyelids glued together with the crust of old tears.

His broad, tattooed back.

In the next room. Is it the same room? In the kitchen area. His massive back.

Where is the door? How do I escape? I rub my eyes. Focus, Tuva. Where is my bag?

He turns around. 'Eggs?'

I recoil. Where is my phone? My truck key?

He spoke. I read him.

'You want eggs? Scrambled or fried?'

My head is clamped in a vice.

'Did we?' I ask, trying to stand. 'Did you . . .'

He looks appalled. 'What? No. God, no. Tuva, please, come on. I slept on the sofa. You snore like my uncle.'

'Why am I here?'

He turns his attention back to the hob for a moment. I can't hear him well enough to make out what he says.

'Sorry?' I say, and I am aware of how agitated I must sound. How unhinged.

He turns around and adjusts his apron.

'You said you had nowhere to go, remember? You told me the Golden Paradise had no rooms and you didn't know anybody here in town. The chairlift was closed for the night and so was the tunnel.'

'So you were a good Samaritan. No ulterior motives.'

'You threw up on the club's outdoor candle, Tuva. Extinguished it with rum and what looked like . . . beef stew?'

I frown.

'With carrots. Listen, I've worked the doors of Wrath for three years and I have never seen anyone manage to puke on a candle.'

I have no recollection of this. Do I trust him?

'I'm sorry,' I say.

'Fried or scrambled?'

'Coffee,' I urge. 'Just coffee. Please. Thank you.'

I sit down at his IKEA table and I am aware of how hideous I must look in this moment.

'Did I, you know, do anything awful?'

He says, 'Apart from the candle drama and calling the Golden Paradise the Golden Shower? No. You were good as gold.'

'I need the bathroom.'

'First on the left.'

I spend ten minutes in the bathroom washing my face with cold water and checking I have no injuries. A bruise on my knee. That is all that is wrong with me. No injuries. He is telling the truth. I borrow some of his spray-on Slazenger antiperspirant without clearing it with him first, because sometimes it is better to seek forgiveness than ask for permission. I emerge to a table full of fried food.

'I'm sorry I kicked you out of your bed, man.'

'Don't worry about it. I have a very long sofa.'

'You didn't even try to part-undress the drunk girl like they do in creepy movies?'

He frowns. 'I didn't want to get covered in . . . stew. To be honest it was more *The Exorcist* than *When Harry Met Sally*. Were you aiming for the candle? I've made your coffee strong.'

I sit down and sip it.

'Fried eggs,' he says.

'What?'

'You never answered so I fried them. Sunny side up. Hope that's okay.'

'All right, Mr Perfect. Calm down.'

He starts to cut into his bacon.

'What's that?' I ask, pointing at my plate.

'I regret to inform you that it is my attempt at a hash brown.'

'Fucking hell.'

'I've never tried them before.'

'I can see that.'

'They taste better than they look.'

'I bloody hope so. Can I charge my phone?'

He passes me his cable and I eat the delicious fried breakfast.

'You're a decent man.'

'Whatever.'

I chew, and ask, 'Any theories on who is terrorising your town?' And then I wonder if it is him. Nice to me, not so nice to the others.

'Theories? I don't know. The guys fascinated by true crime worry me a little. They take their interest to an unhealthy level in my judgement.'

'Johan?'

'For one. And Ingvar. The man who owns the hotel on the summit is also an enthusiast.'

'Eric?'

'You know him?'

I shrug awkwardly and come to the realisation that I need to work harder to connect dots in this town.

'Headache pills?' I say. 'Any chance?'

He stretches and passes me an almost empty pack of paracetamol. I take two.

'I wish I could charge my hearing aids with this phone charger.'

'Running out of juice?'

'One's dead. The other might have an hour or so left.'

'Can't you buy replacements in Willy's? I've seen them for sale in there.'

'I need to charge them. The battery's built in. Big improvement on my old ones to be fair.'

An hour later, after I have washed up all his pots and pans and stripped the sheets from his bed, I'm standing in his doorway. He is twice as large as me and half as obnoxious.

'You did a kind thing looking after me, Ulf. I'll never forget it.'

'You owe me for the eggs.'

'I mean it.'

'You look after yourself, all right? Go easy on the rum, Tuva.'

I give him an awkward hug and leave into the cold, crisp day.

More coffee at the tattoo-parlour coffee house. My head is still sore but I can operate again. I am steeling myself for the ski lift up the mountain. My new plan is to only ride it with another person, a skier, I guess, which is frankly absurd considering there is still danger in this town, on the loose, walking around in plain sight, but what can you do.

I check my emails. There is one from Johan, formally inviting me onto his podcast. He says he has had a guest cancel, a semi-professional kickboxer and former prison guard from Full Sutton – a men's high-security prison in the UK – so he is offering me the slot. He says the prison guard probably cancelled because of safety issues in Esseberg. That says it all, really.

Normally I'd reject a man I have noted on my shortlist of people of interest. But I'm at the point of desperation now. This case needs to be resolved and quickly.

I read through the waivers, contracts, NDAs and tips he includes as PDF attachments. All standard terms, as far as I can tell. It is the kind of document where I can sign it on the screen and save myself a copy. I reply saying I will do the podcast as long as I can ask him direct, pertinent questions at the same time: about the town, the local police, and crucially, the current multiple-homicide case. He replies saying he is fine with that. He also says he wants to ask about the Medusa murders, the Ferryman, the Midsommar kidnappings, the Pan Night events in Visberg, and what happened to the survivalist community two years ago on Rose Farm. My biggest stories to date, each one cited at the award ceremony. I sign the doc and send it. If you don't risk anything you don't get results. Lena taught me that.

As I walk around the rear of the church I catch sight of the deacon and run to him.

'Excuse me, Deacon Sahlin.'

He looks apprehensive. 'I'm so sorry, I'm late for a meeting inside.'

'Just a quick question.' I try to manoeuvre myself between him and the door. 'Two seconds of your time.'

'I would like to talk, but I'm afraid it's not possible. I'm very sorry.' He slips past me and closes the heavy wooden door behind him.

The chairlift is fine, as it goes, but I am getting restless for answers. There is nobody else to ride up with but I am not afraid. Because: daylight. The morning is fresh: crystal blue skies and sun reflecting off the new snow. The mountain looks inviting, not dangerous. And the calm breeze helps soften my hangover.

Eric is sitting in the lobby drinking tea. He has a formal pot, Wedgewood by the look of it, and an antique silver strainer.

He stands and rushes over as soon as he spots me. 'I heard you had trouble on the lift. Are you okay, Tuva?'

And at that very moment, my one remaining operational hearing aid fails me. 'I'm fine. My hearing aids are out of battery. I need to go charge them.'

I focus on his mouth.

'I'm so sorry you were caught out there in the storm.'

All of a sudden I feel like bursting into tears. I have no idea why.

'It's fine. I'm fine.'

His mouth is more like mine than I had realised. It is like staring into a mirror.

Eric says something else but his head is part turned towards the TV at reception so I can't read him.

'Sorry,' I say. 'Repeat that, please.'

He just points at the TV.

It shows a photo of a man in a black coat. He has white-grey hair and a grey moustache. I think it's the Einstein lookalike from before. The words on screen read *Have you seen this man?* I can read the newsreader's lips fairly well, they always enunciate clearly, but I don't need to because the captions are shown on screen as the TV is muted. *Police wish to talk with Bertil Lind in connection with the Esseberg deaths in order to eliminate him from their enquiries. Police reiterate that Lind has not officially been named as a suspect.*

'Who is that?' I ask.

Eric turns to me. 'Bertil Lind? He's the choirmaster at the church. And cousin of the deacon.'

56

An hour later, there are rumours circulating all over social media about Bertil Lind. A post on Facebook suggests he was questioned about an inappropriate relationship with a local teenager back in the late nineties, but the girl vehemently denied any wrongdoing on Bertil's part. She said he never even held her hand, they just talked. The post has since been deleted by the admin of that particular group.

Three missed calls from Tammy. I call her back and it goes straight to voicemail. I call again and she still doesn't pick up. A sinking feeling in my gut.

I know the podcast will be recorded as video as well as audio so I shower and put on mascara for the first time in about a month, and I wear my best winter clothes. My hearing aids are charging. I look as pale as death, the mascara somehow emphasising my lack of zen, wellbeing and healthy, balanced lifestyle.

My journey begins and it strikes me how arrogant mankind is for attempting to inhabit such a barren, inhospitable place as this. Arrogant, and downright foolish. The Sami lived here for centuries, nomadically; existing alongside nature, with the seasons, careful not to damage the balance of wildlife they feel they are a part of. Then we arrived, with our notions and our industries and we think we can dominate these formidable mountains. Cling to their sides and build whatever we want. Mine underneath them, ski on top of them like blood-sucking parasites clad in Gore-Tex and polyester. To reach Johan's place I will need to negotiate the chairlift down, again, walk to my Hilux, then drive as close as I can to his home studio.

I use my pass to access the lift and sit, my feet dangling, as the cable drags me down the escarpment again. My aids are charged and my phone is charged. I wouldn't even countenance an interview like this one if it wasn't for the fact that Johan's podcast is one of the most prestigious of its kind in Europe. He has an agent and a manager and legitimate blue-chip sponsors.

The town looks almost beautiful in the pale, glacial light of late morning. I spend ten minutes with my truck engine running as I scrape the windows and lights, and then I set off, salt snow crunching under my studded tyres. A man with a fluorescent yellow hat crosses the road in front of me. He waves, thanking me for stopping. I saw him a week ago out walking his little dog. And then, once he has passed, I notice that his backpack has an integrated window and the dog is snug inside. Such is the reality of living at this latitude.

Rushed and stumbling over my words, I set up a meeting for tomorrow morning with a man from the other side of the tunnel who wrote a tweet, in vague semi-libellous language, disparaging Bertil and alluding to something that happened in the nineties.

A posse of six Wolverines, each in a matching jacket, patrols the main street in town.

My drive takes twenty-five minutes. The news on the radio mentions Bertil the choirmaster and it also mentions how Camilla Sahlin, the deacon's wife, his third, apparently, is assisting police with their enquiries. The newsreader states that officers have been seen entering the Lutheran church on Fredriksgatan and then leaving an hour later carrying sealed bags and boxes. I will be asking Johan all about this, partly because he was once a choirboy here.

It strikes me, not for the first time, how dastardly it is to commit a crime when holding a position of trust or authority. Any harmful action is abhorrent; of course, but there is an additional layer of immorality when a murder is orchestrated by a teacher, bishop or judge. We afford them a certain level of respect and we expect, in turn, for them to act in our best interests.

I leave the town limits behind.

Unploughed roads and steep drifts each side, smooth and untouched.

The air is dry and it is swine-cold.

On the radio, a local quiz show is interrupted by news that the tunnel has been temporarily closed due to an avalanche. Nobody was hurt during the incident. Teams are working hard to clear the snow.

Trapped.

I pass an abandoned house, the timber joists and beams collapsed in on the main rooms, the wood rotting, the ice and parasites invasive, each claiming its own season. The only item I recognise inside is a rusting cast-iron stove; and bedsprings poke up from a frame like exotic coral from a tropical reef.

No snow in the air today.

Trapped. I can't leave this place even if I want to.

I drive on and cross a river, the water underneath still flowing, but concealed in sections by a glassy crust. Another fifteen minutes, and two bends, and I spot the house. Hidden from the world. Johan described it as a log cabin with a new build attached. He didn't mention that the flag outside would be Norwegian.

Is this the right house? I see no postbox or name sign. This seems an awful long way from Esseberg.

There is a tall, skinny Christmas tree in the driveway and it is covered with white lights. Not the warm variety. The tree is growing in the ground.

I slow my truck but leave the engine ticking over. Inside the house I see a face I recognise. Pointed chin and cropped blonde hair. Johan, peering back at me. There is a snowplough attachment and a bronze-coloured Mercedes parked under a sturdy car port. A steel toolbox stands open next to the snowmobile.

It is important to listen to your gut in this kind of situation. I am here to make a breakthrough, to grill him for information, to add colour to my story, but at the same time I must maintain situational awareness. I keep reminding myself of Johan's success and of how many eminent criminologists and psychologists have been interviewed in this place. One retired National Police Commissioner from Stockholm and a Professor Emeritus from Stanford University in the US.

I step out of my truck and the snow is deep.

'Tuva,' he says. 'Welcome.'

57

'I didn't know you were Norwegian,' I say, walking towards him.

'You didn't?'

I shake my head.

'My parents are from just across the border. They built this place.'

'Did you hear about the avalanche?'

'I did,' he says. 'They need to maintain the mountain better. We tell the Kommun but they do not listen to us.'

I nod. 'Hopefully it'll be cleared soon. Lovely position you have here. Very private.'

He nods and looks it over as if for the first time. 'It's home.'

'They still live here, or?'

'They died.'

'Oh, I am sorry.'

'Dad had only just retired. They had so many plans.'

I stumble as we walk towards the front door.

'I'm sorry,' I say again, uselessly.

'They crashed their car on the E14 motorway the day after Midsommar. Perfect driving conditions. A dry day. The police looked into it and concluded it was wear and tear damage to the brakes. They were extremely unlucky.'

'How awful.'

'That's how I got into all this. Cold cases and unexplained accidents. I think the police often do an excellent job, but sometimes they are constrained by their resources.'

'I suppose so.'

'And also their imaginations.'

What does he mean by that?

'Anyway, thanks for coming, Tuva. Please, step inside.'

His V-neck T-shirt is brilliant white. How come *my* whites never look like that?

He opens the front door. The house is a log cabin, the gaps in the timber walls filled with compacted moss in the traditional style. Inside it is cosy and warm. A log burner glows gently in the corner and the floors are covered with large, thin rugs. It is a tidy, organised home and that instantly puts me at ease.

'Do you know anything about Bertil the choirmaster? Or Camilla Sahlin, the deacon's wife? I hear they're being questioned?'

He swaps his boots for sheepskin slippers. 'Let's save that for the pod. She should be here soon. Do you want a coffee? Tea? Water?'

'Sorry?'

'Coffee or tea? I have a Nespresso machine if you'd like to choose a capsule? I have decaf.'

He hands me a basket full of assorted coffee pods.

'*Who* will be here soon?'

'Astrid.'

I frown and smile.

'I did mention it. I will be interviewing you both together. Two journalists. Comparing your careers and

your processes. How you gather sources, how you interview, liaise with police and local government authorities,
and how you go about gaining the trust of the
community.'

'You didn't mention this to me, Johan.'

'I'm sure I did? I'm sorry if I forgot. I could swear I
mentioned it to both of you. Would it be a problem? If so,
I can record you both separately.'

'No, no. It's fine with me.'

'Are you sure? I want you both to feel comfortable.'

I think about it some more. 'It'll be fine.'

A bleep on the wall.

'That'll be her now.'

He has some kind of driveway alarm. I look out and
Astrid looks back at us both through the window. Rather
than putting my boots back on I let him go out and greet
her on his own. They seem friendly.

The house is attractive: watercolours on the walls, most
of them from the same Danish artist. Johan has put up
Christmas decorations, a green garland of pine branches
adorning the pine banister of the staircase. The kitchen is
dated but everything is in its place.

'Hello again, Tuva,' says Astrid, walking in. 'Have you
heard about the pastor?'

'Hello. No. You mean the deacon? What about him?
What's new?'

We move closer and hug. She is wearing two scarves
again: one maroon, one blue.

'He's being questioned in Åre by detectives. His car's
been taken in by forensics. They got to him before the
avalanche blocked the tunnel entrance.'

'Oh.'

'I'm heading out there right after this is finished.' She looks at Johan. 'Assuming the road is clear by then. You said three hours max, yes?'

'That usually does it,' he says.

'Let's get started then,' she says. 'Busy day. Where's the famous studio?'

He picks up a small wicker basket. 'First I need you to place your phones in this. I'll do the same. We'll pick them up at the end. My sponsors insist on this precaution as we've had alarms and calls in the past. Is that okay?'

We both nod.

He leads us through the kitchen, out the back door, through a short corridor into a light and airy space with a panoramic feature window, the other walls clad in birch. A large desk, three cameras on tripods, four office style chairs, large soft-box studio lights, and four microphones on extendable arms. The walls are covered in some kind of uneven soundproof material. I recognise the bright red 'On-Air' lamp from episodes on YouTube. There is an unframed black and white print of Al Capone. Another of Alcatraz prison. One of Scotland Yard, the famous sign part obscured by fog.

'Are we expecting one more?' asks Astrid, gesturing at the four chairs.

'Just a trio today,' says Johan. 'My cousin may drop by later but he won't be on the show. He's too shy.'

'Your cousin?' I say.

'He drives the snowplough in town.'

'Who is that?' asks Astrid, pointing to a canvas. It shows a clown gurning at the camera.

315

'That is John Wayne Gacy,' he says.

She and I both look none the wiser.

'Clown.'

We both frown again.

'True-crime icon. Sad to say, but true. American sex offender and serial killer. Gacy assaulted, tortured and killed at least thirty boys and young men in Illinois during the sixties and seventies.'

'Not sure I could live with that on my wall,' says Astrid.

I agree with her. This aspect of true crime, the obsessive focus on perpetrators, troubles me.

'Gacy would lure victims to his ranch-style home,' says Johan. 'He'd suggest showing them a magic trick that entailed them donning handcuffs. Awful. I'll leave the rest up to your imagination.'

My stomach gurgles. Acid and regret.

Johan goes on. 'He buried twenty-six young men in the crawl space of his house. During his killing years he performed regularly as Pogo the Clown, appearing at children's hospitals and local parties. It is important we remember the horrors of that case.'

Astrid stares at me.

'And him?' I say, pointing at another print, this one sepia tone.

'Billy the Kid,' he says. 'And that's Quantico, and that one's a still from the O.J. Simpson trial.'

'The glove,' says Astrid. 'I recognise that.'

'Take a seat. Tuva, you there, please. Astrid, you sit there. Make yourselves comfortable.'

He seats us next to each other in the far corner of the studio, well away from the corridor. But he doesn't sit opposite, behind the desk, he pulls his chair so he's only a metre or so from us both, penning us in, and pulls his microphone close to his mouth.

'Is this live?' asks Astrid. 'Have we started yet? Apparently police have been spotted taking files from the deacon's house.'

'We're rolling but it isn't live. I'll record everything and I'll publish from when we start talking properly. You two ready?'

We both nod.

'Let's get into it.'

58

He offers us both headphones with disposable covers. After some discussion back and forth we opt not to wear them. I don't want any interference with my aids. Johan starts off nice and easy. He asks us both to describe our morning routines. Astrid lets me start and so I detail my extraordinarily dull wake-up routine, the vibrating alarm under my pillow, how I put my hearing aids in after I shower, the fact that I don't eat a healthy breakfast or do yoga or meditate. I tell them I am watching my phone pretty much as soon as I wake up, much like the rest of the world. Astrid says she doesn't have much of a routine, either. She tries to jog to work once or twice a week and she likes a hot breakfast in the wintertime. When she was younger her mother made the best porridge in the world. She tells us how she'd mix in an egg and that made it rich and creamy. I won't be trying that in a hurry. Johan goes on to ask us about our favourite TV shows growing up and I know exactly what he is doing because I do the same thing. You go in soft and gentle. Lena taught me never to ask a *high-trust question,* as she calls them, too early. As humans we need to establish rapport. Establish basic boundaries. I tell him I enjoyed weird TV, mostly reruns of shows like *Eerie Indiana* and *The X Files.* Astrid is younger than me so she talks about *South Park* and *Beavis and Butthead*. I am kind of impressed with her TV taste and I can tell Johan is as well.

He says he is fascinated by journalism, especially how it is changing in the digital age.

'Tuva, you've been involved in some high-profile cases over the past half decade. What have been the high points and low points?'

I take a moment. 'High points? Whenever I do my job well. Usually I fall short but sometimes I will come across a detail or angle other people missed. I like it when I can contribute something to the case being investigated, but also, crucially, write about it afterwards and do the victims and their relatives' justice. As for the low points, I don't know, maybe sharing an office with a guy who reads books on the history of the Rubik's Cube and keeps a pet Tamagotchi.'

'They're still *alive*?' asks Astrid.

'His is.'

'That's the low point?' asks Johan. 'Because I know you've been through some real trauma, Tuva.'

I shift in my chair. 'I'm not going into that.'

Johan nods. 'I understand. Astrid, then. Highs and lows.'

The atmosphere in the room cools.

'Highs are every time I land a scoop, if I'm honest. That feeling of being first. And then, like Tuva said, writing a well-constructed piece that people will take in as they read their paper over breakfast. We're letting our readership know what's going on in their area.'

'And the lows?'

'I often find it harrowing to talk to relatives. Spouses and parents. I mean, I can manage it. I have done it many times. But it's tough, especially so if the incident involved a child.'

I shudder. 'That's the worst.'

Johan nods. 'Have you had to investigate many cases like that? Involving children?'

I say, 'Mercifully, very few.'

'I've done several,' says Astrid. 'It's very hard. Takes a toll.'

He adjusts something on his laptop.

'You both work for smaller newspapers,' says Johan. 'Tuva, your paper is particularly rural. How do you find balancing the major stories – corruption, political scandals, violent crime and so on – with everyday stories of school tennis matches and fun-runs?'

'I love that aspect,' I say. 'I never had that when I interned for a national paper in London. The stories were narrow and deep. I've grown to enjoy the balance. Those small stories can seem irrelevant or facile at first glance. But they are the glue that holds a community together. The small victories and personal updates.'

'She's good, right?' says Astrid. 'See, this is why she wins all the prizes.'

'No,' I say. 'I had to pay significant bribes for that.'

'Let's talk about that, though,' says Johan, adjusting his microphone. 'How does it feel to be acknowledged for your work, Tuva?'

'More people hate my work than admire it. My editor says you should do your level best to ignore all criticism and ignore all praise. Stick to your principles and work you ass off.'

'I like your boss already,' says Astrid.

'And you?' says Johan. 'What goals do you have, Astrid?'

'Goals? Oh, I don't know. I don't like to look too far in the future or make detailed plans. Maybe that's why I'm still single.'

'Does being single help you in any way? You both came here to investigate the Pepper Spray killings and you've both been able to stay for an extended period. Would a relationship hinder that ambition?'

'Are you suggesting if I had a husband at home and a couple of rug rats I'd be chained to a kitchen sink?' I say.

He smiles. 'No, not at all. But there would be a need for balance, right?'

'The best journalists I've seen,' I say, 'Have been committed to their stories regardless of marital status, gender, age, or any other factor. If you have a nose for a story you have a nose for a story. It's that simple.'

'What she said,' says Astrid. 'When my boss told me how Peter Hedberg had gone missing in Ice Town, and he told me about the unusual tunnel, I practically begged to cover the story.'

'Same,' I say. 'These kinds of stories don't happen very often, thank goodness. I jumped in my truck and drove straight up here.'

'Let's go into that,' says Johan. 'You've both been in the town for a week or so. I'm curious. The Pepper Spray Killer appears to be highly intelligent. Do you think he or she will ever be caught?'

59

We both shift uncomfortably in our chairs.

The podcast studio is a little too warm and a little too airless.

'I think they will be apprehended in the coming days,' I say, breaking the silence. 'A spree of crimes this audacious. The perp will have missed something, or left something identifying behind: an eyelash or the use of a credit card, maybe an online search.'

'We hope so,' says Astrid, pouring water into her glass. 'The police seem to be making progress.'

Johan smirks.

We both look at him.

'You don't think the local police are up to the job?' I ask.

'Do *you*?' he says. 'If they were up to the task surely they'd have at least arrested someone by now? This isn't Detroit or Cairo. Esseberg is a small place.'

I look him in the eye. 'Maybe the killer is very smart, like you said.'

'Even so,' he says. 'The Wolverines are of more use, that's the way I see it. They are imposing a kind of voluntary curfew and they're patrolling at night. Yesterday they checked two citizens, asking them what they were doing on the streets at night, patting them down. What would you say if they caught the perpetrator before the police?'

Astrid and I both look at each other again. A three-way conversation is a little awkward.

'I'm not entirely sure they can pat people down. I guess if they ask, and it's voluntary, that might be okay? I don't know. If they find the person responsible, as long as they hand him over to the authorities immediately, who cares who catches him?' I say. 'The priority is that nobody else is murdered.'

'It's possible the police are working in tandem, unofficially, with the Wolverines,' says Astrid. 'I heard their second in command has a brother on the force in Åre. They're supposedly unarmed, though I find that hard to believe, but I've heard they have intel from ... somewhere.'

'And why do you think the killer chose this particular location?' asks Johan.

'Most likely because this is home,' I say. 'It's convenient. They feel safe on these streets. Most violent criminals are lazy and lack ambition. They work where they feel secure.'

Johan raises his eyebrows. 'Lacks ambition? I'm not sure others would agree. Bear in mind it's possible there are more bodies out there hidden under snow.'

'You don't think the killer is lazy, Johan?' asks Astrid.

'No, I don't. This is an ambitious spree. It has the attention of most of Europe and it's been discussed on American TV.'

'Is that *impressive*?' I say.

'It's merely a fact,' he says, maintaining his composure. 'Both of you, move your microphones closer to your mouths.' We do as he asks. 'That's better. Now, I'm curious. What do you think his or her motive is?'

'From what I've read and seen in documentaries it's usually sexual, sadistic, revenge-based, or financial,' says Astrid. 'One of those four.'

'I don't think it's financial,' I say. 'Or sexual, unless the killer gets a thrill out of the asphyxiation process, which is certainly possible. I think revenge or sadism, which overlaps somewhat with the concept of a thrill killing, is most likely.'

Johan moves closer.

I feel pinned into the corner.

Astrid crosses her legs, then her arms.

'Why did he choose these particular victims?' he asks, and he's starting to get red in the cheeks. It's too warm in here. 'Any connection between them and the local parish church?'

'I can find no logical connection between them,' says Astrid. 'I thought I had discovered a link through the choir and hockey teams going back years. But it fell apart with the later incidents.'

'We've seen spree killers before,' I say. 'It is the act of killing that is often most important to them rather than any particular victim profile.'

We talk about this in detail for another ten minutes before Johan asks, 'The modus operandi. We're not privy to all the details yet but we do know the killer strangled each victim after attacking them with bear spray. Is this the first you've heard of this technique? Could it be a copycat killer?'

I look at the photo of Al Capone on the wall. 'Not that I can think of, but I'm no expert.'

'Perhaps indirectly,' says Astrid. 'My editor told me of a case where sex workers were being incapacitated with spiked drinks. Then the killer would strangle them. I think he killed three women in total.'

'There are many such cases, sadly,' I say. 'You're right. This is different but it's also similar.'

'I think he's an original,' says Johan. 'Even if there are similarities. I mean, *bear spray*? I've never heard of anyone using that before in Sweden.'

'A woman was arrested for using it to scare off a potential mugger in Hisingen, Gothenburg,' I say. 'She received a fine. Bear spray and pepper spray are classed as offensive weapons according to Swedish law.'

We discuss the semen found on the ski trousers of one of the victims. And how the police haven't yet managed to ascertain the identity of the person who bought the sample from Philip Wallin.

'What do you think Ingavar Persson, our resident celebrity, thinks of this situation?' he asks.

I shrug. 'I don't know him well at all. Is he a celebrity?'

Astrid says, 'I think he is justifiably concerned that people are pointing their fingers at him because of his past. As far as I know he is cooperating with police.'

'Do you suspect he's impressed with the scale of the killings?'

Astrid shifts awkwardly in her seat. 'What do you mean, *impressed*?'

He sticks out his lower lip. 'I don't know if impressed is the right word. I'm surprised something like this could happen in this area, that's for sure. And I'm unimpressed with the efforts of the police and prosecutor.'

'They seem to be focused on the church at the moment,' I say.

'Ridiculous,' says Johan. 'Those people do a lot of good in the town. I'm not religious anymore but I support the deacon and his team.'

Astrid frowns. 'Dude, are you familiar with the history of the Catholic church?'

Johan sighs. 'Not relevant in this town. And the deacon and his wife aren't Catholic. There is nothing that I can see linking our church to these incidents. There's always whispers and gossip. The deacon is extremely shy and that means people talk.' He moves his chair so he's even closer to us. His knees are almost touching ours. 'Do you think the killer has fantasies? Do you think he replays his crimes after the fact for repeat gratification? Do you think he could be replaying them right at this moment?'

'What I think,' I say, standing up. 'Is that it's time for a break.'

60

Astrid and I glance at each other as we walk out into Johan's kitchen. It is a look that women have given each other for millennia.

'Where's your toilet, please?' she asks.

He points to a door. 'Through there, down the stairs, hit the light switch, door in the rear-left corner. Guest bathroom.'

She leaves, her eyes lingering on mine and I know exactly what she is thinking.

'Tuva,' whispers Johan as she walks down out of sight.

'Yeah?'

He checks the screen of his phone. I see a grainy black and white image of Astrid passing, then walking down into the basement.

'I'm concerned. I think Astrid is deceiving us.'

I frown at him. 'Sorry?'

He moves closer. A hint of stale coffee breath. 'We can't rely on any one indicator, any one body-language sign. But there are multiple indicators.'

'What are you talking about?'

He urges me to lower my voice. 'Her rise in vocal tone, fidgeting, change in speech patterns. All signs. She is self-soothing when she answers difficult questions. She vents from her neckline, moving her shirt, a sign she's literally becoming hot under the collar.'

'Now, come on,' I say. 'Wait a second.'

He goes on, still hushed. 'She covers her mouth and sometimes her eyes with her hand. A blocking technique. She shifts her anchor points, her position in the chair and her feet when I ask her something directly.'

'So? I must do that as well.'

He shakes his head. 'I study this, Tuva. It is my one obsession. She's stuttering, breaking eye contact, locking her arms. One time she moved her eyes from mine directly to the camera.'

I back away from him. 'I'm not comfortable with this approach. This is supposed to be a casual podcast recording.'

He lifts his index finger to his lip. 'She'll hear. Listen to me. She points away from herself when she needs to deflect attention. She is telling me one thing with her mouth and another thing altogether with her body.'

'If you're so sure of yourself, let's call the police and let them talk to her. Go on, call them. But if you're wrong she is going to write one hell of a scathing piece about your podcast.'

He checks his camera feed. The low-lit room downstairs. The staircase.

I see movement on the screen.

'We can't do that yet. I don't have enough on tape. Not nearly enough.'

'Sometimes justice is more important than your audience metrics and sponsors.'

'No, I mean she might clam up or ask for a lawyer. She is a sophisticated communicator. We might never discover what she knows. I'm not saying she's responsible for anything directly, but she *knows* something.'

'You think a professional journalist knows the identity of the Pepper Spray Killer and chooses to protect him?'

He shrugs. 'I intend to find out. Look, she's coming now.'

Astrid walks into the kitchen. She has splashed water on her face and I can see from her shirt she's been sweating.

'You sure do have some pretty rabbits down there,' she says, giving me another purposeful look like before. A glance that says: *watch your back.* 'How many rabbits do you have living in your basement, Johan?'

'Twenty-six. You two ready to record again?'

61

When we sit down again in our previous positions, Johan seems even closer than before. The room is stuffy. He checks his equipment, the mics and sound levels, and then he says, 'We're on.'

Astrid and I wait for the next question but there isn't one. He stares at us.

'Why did you start this podcast?' I ask, tentatively. It feels good to take control of the conversation. It's where I prefer to be.

'I was obsessed with internet radio, digital, the early days. The Wild West, I used to call it. Howard Stern's heyday. Those uncensored shows were amazing after decades of asinine, scripted TV. No gatekeepers. And then, one day – and I was quite satisfied as an apprentice piste-basher, honestly I was, I never expected a side-hustle that would eventually turn into a career – but, one day my life changed.' He glances at the camera. 'Long-term subscribers and Patreon members have heard this already. Sorry for repeating myself, guys. Anyway, one day Howard Stern had a call-in from a self-confessed serial killer. Late nineties, I think it was. I listened to it live and I was completely and utterly mesmerised. The caller sounded like a normal guy. He didn't give away any personal details but he said, calmly, he'd killed twelve women. He went into quite some detail about how he did it. You can still listen to the conversation online if you look for it hard enough. Stern was a consummate professional. He tried, in a gentle, probing sort of way, to ascertain details that may assist police. He asked about the man's age, whether he had any tattoos, when his first kill was. And there I was, some random ski-bum kid in Sweden, listening to all this. There were no broadcasting authorities or regulators checking it. No censor to cut the feed or bleep words. The chat was live and unedited and it blew my fucking mind.'

'The police arrested him after?' asks Astrid.

Johan shakes his head. 'That caller has never been caught.'

Astrid and I look at each other.

'That's horrific,' I say. 'This is what inspired you to start your podcast?'

'New-form media. I start it, I run it, I work at it, I control it.'

'Is it important for you to control things?' I say, keen to put more heat on him for a change.

'Sometimes,' he says. 'Astrid, what do you think about it?'

She waits a moment. 'I think you were ahead of the curve. Here's me and Tuva sweating away for our bosses on traditional newspapers that are under constant threat from tech, governed by journalistic rules and principles, held to account by readers and advertisers and shareholders. You can do what you like and make a good living from it.'

Will Dean

'I meant,' he says. 'What do you think about the serial killer calling in to the radio show?'

I observe her.

'I think it's a damn shame they couldn't triangulate his call. It sounds like the bastard was taunting everyone. Playing games for his own sick amusement.'

I saw no hand in front of her mouth. I detected no stutter or change in pitch.

'Have you ever bought bear spray, Astrid?' he asks.

'*Excuse me?*' she says, her mouth wide open.

'I asked if you have you ever bought a can of bear spray?'

She frowns, peering round the studio. 'Are you serious right now?'

'I'm not interrogating you. I'm just seeing if anyone, any normal, law-abiding civilian, any random Swede, has bought or come across this stuff. I mean, we have plenty of bears here in Jämtland and maybe it's a sensible thing to have on your person.'

'No, I have never bought bear spray. I hate those macho hunting shops, anyhow. All the guns and camouflage. All that indecipherable jargon. I love animals. More so than humans. Do I look like I go hunting?'

'They don't sell it in hunting shops,' he says. 'It's illegal, remember. Nowhere in Sweden sells it.'

'Tuva and I are here, sent by our respective newspapers, to investigate and write stories. Professional journalism. What are you here for, Johan?'

I notice him wince at the insinuation that he is an amateur compared to us.

'I live here,' he says.

'Yeah, you do, don't you. You know these quiet trails and back roads like the back of your hand. And you drive the pistes each and every night this time of year. Have *you* bought bear spray?'

The studio feels even smaller like the walls are moving in slowly and the ceiling is coming down on us.

'I've lived here all my life,' he says, and I notice him move his hand in front of his mouth. Then he moves his chair and shifts position.

'How well,' she asks. 'Do you know Bertil Lind, the choirmaster?'

He crinkles his mouth and says, 'Hardly at all.'

Johan checks something on his laptop again.

'Tuva,' asks Astrid. 'Where would you guess the killer is based?'

I point to myself and then I am intensely aware I shouldn't make any bodily movements at all in case he determines them to be indicators of deception or guilt.

'Here, or close by,' I say. 'Police suspect the culprit knows the area well enough that they can be confident of quick egress.' It feels good just to say the word *police*. I do not feel at all comfortable with this kind of amateur behavioural psychology.

'How do you think it *feels* to choke someone?' Johan asks, looking at us in turn. 'This is for both of you. How does it feel to asphyxiate someone, a stranger, with a medical tourniquet designed specifically to save lives. What do you think that sensation might be like? With each turn of the windless mechanism, you are supposed to increase the chances of survival as you slow down the blood loss suffered on an injured extremity. Instead, you use that same mechanism, in a gradual and measured way, to close the airway and blood flow to their brain.'

We don't speak.

He comes a little closer still in his chair, the wheels squeaking.

Astrid angrily moves her microphone to her mouth so it's touching her lips, and says, 'You seem to have given this a lot of thought.'

Johan leans in. 'I have.'

I say, in an attempt to cut the tension and bring things back to a civilised tone, 'That's the kind of attack that worries police the most, I'd imagine. It's not a crime of passion. It's pre-meditated, at least after the first killing. Slow and steady. The killer is literally laying their hands on each victim. Squeezing the life from them.'

'Reminds me of the majestic snakes,' says Johan, staring up at a picture of Quantico, Virginia on the wall. 'The anaconda and the python. The mighty boa constrictor. Squeezing the life out of their prey. That would have been a much more appropriate name than the *Bear Spray Killer*. Don't you think?'

62

We talk for twenty minutes about the locations of each homicide, and in depth about the slightly different, lakeside location of the most recent body, and who came to observe the crime scene. The mood has shifted. Part of me thinks that if we weren't being filmed and recorded, Astrid and I would have made our excuses and left already. But there is something about having yourself captured on film that makes you unwilling to countenance the idea of walking away. When you see guests on TV shows stand up and walk out, they look, at the very least, weak and out of control, and sometimes they look guilty.

I let Astrid give a genuinely excellent answer to a question about the ethical considerations pertaining to photographing active crime scenes. She talks at length about how and when to approach, how close to get, how to deal with law enforcement, how to take the statements and contact details of fellow bystanders, what's publishable and what isn't.

And then I request another break. Partly because I need the bathroom but also because I feel an urge, a gut instinct, to text Lena my whereabouts. Johan looks aggrieved but he agrees to the pause and escorts us out of the studio again. It is beginning to snow heavily outside. Large, flat flakes floating down from above. What Noora used to call 'Disney snow'.

He points downstairs to the basement. 'Through the door, down the corridor, down the stairs, hit the lights, door in the rear left corner.

Discretely, I take my phone from the basket outside the studio door and make my way down. When I glance back Astrid is talking to Johan but I can't make out her words.

The corridor is dimly lit. The lights are down by my feet and they illuminate automatically with every step down. More sensors. It makes the stairs seem like they are floating.

I turn into the basement proper and find the switch. One naked bulb in the centre of the room, dangling from a ceiling.

The rabbits are silent.

Twenty-six of them living on a wall.

A wall of meat rabbits.

They smell sour. Each one has a small cage with water bottle and food bowl. They do not move but they are alive. Whiskers twitch and soft bodies rise and fall with each breath. I can't see them well in this murk. Fur covered future meals. This place looks more like an animal-testing laboratory than a homestead project. He eats these? I am tempted to open each and every cage and then run away with them.

That is the irony.

They would perish out there in less than a day, and so would I. They're not built for these temperatures. They'd freeze or else they'd be hunted by a vicious wolverine or lynx cat. This gloomy wall of cages is, somewhat tragi-cally, the best life they can hope for.

The bathroom is small and spotlessly clean. Smells like bleach. It's overpowering. Like many Swedish bathrooms it has a shower head because it doubles as a wet room. There is a drain in the corner flush with the dark-grey floor tiles.

Framed photographs on the walls. I recognise some of the names listed. Joe Rogan in his studio with Bernie Sanders. Lex Fridman with Kai-Fu Lee. But they're not all podcasters. There are photos of Johnny Carson with Danny Devito, Terry Wogan with Madonna, Graham Norton with Meryl Streep. I ponder if Johan was an enthusiast of interviews first, of the art of interviewing, and then, when he stumbled upon his niche, went deep into true-crime podcasting.

I text Lena where I am. I tell her I'm fine and I plan to be here for another hour. She knows what this means. I have texted her similar messages before.

When I flush and leave I notice boxes in the corner of the room, barely visible beneath a black bed sheet.

I know Johan can see me via the camera linked to his phone but I step closer to the boxes, anyway. My heckles are up. I do not like being in a dim room like this one but I cannot ignore the things I have seen.

I hold up my phone for its light and notice that my message hasn't sent. It is sitting there in purgatory because I have no reception. I take three steps and peer under the sheet.

Hundreds, if not thousands, of DVDs in clear cases. A sack of shredded rabbit bedding. Three holdalls with locked zips. A carton holding three spray cans, each one painted black. I look closer. They're not painted; they're covered with layers and layers of black tape.

A bang from upstairs.

My heart pounds against my ribs and I walk briskly up the stairs, each one lighting up again as I ascend. I open the door and Johan is gone.

Astrid is standing all on her own and she is staring at me, silently repeating one word over and over.

I read it on her plum red lips.

'Hurry.'

63

'Where is he?' I whisper.

Astrid points to the stairs leading up to the next floor.

'You okay?' I ask.

She glances over at the front door, at the stairs, at the window. Then she beckons me closer. 'He . . . he told me – and I don't believe it, okay, I do not believe it for one second – but he told me you were showing indicators or something? Signs that you're not being truthful?'

'What?'

'Not so loud.'

'What exactly did he say?'

'He said you were sweating, flaring your nostrils, not looking him straight in the eye. He said you were showing classic body-language indicators of dishonesty.'

'He is mistaken, Astrid.'

She bites her lip. 'I know that.'

I want to tell her he has implicated her as well, on the basis of nothing except so-called indicators, but something stops me.

'I think I need to leave now,' she says. 'This is too . . . unorthodox.'

I nod.

'Are you coming?' she says.

'Listen. I know what you mean. He's playing some stupid game with us. Trying to make this whole thing more attention grabbing. I've listened to his podcast, and I've watched a few of the videos. He likes to throw out some pretty wild and baseless accusations in the second half. He craves the watch-time and the clicks. He needs outrageous clips for his social media. I think that might be what this is.'

'I don't care what he *wants*,' she says. 'I'm going.'

'I'm taking my phone into the studio this time. He hasn't noticed I've taken it back out of the basket. If things get too uncomfortable I'll hold down the buttons and it'll send out an SOS call. Okay?'

Footsteps on the stairs.

'Okay?' I say again.

Louder footsteps.

She nods to me.

I see his sheepskin slippers.

Then his legs.

Then his torso.

Then his face.

'Sorry that took a while,' he says, moving his hair away from in front of his eyes. 'I had to take care of something for an old friend. Shall we get back to it for the final section?'

64

My phone is bulging from my jeans pocket but he doesn't seem to notice.

He brings us both fresh paper cups of coffee from his machine, and there's a plate of Haribo sweet liquorice on the table between us.

The red 'On Air' sign is still lit. I don't think it's connected to the recording in any way, I suspect it is simply a decorative light.

The studio is even clammier than before. I don't know how Johan can stand it in his slippers. I wipe my forehead and Astrid moves her shirt away from her neck.

'It will be dark in a few hours,' he says. 'Not long now until the longest night. We're on.'

'If you had to implicate one person in this town,' says Astrid, quickly, seizing the moment. 'Not necessarily someone who is guilty of the actual crime, but perhaps of conspiracy to murder, of covering-up or holding back, who would that be?'

'You're asking me?' says Johan.

She nods her head.

'Not gonna take the bait, sorry. I have to stay living in this town after you two have both gone home. And

341

anyway, if I suspected someone was involved, even in a minor way, I'd take that to the police immediately.'

'What if it was your own father,' she says, calmly.

'My father died years ago,' says Johan.

'Hypothetically.'

'*Hypothetically*? Sure, I'd go to the police. Jesus, we're talking about multiple murders here. It would be tough but I would do the right thing. You wouldn't go to the police?'

Astrid says, 'I would. But we're not talking about me, we're talking about you.'

'I'd do the right thing,' he says, frowning. 'But, back to you, Astrid. Hypothetically, let's say *you* are implicated in some way, by virtue of the fact that you witnessed something but never came forward. Maybe because you wanted to use that information in your stories in order to win the kind of prizes that Tuva has won in recent years. Perhaps you wanted the scoop, as you mentioned earlier. The kudos of being first. Hypothetically, would you throw away those chances in order to tell police what may well turn out to be useless information?'

She frowns. Pauses. 'I'm not going to scupper a major investigation just to have a chance at some random journalistic prize.' She turns to me. 'No offence.'

I smile.

'Here's a question,' says Johan, taking back control. He looks at the camera for a moment. 'Tuva, Astrid, I haven't mentioned this possibility to you but long-term subscribers know I throw it into the mix occasionally.' He turns back to look at us and wheels his chair closer. 'How would you both feel about doing a polygraph test on camera?'

My eyebrows shoot up. I cannot stop them.

Astrid mouths out, 'A what?'

'I have all the equipment here. I'd start with some basic questions about your names, date of birth, employers. Verifiable information. Then move on to more direct questions about the cases you've each written about and so on. Nothing too personal.'

'Fuck, no,' I say.

'I'd . . .' says Astrid, looking at the pictures on the wall. 'I don't know. I'd consider it. As long as I can write about the experience in my paper afterwards.'

'Well I wouldn't,' I say, butting in before Johan can respond. 'Polygraph? For what purpose? On whose authority?'

'It's merely another way of me asking you questions if you think about it,' he says. 'My audience are sophisticated. They judge and appraise the veracity of your answers in the comments section. Happens in every episode. I'm merely suggesting we take that one step further. I conducted such a polygraph with a Scottish prison officer last year and it was most illuminating.'

Suddenly, there is feedback from the audio system.

Pulsing white noise in my hearing aids.

Johan looks furious. His face turns from mischievous boyish good looks to pure fury.

'Who brought a phone into my studio?'

65

Astrid and I look at each other.

'Oh, I do that all the time,' she says. 'It's like a reflex to have your phone with you these days.'

'I'm sorry, Johan,' I say. 'I apologise.'

'Get it out of here.'

'I took mine into the theatre just last month in Stockholm,' she says. 'The alarm went off halfway through and I was mortified.'

I can't exit the studio without Astrid moving, so after some awkward back and forth in the tight corner, she takes the phone from me and steps outside into the corridor to place it back in the basket. I'm not sure if Johan is angry about her leaving for a moment or because he hasn't recorded any kind of scandalous breakthrough from either one of us, or maybe it's simply because there have been too many interruptions for his liking.

Astrid steps back inside.

Johan says, his face tense, 'Tuva, why don't you tell us about your relationship with Police-Chief Skoglund. I have it on good authority that you two have been spotted eating dinner together in a private residence on Nygatan.'

I start to protest when I notice a flash of white light.

344

A reflection of the ice-white brightness outside.

I squint and Johan splutters. I retreat instinctively, pushing my wheeled chair back into the wall.

Astrid is standing behind Johan and she is holding a kitchen knife.

66

'I know it's you,' she says, her lip quivering, moving the blade towards his throat. 'I know it is you, you bastard. The police are on their way. This is over.'

He tries to protest, to struggle, but her knife grazes the thin skin of his neck and a spot of red appears. It trickles down beside his Adams apple and soaks into the V-neck collar of his pristine white T-shirt.

Astrid sees the panic on my face.

She looks down at the blood. 'Oh, God,' she says, looking at me. 'I'm sorry. I didn't mean to cut him. I just don't want him to hurt us.'

'What did the police say?' I ask, my hands tight on the arms of my chair.

'I gave them this address. They're on their way.'

'Bitch,' says Johan, through gritted teeth. 'You fucking stupid bitch.'

'Tuva,' says Astrid. 'I need your help. Come here. Be careful, don't get too close to him.'

Johan is snarling, the knife tip digging into his neck, and his bright white T-shirt is darkening with every passing second.

'Take one of my scarves,' she says. 'Tie his feet to the wheeled base of his chair. Tie it tight.'

I take her scarf and I can tell she is very afraid. It is an intimate act, removing a scarf from around someone's neck, from their face, holding their warmth, their scent. I haven't been this close to another person for a long time.

The scarf is dark blue lambswool. I bend down and rest on my knees.

'You're making a big mistake,' says Johan.

'If you kick her,' says Astrid. 'Or so much as move a muscle I will not hesitate.'

I reach in around the chair's base with my arms and gather his calves together and then I thread the scarf around them and behind the stem leading to the wheels and I tighten it.

'That's way too tight,' says Johan grimacing. 'That hurts.'

'Don't listen to him,' says Astrid. 'If it's not tight he'll work free and do to us what he did to them. I found a printed Amazon receipt downstairs in a stack of papers. It was from Amazon Germany. They delivered a six pack of tactical tourniquets here two weeks ago. If that was his only order it means he has one left.'

I stand up, my cheeks flushed. I can't hear every word but I understand enough.

'You don't get to do this to me in my own home,' says Johan, more control in his voice now.

'You think you're the one who gets to decide the fate of others?' says Astrid. 'Tuva, take my other scarf and tie his hands behind the chair.'

I remove her scarf, this one dark red, cashmere, and bind his wrists behind the back of the seat. His nails are manicured to perfection.

Astrid takes the blade away from his throat now that he is safely tied up, and she inspects his wound, grimacing as she looks at it.

'It's a shallow cut,' she says, cringing. 'The bleeding has stopped. I didn't mean to cut you.'

'Bitch.'

'I found bear spray canisters downstairs. He'd taped over the labels with this.' She takes a loose spiral of black duct tape from her pocket. 'He has three cans left. How long for the police to get here, Tuva?'

'I don't know. We're quite a way out. Ten more minutes? Fifteen?'

She walks back to Johan and gently places the blade against his throat again.

'No,' I say. 'Leave him for the police.'

'Tuva,' she says, pushing the edge of the blade deeper into his neck, once again drawing blood. 'Why don't you tie yourself to your chair over there.'

'What?'

'It's time. Tie yourself to it or I'll cut him.'

67

'Run,' croaks Johan. 'Run away.'

'I had nothing to do with any of this,' I say to her. 'I'm not with him. You think I'm his accomplice?'

'Tie yourself to the chair.'

'Tuva,' says Johan. 'Go.'

Astrid slices a deep gash across his left cheek, just beneath his eye.

He screams louder for me to run away but I am frozen in place. What is happening? I couldn't run even if I wanted to. They are blocking the way.

'If you leave, I will kill him,' she says. 'This is in your hands, Tuva.'

The camera is running. The mics are picking this all up. I can't breathe.

His shirt grows redder with every passing second. There is no white fabric until you reach his chest or his arms.

I sit down heavily on my chair.

'Okay,' she says. 'Take that cable from under the desk, the long white one. Tie it around the chair with you sat in it. Knot it tight. I will be able to tell if it is not tight. I will cut his throat if it is not secure.'

Now is the time for the police chief and Carlsson and

a dozen uniformed police officers to run in with their pistols drawn.

Silence.

'Do it now or I will cut into his voice box.'

My chest is tight. Tying yourself up isn't easy. The cable has attachments on each end. I think it's an Ethernet extension cable. Ten metres or so. My hands are unsteady but I manage to pass it behind myself and wrap myself, binding my body to the chair, tying a double knot at the front over my chest.

'Tighten it.'

'It's tight,' I say.

She cuts his other cheek and he lets out another shriek. 'Knot it again or he dies.'

I cannot look at his face. He has what look like scarlet tears pouring down from under his eyes, dripping off the point of his chin.

I tighten the Ethernet cable to the point where it cuts into my flesh like cheese wire, and then I secure it with another double knot.

'Fine,' she says. 'Excellent.'

And then she cuts his throat.

68

Johan writhes in his chair, flexing his arms and spreading his fingers like starfish.

His eyes bulge.

The noise is indescribable.

I clamp my eyes shut.

And then I reopen them and scream, 'Call an ambulance! You can undo this. Tell them to come now.'

They'll need to drive through the tunnel, though, won't they. They'll need to wait, with their lights flashing and their sirens blaring, at the front of the queue, until the train, or the oncoming road traffic finishes making its way through from Esseberg. Even with an emergency protocol to let them through, they'll need to wait for the tunnel to empty.

This whole place is a death trap.

His neck is red.

Astrid looks the other way and places down her knife on the table next to Johan's laptop. She looks faint. Her face is pale.

Maybe they'll send a helicopter from Östersund hospital.

That might be quicker.

Not quick enough.

Through gritted teeth I say, 'You need to hold pressure against the wound right now. He can still make it, Astrid. You can still do something good here. He deserves to live even if he hurt those people.'

I expect him to pass out but he remains conscious the whole time.

'Oh, Johan will survive,' she says. 'Look at him carefully. There is no arterial bleed. No spurting wound. God, I loathe blood. It's disgusting. There is no risk of him bleeding out, Tuva. I detest the whole concept of exsanguination.'

I recognise that term from a forensic report I once read about a farm worker who injured his leg out in the fields feeding livestock. The blood loss was massive and it was horrifically rapid. Within a minute or two he had lost so many units of blood there was no longer sufficient pressure within his vascular system to keep his vital organs functioning. A minute later he was dead.

'He can still die, Astrid. Please.'

The cords dig into the flesh of my wrists.

'If he dies, who'd upload this video?' she says. 'Johan is an important part in this. He needs to survive. I will make sure of it.'

He stares at her with his wet, wine-coloured T-shirt and his bulging, panicked eyes.

'I slit your trachea, Johan.' She speaks slowly and loud, as if to a child. 'Your windpipe is open now, okay? You will need a short procedure to remedy that. No significant hospital time required, you'll be able to stick to your podcast schedule, don't worry about that. But you won't be able to talk for the remainder of this particular episode.

Think of yourself as a member of the audience from this point on. Okay?'

I shake my head.

If I hadn't scrimped on my hearing aids I could have used an integrated voice-activated microphone. That would have enabled me to say a particular word and so call emergency services using just my voice. Instead, I'm helpless.

The On-Air sign glows red and the scene outside the window is absurdly idyllic. Fresh powder snow settling on pine branches; the landscape serene.

Rabbits a floor below us munch away at their food, oblivious.

'Better get started, Tuva. We won't have much time.'

I frown at her. 'Get started on what?'

She smiles. 'Go on. I know you're dying to ask me your own questions. You're the interviewer now. Begin.'

69

'I'm not asking you anything,' I say. 'I'll leave that to the police.'

'No, you won't,' she says, standing over me. 'I won't tell *them* anything.'

I gesture over at Johan. 'Help him, please, for God's sake. He can't breathe.'

'He *can* breathe. He's breathing adequately out of his neck. He can't talk but he can breathe. Now ask.'

I scream from exasperation.

And then I take a deep breath.

'Did you kill five people in Esseberg?'

'No foreplay with you, is there? You just ram it in dry.'

I scowl.

'I did what I had to do,' she says.

I let out another scream because Johan is spasming. He might be having a fit. 'Help him. Do it now. I won't ask you any more questions until you help him.'

She rolls her eyes and checks on him by licking the back of her hand and holding it to the slice in his trachea. She waits, a bored expression on her face. Then she removes her green jacket and turns it inside out. It is a reversible jacket. It's now black. She lays it over him, concealing the bloodied shirt.

'Our gracious host was a tad cold. Perhaps a little in shock. Better now.' She sits down again in her chair and swivels it to face mine. 'Proceed.'

'What do you want me to ask you?'

'No, no. You do this for a living, Tuva. And you're so very, very good at it. Renowned and respected all over the country. So put some effort in.'

'Why did you kill them?'

Astrid smiles for the camera. Adjusts the angle of her chin. 'Life is complicated, I guess. For some of us, it is. I have never had an easy time of it. My parents didn't beat me or anything like that, but they were always, I don't know, *detached*. I grew up alone in a household of three. The only child. I never made friends easily.'

Her words sound rehearsed. When I glance at Johan he gives me the most hopeless look of abject desperation I have ever seen and I am forced to avert my gaze.

'Are you listening to me?' She snaps.

'Yes. Of course. Go on.'

'I have explained this to myself a million times and it usually sounds more coherent than this. So, my life, at school, at parties, at work, at university, at home even. Nobody ever noticed me. Not one person.'

'I noticed you.'

She starts scratching at her temple. 'That's different.'

'I noticed you, Astrid.'

'Don't.'

'I noticed you from the moment I saw you.'

'Don't even try.'

'You killed the others. Why kill them and not Johan?'

He starts shaking his head and groaning at my question but I keep my eyes on hers.

'He is not meant to die. He is meant to upload this to the world. That is his personal destiny. It is one of the most downloaded podcasts in Europe. You know that, right?'

'So why did you kill the others? You could have tied them up and sliced their airways. You could have let them live.'

She laughs. 'You have no idea what you're talking about.'

'So, tell me.'

'They were *meant* to be asphyxiated. It was ordained. That was their shared destiny. They fit the list, you see.'

70

I ask her for a sip of water and she tells me there is no time.

'Tell me about the list. Whose names were on it? Have you completed the list now?'

'There are no *names* on it,' she says, dismissively. 'You don't understand, do you?'

'Why don't you explain?'

'I had a master list of characteristics in my mind. On my iPhone as well. Vital characteristics. Traits I clearly didn't have. Never had. Still don't. Traits that would have made me special.'

'Like good looks or something?'

'No, Tuva. Not like good looks. I have good looks and they never got me noticed.'

'Okay.'

I need to keep her talking otherwise God knows what she'll do next. Johan is slumping in his chair. He is not dead but I fear he is dying. We need police.

'I had a job, a family, an education, a circle of associates. I used to have a flat that I rented. I had neighbours and hobbies. I should have been visible.'

'Had?'

'Have. Whatever. This is closure for me and I can't tell you how relieved I am about that. Do you have any idea how exhausting it is to carry all this around with you on your shoulders? I crave a quiet life in a nice, comfortable Swedish institution.' She closes her eyes. 'I've dreamt about it. I'm ready for routines, and for simple tasks to be assigned to me. I want the same four walls. I want zero expectations of me. Zero resolutions missed or decisions to make. Nobody will compare me to my peers and find me lacking. Not after Esseberg. That feeling of being insignificant will never plague me again. I will be peerless.'

I'm relieved she's talking about prison.

As much as I loathe the realisation, the memory of my earlier conversation with Astrid returns to me. The responsibility of war reporters. To capture battle but also humanity. Lovers saying goodbye as one catches a train to the front line. Civilians carrying water for their elderly relatives. Our lives, distilled. Love and hate. Sometimes we journalists have to do the unthinkable in order to report on a story and bear witness. Forcing yourself to do something that conflicts with every instinct you have in order to record events for posterity.

I have no choice right now but to do my job.

71

'How did you manage to evade police for so long?' I ask.

'I understand exactly how they work,' she says. 'Protocols and procedures. I have investigated criminal cases for years. I have interviewed many competent detectives on the east coast. I couldn't do their jobs but I comprehend enough to be able to put them off the scent. The list principle is something I have pre-played in my mind for a long time, you need to understand that. Not the specifics, I didn't build out my list until this year, but I knew I'd check out in Ice Town.'

'What do you mean by *check out*?'

'Check out of civilised, domesticated life. Leave all this toxicity behind.'

I glance at the camera. 'You knew you'd do all this here in Esseberg? Why?'

'I had my childhood here, that's why. Every winter we'd come up here to my grandpa's cabin. We'd ski and sled and have snowball fights. I went to the church for St Lucia and for Christmas. I really liked it here.'

I want to quit asking her polite questions and check on Johan but I know that won't help him.

'So you chose to murder *strangers* here?'

'No. They didn't feel like strangers to me.'

'You knew them?'

'I knew their *characteristics*, Tuva. I knew their characteristics intimately. I have studied them for several years, month in, month out.'

'The list.'

'Right.'

'Who was on the list?'

'Not who, *what*. I have already told you. Traits. Listen, I have only good memories from this town. It felt manageable to end it all here. I knew the trails and woods, the lakeside walks and paths. When I went out to work on the list I would wear the size forty-five boots my dad used to wear. They don't make them anymore so I hoped they'd lead police to think they were dealing with a man. I would wear four pairs of winter socks inside them. I never felt the cold, not one time.'

I sigh.

Exhausted.

Johan wheezes and I hear some kind of fluid bubble from his throat but he is still alive.

'The semen? What was that about?'

'I ordered it from a local idiot online. Easy diversion. I needed to buy myself time to complete the whole list. Throw shade on someone else. It worked.'

'Would you tell me more about the list?'

She smiles.

'Please?'

'You're so wily aren't you, Tuva?'

'Me?'

'You're so, I don't know, quietly capable.'

'No, I'm *really* not.'

'So humble with it.'

I close my eyes tight. Am I next in line on her list?

'When you won a place on the prestigious *Thirty under Thirty* ranking in *Journalisten* I became fascinated by you and your career. How you managed to achieve so much in so few years.'

'My career?'

'Oh, don't act so coy. You've done amazingly well. University College London. The internship. Your work at the *Posten*, but also in Malmö at the *Sundhamn Enquirer*. Your promotion. I became quite fascinated by you.'

'It's nothing.'

'You don't mean that. I read every word you write, Tuva. Every single issue of the *Gavrik Posten*. Check with your subscriptions guy; I'm probably the only person in Norrköping who buys your paper each week. And then, through your interviews and articles I came to under-stand about your personal losses. I came to *know* you. Understand about your parents, and then Noora.'

I look down and the cable tightens around my torso.

Do not bring her name into this, you demon.

'And my list formed all by itself. You were so very noticed and admired.' She smiles. 'Like I said, the list appeared in my head fully formed. It felt natural. I knew I would need to put serious work in. One deaf person, obviously. Peter. Box ticked.'

I am slackjaw with horror. *Box ticked?* She literally hunted Peter *because* of his deafness?

'One bisexual,' she goes on. 'Check. One orphan. Done. I had plenty of those to choose from but I wanted someone youngish. One who'd lived in London. Yes. One writer. Found him. An old woman stopped me in the street and said she recognised me from the town decades ago and I thought I might have to spray her as well, which displeased me as she didn't have any of the characteristics. She didn't fit the list. Eventually she agreed she knew me from the TV, from my reporting, and I let her go. Completing my list satisfactorily is my one genuine noteworthy achievement and now I have confidence I will be noticed and remembered for decades to come.

My name will finally mean something, like yours does.'

72

She is utterly insane. I can't ask her more questions.

'Check his pulse. Please.'

'He is fine. Focus on me. This is about me.'

I bite my tongue. 'Why did you spray them and then strangle them? It's appalling.'

She smiles and looks at her hands. 'I sprayed them because I needed to take complete control over them, and that was, in my mind, the cleanest way to do so. I never considered guns or knives. I detest mess. I briefly pondered poison but it was too complicated and slow. Too unreliable. Once I had incapacitated them with bear spray, careful not to breathe it in myself, I could control them. The tourniquets allowed me infinite levels of adjustment. I could use the windless to stop both blood and airflow, and then, on the very edge of unconsciousness, I could relieve them for a moment. Bliss. Such power. I could turn the windless anticlockwise, just a few degrees, and that would afford the person a trickle of oxygenated blood and a short unexpected breath. Then I would tighten it again. Loosen it. Play with them a little. I was in the driving seat for once.'

'You know a lot about medical procedures and equipment.'

'I don't know a lot.'

'Compared to me.'

'My mother runs a first-aid course in Norrköping, associated with the Vrinnevi hospital. She'd give basic courses to teachers, stadium security, that kind of thing. She taught me about tourniquets, arterial bleeds, choking, hypothermia. She always emphasised to me how vulnerable we all are. She'd say the watershed between life and death is paper-thin.'

'She gave you the tourniquets?'

'No,' says Astrid. 'She has always been meticulous with her equipment, and she never really trusted me. She doesn't think I'm capable of being responsible for precious things. So I bought them online.'

'And the bear spray?'

'Same thing, eBay; sellers from Poland and Germany, or wherever pepper spray is legal. They'd write something vague like *wildlife repellent* on the package to make sure it sailed straight through Customs, not that there is much Customs within the EU. They wanted their review and their money and their five-star rating. And to be fair to them I never had any problems or delays.'

'And you brought all this gear to Esseberg?'

'I didn't know it would work satisfactorily.'

'You mean, the bear spray?'

'No, I believed that would work. If it can stop a bear it can stop a miserable kindergarten teacher. But I didn't know if any of it would be enough to attract *you*, Tuva.'

'I don't understand?'

She moves her mouth closer to her microphone. Looks over to Johan for his approval. 'I decided to deal with

Peter Hedberg first, as he was the only deaf resident I could find in Esseberg over the age of sixteen and under the age of fifty. You see, I would never harm an animal or a child. I am not a monster, whatever my mother thinks. I researched Peter and I hoped you'd discover he was missing or dead and you'd drive up here to cover the story.'

'Am I that predictable?'

She ignores my comment. 'I had the rest of the list figured out. Some would need to be struck off because they never ventured out alone or maybe they'd gone away to the Canaries for some winter sun. I had backup options and contingencies. I figured eventually you would come up here.'

'And so I did.'

'Like a puppet on a fucking string. Because you're the best in the business, baby. You're ambitious and you won't stop until you get your story.'

'I'm an idiot.'

'Far from it. You're the one everyone notices. Johan noticed you, didn't you, Johan? She kicks his chair. 'It was you he really wanted on the podcast.'

'I'm nothing special.'

'You are!' she roars, her nostrils flaring. 'You are the chosen one. You're the reporter everyone talks about, at least in our age group. They can't *stop* talking about you.'

'I really don't think you're right about that.'

'I am right,' she snaps again, narrowing her eyes. Then she softens and smiles. Let's out a laugh. 'Let me put it this way. I have never been a confident reporter. I've never had that ability to assert myself, to deal with politicians and local community leaders and councillors. But here, with you, working as peers, a kind of team, Thelma and Louise, I felt that self-belief for the first time. Rubbed off on me, I guess. Working on the list, being in control, it lent me some of that kudos and respect. Which, I think, is all I've ever wanted.'

73

Johan is deathly pale.

'Can you let him go now, please? Let him get patched up? He's not on your list, Astrid.'

'He needs to be here.'

'Why?'

'This is his show. He needs to process the footage. Edit it. Check for sound levels. Add in his sponsored ads and so on.'

'What he needs is the hospital.'

'Oh, he'll get that, too.'

'Are the police really on their way, Astrid?'

She smiles at me.

My heart sinks. 'What?'

'We don't need any silly police.'

Ice runs up my spine and settles at the base of my brain. There is no one coming here to help us.

'Interview me,' she says, greedily. 'Come on. Work. Ask me things.'

I stare at her.

'I said *interview me*.'

'Okay. I still don't understand why you did this. Was there anything in your childhood? Abuse? Neglect?'

'Good question. No. Next.'

'No?'

She chews her lip and then clears her throat. 'Fine. When I was eight my dad killed a chicken. There was that, I guess. She was one of our layers, we had half a dozen. He wrung her neck and then Mum cooked her. We ate her later that weekend. I felt, I don't know how to describe it, really.'

'The more you can tell me, the better the interview will be,' I say.

'Right. I felt shame, I suppose. Well, honestly, I may as well be honest, I felt kind of aroused when he squeezed her neck. She stiffened right up. I saw her pass on, the exact watershed moment of it. His hands around her scrawny neck. But this isn't a sexual thing.' She looks directly at the camera. 'I'm not a pervert. This is something else. I'm not sure why it excited me. Immediately afterwards I was ashamed.'

'Because you felt aroused?'

'Yes, and because I love animals. I really do love them. I think they are much more valuable than us humans, objectively speaking. And I was exhilarated when that chicken died.'

'It was just a chicken.'

'No,' she says, firmly. 'She was an innocent.'

I start to wriggle a little. I try to surreptitiously loosen my bindings.

'Much like your victims, then,' I say. 'Innocent.'

'None of *us* are innocent,' she says. 'Not us. We both know that from our years of reporting. There isn't a sinless adult in the country. That is why I have never harmed a child or an animal.' She kicks Johan's chair again and he groans. 'Why do you keep rabbits like that you fucking sicko? You know how cramped they are down there? That's no kind of life.'

'Do you get on well with your editor?' I ask, desperate to keep her attention on me.

'He was useless. Never gave me enough support. Never put me on the most interesting stories. He assigned me to things that he knew would never garner much attention. I don't think anyone in Norrköping even knew I was a serious journalist. It's as if people see right through me.'

The police aren't coming.

When the tape stops running or she runs out of things to say I have no idea what will come next.

'Your editor wasn't all bad,' I say. 'He let you come here to Esseberg to work on this.'

'Yeah, right.' She frowns at me. 'That bastard fired me three months ago.'

74

The snow has stopped.

The world beyond the glass is darkening.

'You ... you pretended to be working at the *Norrköping Nyheter* all this time? The press conferences and such?'

'Nobody ever checked.'

'Jesus.'

'We're peers, Tuva. We have the same profession and we have been working on the same story, only from different angles.'

I don't reply.

'I'm not unhinged.' She looks directly at the camera again. 'I am not insane, I want that noted on the record. I may have ice in my heart, but I am perfectly sane. Listen carefully: I am coherent. I know exactly what I am doing. None of the people on the list were blameless. They sinned in life. I sinned. We have all done it. I have not harmed a single innocent.'

'You need to let us go, Astrid. Johan and me. Do that one redemptive thing. You have the power to make that happen.'

'I know I do.'

'Good. It is in your control.'

'My time has come, finally. It is time that I am discussed and analysed in great detail; by academics and investigators alike. This will happen, I truly believe that. I have done enough now and that knowledge brings me peace. There will be shows, not just YouTube and podcasts, there will be primetime TV shows, documentaries, books and dissertations written. I am clearly far more capable than they ever gave me credit for. There is no doubt.'

'I see that.'

'Everyone else will see it, as well.'

I take a deep breath but my bindings make it difficult.

'I can't breathe properly, Astrid. Can you loosen the cables, please.'

She ignores me. 'I will require a Wikipedia page, a thorough one with citations and sub-headings. As for the photograph, I have already selected one and left it in my apartment, together with my insurance and banking documents. I've left my affairs in good order. I believe I'll go viral. It is time the world saw my face and heard my story.'

'My cables, Astrid.'

She looks back at the red On-Air sign, and then she nods.

She walks away and pulls a long extension cord from the wall.

The On-Air sign switches off.

She ties the extension cable around her own neck.

This doesn't compute. What is she doing? I don't know why but I am stunned into silence.

She sits on her own chair and pushes it gently to meet mine, and then she spins it around so we are back to back.

Will Dean

I can't see her directly but I can watch her in the window. She places another cord around both our necks.

'What . . . what are you doing?' I scream.

'I must be seen.'

75

I can't view her clearly in the reflection. It's like I am watching this unfold on a wall-size TV screen with a low-resolution picture, the screen pitched at an awkward angle.

The tranquil scenery beyond – pine trees and snow drifts and icicles hanging from the roof – mixes with the horrors on the glass.

I watch as a deeply troubled *former* journalist carefully inserts a bright-blue ski pole into the knotted length of extension cord she has secured around both our necks.

'Astrid,' I say, as calmly as I can manage. 'Please listen to me now, very carefully.'

'Everyone listens to you, Tuva.'

'You don't need to do this.'

'The last two on the list. The closure. We are not innocents.'

'Ignore the damn list. You're in complete control.'

'I know.'

Johan is trying to shift his chair now she has tied herself to me. He shuffles and shunts with his bodyweight and a new bubble of blood and mucus froths from his gaping trachea.

Will Dean

She twists the blue ski pole and my head is dragged incrementally closer to hers.

Our hair meshes together.

'Astrid!'

The pressure builds as she twists because I realise she is using the ski pole as an oversize windless. Winding tighter and tighter. I will it to snap but I know that wish is pointless. These poles are hardy. They are built to withstand large forces on the slopes.

Pressure builds.

The cable digs deeper into my skin and I gasp for air.

A crushing sensation.

Panic.

'No, Astrid. I beg of you.' But my voice is weak and wheezy. 'Stop it. Please. Stop it right now.'

'You and me are equals,' she gasps. Her voice is as strained as my own. 'Mirror images.'

Johan bangs his chair against the podcast desk.

She struggles to tighten the pole, twisting it, and the cables pull us together. We are as one.

My peripheral vision darkens.

Black snow.

An image of my father in my head.

Help me.

'We leave here today,' she gasps. 'As equals.'

76

I fight to breathe but there is nothing.
  No air.
  My blood flow has stopped.
  There is no space. No hope. I am so very cold.
  We will leave this life together and that is a travesty.
  The window darkens.
  Everything to black.
  But then it lightens again and I force my eyes to stay
open.
  Movement out there in the snow.
  Shouting voices.
  Commands and lights.
  I can't hear them.
  Darkness.

77

I am sat on the sofa in Johan's open-plan kitchen-living room being attended to by a tall paramedic. Johan is being patched together, a drip in his arm; no, wait, I think it's a bag of blood, and there are two people wearing gloves working on his neck.

They give him an injection and wheel him away on a gurney.

I touch my neck. It is red raw but she never broke my skin.

Carlsson checks on me quickly before moving to the podcast studio. Just looking into his unusual eyes is reassuring. He tells me they received a call to drive by the address. A welfare check. He says he used his multi-tool to cut the cables knotted around my neck. Around *both* our necks. The tool sits next to me on the sofa, along with discarded wrappers from medical gauzes and syringes. I suspect they considered Johan the threat when they entered and saw two woman bound together.

The tall paramedic checks my pupils with a light. Checks my pulse. Asks me simple questions. *What year is it? Who is the Prime Minister?* He offers me a sip of water.

And then Astrid is dragged through by four police officers. She is conscious. The paramedics must have revived her in the studio. She is handcuffed and they are not being gentle with her, considering she almost died. She does not struggle or protest. They pull her through Johan's kitchen and she turns to me and she does not smile, but, in the most unnerving way imaginable, she now looks completely at peace.

78

Yesterday, when the last of the day's light was draining from the skies, I was taken to Åre to be checked over thoroughly by a doctor. Chief Skoglund wanted me to spend the night in Östersund hospital but I told her that would not be necessary.

After thorough medical checks I gave my statement at the police station. It took a long time. They offered me a sandwich but it still hurts to swallow. By the end of it I was exhausted. Living through the ordeal again in great detail. Not only the podcast, but the days leading up to it. I have lived the past eighteen months quietly, with little deviation from my standard routine. No serious crimes or incidents to report on. And then a whole year, a decade, a lifetime, happened in a single week.

My text message eventually went through. That must have been what caused the feedback that irritated Johan. Lena called the police after receiving it.

I owe her my life.

She talked to Chief Björn, who then contacted Chief Skoglund to request a welfare drive-by. She saved all three of us with that quick thinking.

And thank God the tunnel had reopened in time.

I dread to think of the alternative.

Last night I slept in a basic chain hotel in Åre. My neck was still very sore. The doctor was reluctant to prescribe me a sleeping tablet to go with my pain killers but in the end I didn't need one. I slept as soon as I curled up on the bed.

I am travelling back to Esseberg to collect my Hilux. This time I am in the back of a taxi and we are midway through the tunnel. *Ice Town. Twinned with Whittier, Alaska.*

I hold the seatbelt well away from my neck. The friction burns are still raw.

The town seems different as it passes by my taxi window. It is only four below and there are people out and about pushing buggies and dragging sledges, making the most of the clement weather. Children play on the shallow hills outside town; taking turns to sledge on the smooth slopes like children have always done.

Astrid diligently left reviews on various European Amazon sites for her tourniquet and bear spray purchases. Five-star anonymous reviews where she went into great detail about the effectiveness of the items. This is all over the news. She wrote how the tourniquets *tighten with ease to satisfactorily cut off all blood flow* and the bear spray could *stop a full grown man, or several full-grown men, in their tracks.* The most recent review was written two days ago.

I pass Willy's on my left and Wrath on my right. I smile when I think of Ulf, the gentlest, most poetic bouncer of them all.

I have seen Ingvar interviewed on the TV. He talked eloquently, still dressed in his red ski jacket, about how Astrid fits the profile for an *attention-seeking* serial murderer.

How there have tragically been many such cases across the globe. How the perpetrators are usually the architects of their own downfall, and how, if they deem themselves successful in their horrific endeavours, they can appear oddly at ease with their actions and punishment.

So far Astrid has been charged with Attempted Murder. She is being held in custody in Östermalm following medical treatment and it is expected that she will be charged with five counts of murder.

After paying the driver I head to the lift station. Eric is already waiting for me. He has come alone and he is holding my bag in his hand.

I smile. 'Good of you to bring it down.'

'This infernal wind,' he says, blinking hard. 'Making my eyes water.'

'I will be in touch again, you know,' I say, patting the sleeve of his wool jacket. 'Let's get to the bottom of what happened all those years ago in Stockholm and take it from there. I am glad you told me. Let's just see what happens.'

'I want you to be very careful,' he says. 'Please, Tuva. With your job, I mean. We nearly lost you.'

I smile. 'I'm tougher than I look.'

A twinkle in his eye. 'Would you ever consider a less dangerous career? Hospitality, perhaps?'

My smile broadens and I shake my head. 'I'm not very hospitable.'

'Drive back safely. Do you have good tyres?'

I nod. And then I approach him. I say, leaning close to his ear, 'Goodbye, Eric,' and I hug him briefly and he pats me on the back with gloved hands.

'Call me anytime you like,' he says. 'Whenever it is convenient for you.'

I turn and walk away, and, not for the first time, I am unsure of both what I am leaving behind and what lies ahead.

79

I have a little over an hour.

When I drop off my bag in my Hilux I spot the lady who owns the Golden Paradise B&B.

'She strangled you?' she says, probing my scarf with her eyes.

'I'm okay. I'm glad she's safely off the streets.'

'I heard you medically died.'

I frown. 'You heard that?'

'You died, medically, and they resuscitated you. You look fine now.'

'I am fine.'

'I'm not letting journalists stay in my B&B again.'

'I don't blame you.'

'She looked so normal!'

I nod. 'They always do.'

After dropping off a box of Christmas chocolates I bought in Willy's at Peter Hedberg's grandma's apartment, and enjoying her vastly superior home-baked gingerbread cookies, I walk into the Vårdcentral surgery near the pensions office, avoiding reporters as I go. Carlsson's here with someone who looks like an intern or trainee. They are packing up their makeshift police outpost.

He steps out to talk with me.

'You okay?'

'I've felt better,' I say.

'Look at them.' He gestures to people walking in and out of the church community centre. Others dragging groceries from Willy's on sledges or in their backpacks. 'They are at ease once again. You can feel it, can't you? Something in the air. Quiet small town folk going about their business.'

'Is the chief here today?'

'No, she's busy with paperwork and the press. Plenty of loose ends. Lots more work to do.'

He notices my disappointment.

'She passed on her best wishes to you, Tuva. Said she wants you to have a safe trip back home and to say hello to Chief Björn from her.'

'I'll certainly do that.'

We chat for a while about the coverage of the story. How journalists from further afield are pouring in just as I am leaving. Reporters from Berlin and Oslo are already here. He says they are all making a concerted effort not to name the perpetrator more than they have to, and never in the headlines. He said they're trying to focus on the victims and give her, the attention-seeker, as little column space as possible. I expect that will change in the coming days but I am glad to hear it regardless.

The deacon and his wife step out onto the broad granite steps of their church and the bells begin to ring. Sometimes a shy deacon is just that. I've seen the same thing time and time again in Gavrik and Visberg. Unfounded rumours can cause real harm. I need to work harder to make sure I don't accept them as fact. I need to work harder in so many ways. The deacon and his wife both smile at me and she raises her eyebrows in a gesture I take to mean *are you all right?* I smile back. *I will be.*

A red Saab pulls up outside the church.

There aren't many editors who will drive through the night to check you're okay and ride with you all the way back home.

But there is one.

80

We are on the road for almost eight hours.

She never once asks me about what happened in the podcast studio. She knows how this works. She understands that I will tell her when I am ready.

We take it in shifts, two hours at a time, in my Hilux. The motorway has light traffic – Volvos with mattresses of snow affixed stubbornly to their roofs, and lumber trucks transporting felled pine trunks to lakeside pulp mills. I am grateful to Lena Adeola for so much. As I watch her face as she drives, me wrapped up in a blanket on my passenger seat, I'm also grateful to her husband who's making the journey back down to Gavrik alone in their Saab. She says he enjoys the solitude and then she glances at me with a naughty look and tells me he likes to listen to long podcasts. I love them both like family and I will never forget his unspoken, unshowy kindness.

So many versions of the elk mother and her calf. I see them mirrored everywhere I go.

A message from Khalyla. Direct, not through her agent or manager. She thanks me for working on the story. She says she felt I was there to help, and she recognised we both shared the same *eternal outsider* perspective that Peter also had.

I spot the twin chimneys of Gavrik town on the horizon as we drive down the E16 in the slow lane. We take the turn off and pass through the landmark gateposts of McDonald's and ICA Maxi. The town is dark. Light fog. I spot Tammy's food van parked in the supermarket car park, lit by floodlights. Lena drives me home and I sleep for thirteen hours straight.

The next morning I have butterflies in my stomach.

I dress in my best merino wool sweater and jeans, and I spray perfume on my wrist and dab it behind my ear, something I almost never do. Vague memories of Mum doing this in our Stockholm apartment when I was very young. Perhaps she did it for Eric.

The Lutheran church on Eriksgatan is packed when I arrive. The car park is full so I leave the truck in my slot behind the *Gavrik Posten* office and walk over, careful not to slip.

The bells ring and the long-life candles in the graveyard sparkle and shine because this is Santa Lucia, the remembrance of light and hope. It is exactly what we all need to make it through each winter.

Most of us aren't regular churchgoers. Some of us aren't even religious. But we all come together for this occasion. When you live in a cold, gloomy, distant corner of the world you relish any opportunity to meet up and quietly, solemnly, in true Nordic fashion, give thanks for whatever light we all have to share.

The procession has not yet begun.

I recognise everyone. And I mean every single person. It is so good to be home.

Some people stare but most are busy keeping their

children from wrecking the place or running outside to play in the snow.

And there she is.

Tammy stands up and winks. I make a bee-line for her pew and apologise as I squeeze past the other Gavrik residents in their multi-layered finery.

She holds out her arms and I open mine and we hold each other tight for a long time. She smells like safety. She smells like all the very best things in the whole world.

Organ music begins.

The procession.

Candles flicker all over the church and the distant sound of angelic children singing makes the hairs on the back of my still-sore neck stand on end. When I turn back to see them walking with their lights and their white dresses I notice Chief Björn seated directly behind me with his wife and it takes everything I have to stop myself from crying. There is no one particular reason. He understands that. He nods curtly and then he pats my gloved hand and his wife smiles.

Tammy couldn't be sitting any closer. She is looking after me as she has done a dozen times before.

The ceremony is beauty and goodness concentrated to its ultimate quintessence.

As we file out, I manage to talk with Benny Björnmossen and his wife, and Thord, and Luka Kodro, and then I chat with Lars and Nils from the office.

Two hooded figures in the far corner of the church-yard, over by the noticeboard.

I say my goodbyes and head over in their direction.

They stand on shovelled snow. They appear taller than they really are.

'Heard you had some bother up north, girl,' says Cornelia, one of the wood-carving sisters from Utgard forest.

She is holding a troll but she's keeping it under wraps. Perhaps she is delivering it to a private customer. They sell a lot of carved trolls this time of year.

'Bother,' says Alice, the quiet sister. She's wearing a hunting cap with ear flaps and I can see she's completely bald underneath.

'Are you both okay?'

'We okay, Alice?' says Cornelia.

Alice blows a raspberry.

'We're always okay, girl,' says Cornelia.

'I think I saw one of your chessboards up in Jämtland. Pieces with ribs?'

They look at each other and smile.

'Lots of work, wasn't they, Alice?' says Cornelia. 'Them chessboards, back in the day.'

'Check mate,' says Alice, under her breath.

And then they turn and walk away, Alice with a noticeable limp.

I unzip my coat and climb into my Hilux.

Ninety minute drive.

My hands are shaking as I grip the wheel. Amy seems so perfect on the phone, so likeable in every way, but I am not sure if I am ready. When are you ever ready?

The drive passes in a blur.

The snow has abated.

When I walk inside the building I am directed to a family room. There is a watercolour outside and I stop to look at it. A sheltered lily pond with shade from weeping willows. Springtime. Wild flowers and birds in flight.

I knock on the door and go inside.

Amy is sitting with Noora's parents. After she was shot we took it in shifts in the hospital. When Noora was released home, no signs of awareness, no blinking to answer our questions, we took it in shifts to be with her. My own family was fractured and complicated but Noora's parents absorbed me into their unit in an impossibly kind and generous way. We cared for her together. Until it was time to let her go.

There are empty cups of coffee on the table because they wanted to be here half an hour before me and I agreed that was a good idea.

They have cried their tears.

Seeing them with Amy thirty minutes ago would have most likely broken me.

She smiles. Red hair and freckles. A long, elegant neck. Her scar by the open top buttons of her gingham shirt.

'Tuva,' she says, smiling with her eyes and with her mouth.

'Thank you, Amy.'

She shakes her head. 'No, it's me who is thankful.' Her voice cracks. 'So very thankful.'

We hug gently and I struggle to let go of her because we are together once more.

She understands. She lets me hold her.

I pull away.

'Do you want to hear?' she asks.

I nod and inhale deeply and then I take the stethoscope from Noora's mother and she nods her encouragement. I take another breath and place the earpiece up to my ear.

Amy guides my hand, holding the cold end of the stethoscope to her chest.

I exhale properly for the first time in years. A true breath. I sob and smile and listen to the beautiful heartbeat of my beloved. It is strong and true and pure.

Her heart.

Her perfect heart.

Acknowledgements

To my literary agent Kate Burke, and the team at Blake Friedmann (Isobel, Julian, Conrad, Anna, Juliet, Sian, Lizzy, Nicole, Daisy et al): thank you.

To my editor Jo Dickinson, and the team at Hodder (Alice, Alainna, Sorcha, Kate, Jenny, Nick, Sarah, Catherine, Richard, Sinead, Dominic et al): thank you.

To my international publishers, editors, translators: thank you.

To Maya Lindh (the voice of Tuva): thank you.

To all the booksellers and bloggers and librarians and reviewers and fellow authors: thank you. Readers benefit so much from your recommendations and enthusiasm. I am one of them. Special thanks to every single reader who takes the time to leave a review somewhere online. Those reviews help readers to find books. Thank you.

To @DeafGirly: thank you once again for your help and support. In many ways your opinion matters to me more than anyone else's.

To my family, and especially my parents: once again, thank you for letting me play alone for hours as a child. Thank you for taking me to libraries to borrow books. Thank you for allowing me to build (so many) dens, and then letting me read and draw and daydream inside them.

Thanks for not censoring my book choices (too much). Thank you for allowing me to be bored (a lot). It was a special, and increasingly rare, gift.

To my friends: thanks for your ongoing support (and patience, and love).

To the residents of Whittier, Alaska: thank you for inspiring this novel with your tunnel.

Special thanks to my late granddad for teaching me many valuable lessons. He urged me to treat everyone equally, and with respect. To give the benefit of the doubt. To listen to advice even if you don't then follow it. To take pleasure from the small, inexpensive things in life. To protect nature, and to appreciate it. To read widely. To never judge or look down on anyone. To be kind. To grow food, even if that means herbs on a window sill. To spend time with loved ones. To keep the curious child inside you alive.

To every shy, socially awkward kid: I see you. I was you. It will get easier, I promise. You will make it through to the other side.

To my wife and son: thank you. Love you. Always.